In Ole Virginia

Southern Classics Series

M. E. Bradford, Editor

Southern Classics Series
M. E. Bradford, Series Editor

In Ole Virginia

Or, Marse Chan and Other Stories

THOMAS NELSON PAGE

with an introduction by Clyde N. Wilson

J. S. Sanders & Company

NASHVILLE

Library of Congress Catalog Card Number:
91-62457

ISBN: 1-879941-04-X

Published in the United States by
J. S. Sanders & Company
P. O. Box 50331
Nashville, Tennessee 37205

Distributed to the trade by
National Book Network
4720-A Boston Way
Lanham, Maryland 20706

1991 printing
Manufactured in the United States of America

To My People
This Fragmentary Record
Of Their Life
Is Dedicated

Note

The dialect of the negroes of Eastern Virginia differs totally from that of the Southern negroes, and in some material points from that of those located farther west.

The elision is so constant that it is impossible to produce the exact sound, and in some cases it has been found necessary to subordinate the phonetic arrangement to intelligibility.

The following rules may, however, aid the reader:

The final consonant is rarely sounded. Adverbs, prepositions, and short words are frequently slighted, as is the possessive. The letter *r* is not usually rolled except when used as a substitute for *th*, but is pronounced *ah*.

For instance, the following is a fair representation of the peculiarities cited:

The sentence, "It was curious, he said, he wanted to go into the other army," would sound " 'Twuz cu-yus, he say, he wan'(t) (to) go in(to) 'turr ah-my."

Contents

Introduction

In *Ole Virginia* is a memorable portrait of the Old South before its destruction and one of the small company of truly enduring achievements in nineteenth century American literature. Its author, Thomas Nelson Page, was the most popular and most representative Southern writer of his time and one of the few Southern writers of any time to achieve the fullest measure of recognition and worldly success in his own lifetime.

Page was born in 1853 at Oakland plantation in Hanover County, Virginia, the same county in which Patrick Henry and Henry Clay had been born. Four obvious influences can be seen in his origins.

First, an ancestral pedigree that reads like a roster of the First Families of Virginia. Second, a childhood spent in a region north of Richmond during the War between the States that was one of the most heavily fought-over areas of the continent. Third, reduced family circumstances, which gave a spur to industry and ambition. Fourth, a spinster lady relative (remembered in Page's sketch, "My Cousin Fanny," in the 1894 collection *The Burial of the Guns*) who introduced him to literature and determined the direction of his aspirations.

Turning twelve two weeks after Appomattox, Page experienced the war at the most impressionable age, so that the heroism of the men in gray and the women who sustained them, and the hardships of the "Reconstruction" peace which followed, formed the central theme of his experience and thus of his writing. He is the premier interpreter in fiction of those Southern experiences for his generation.

Page knew directly the fall of fortunes entailed by defeat for Southerners, especially those of his class, in an irregular education, interspersed with periods as a tutor. He was able to attend Washington and Lee (then Washington College) for a time when General Lee was president, but could not stay long enough to graduate. After awhile, he was able to attend the University of Virginia Law School. Again he had to leave without graduating, although he enjoyed at Charlottesville a stimulating literary fellowship.

In 1872 he began a law practice in Richmond that was moderately successful and which he continued for some years, even after his literary career had begun to prosper. In 1886 he married Anne Seddon Bruce, whose pedigree equalled his and who is perhaps the model for "Anne" in "Marse Chan." She died suddenly a year and a half later at age twenty.

"Marse Chan," Page's first significant published fiction, appeared in 1884 in the popular *Century Magazine* of the Scribner publishing family. The editors liked the story but delayed publication for two years, apparently because of misgivings about the readability of the dialect. The doubts proved unfounded. When published, the story was immediately popular, and thereafter demand for Page's work on the part of the Northern reading public never ceased.

In 1887 his first book, *In Ole Virginia*, a collection of his earliest stories, appeared, to critical and popular acclaim. It remained his most popular and characteristic book. "Marse Chan" has always been his best-loved story, and Page considered the second story in the volume, "Unc' Edinburg's Drowndin'," to be his best-crafted and most technically perfect tale.

By 1893 he was able to give up law practice and lecturing. He married into a very wealthy Northern family and established a home in Washington, a gentleman of means free to mingle in the highest society, enjoying fame, a Maine seaside cottage, membership in the best New York clubs, and extended European travel. He was a friend of Theodore Roosevelt and Woodrow Wilson.

From 1913 to 1917, during most of the World War I era, Page was, on Wilson's appointment, the American ambassador to Italy, a difficult assignment well-performed. He died in 1922 at Oakland where he had begun.

Even after achieving fame and prosperity, Page continued writing—stories, novels, dramas, poetry, history, social commentary. The collected "Plantation Edition" of his works, published by Scribner's, ran to eighteen volumes. *In Ole Virginia* was Volume 1. This continued productivity, along with occasional efforts to break out of his successful formula and topics, are sure signs of serious literary craftsmanship and dedication. Page must be taken as a serious writer, in spite of the fate of immense popularity in his lifetime followed by neglect afterward.

When asked about his literary career, he wrote, in what is surely a remarkably accurate and guileless writer's confession: "I think the principal thing after my liking for books, was my desire to see myself in print. Emulation of others, the desire to add to my poor income, and ambition afterwards played their part; but I think . . . the first motive was, to use a term for want of a better—vanity."

The fact that a Southern writer, an unequivocal defender and celebrator of the virtues of the South and its people, could enjoy such a successful career is a commentary, of course, on the period of American history in which Page flourished. To put a fine point on it, he could not have achieved such recognition, as Southern writers have learned the hard way in less hospitable eras, had he not been perceived to be performing a service for the North.

Page was fortunate to begin writing at a time when the North had become disillusioned with the failed and misguided crusade of Reconstruction and was experiencing a widespread if not universal impulse for reconciliation and healing of old wounds. Such a reconciliation was necessary if American society was to go on to a higher level of unity. Thus it was a period in which Southerners could receive some encouragement on the national literary scene, and there was an audience willing to believe that there had been, after all, some honor, heroism, and sincerity in the Lost Cause.

Page did not pioneer the fiction of sectional reconciliation, which had already become a familiar mode when he began to publish, but he did become its most successful practitioner. Reconciliation by inter-sectional marriage was a popular theme, holding out the promise of a restoration of pre-war civility, and nowhere more happily treated than by Page in "Meh Lady: A Story of the War."

For Northerners Page provided reassurance that sectional conflict was not intransigent, that the South had accepted restoration of the Union in good faith. For Southerners, he satisfied the desire to establish that they had not been dishonorable in their motives and conduct in the war and that the South had not really been the domain of diabolism of lurid abolitionist and Black Republican propaganda. Both sections got something from the bargain. Page is thus a central cultural figure in American history, in the restoration of that real Union that must rest, as John C. Calhoun had always argued, on consent rather than conquest.

It is customary in recent commentary to dwell impatiently on the alleged disservice Page did the South in casting its history into an attractive and comforting myth. But he performed an equal or greater service for the North, where the preponderance of his readers were, by assuaging its guilt—not guilt over abandonment of the blacks at the end of Reconstruction, as modern liberal historians urge, because there was no guilt about that—but guilt over having indulged in excesses of political fanaticism in the war against erring but honorable countrymen.

A central part of the reconciliation bargain was the North's willingness to leave the problem of race relations to the Southern States. The most recent school of historiography sees this as a kind of moral betrayal of a previous commitment to equality. But it is doubtful if there ever had been such a commitment, except on the part of a very small minority, and hatred of Southern whites had always been a stronger motive for reform than sympathy for Southern blacks. It might be more accurate to say that the North had concluded that it had been wrongheaded to seek anything more than the original war aims—preservation of the Union and economic hegemony.

What is likely to be most unsatisfactory to egalitarian readers of the later twentieth century is the skill and success with which Page incorporated the black people into his Southern myth (and I mean myth here as an imaginative conception formulating a social truth in a way that is not counter-factual but supra-factual).

In Ole Virginia is Virginia before and during the war, as remembered fondly by its black bondsmen after its destruction. Here Page showed his real skill as a writer and a defender of the South, for he portrays the plantation gentry through the eyes of its faithful retainers. He was not the first or only Southern writer to do so—Joel Chandler Harris and others were about the same mission—but he perhaps did it best.

Much can be said about this before we dismiss it as no more than an imposture upon black Americans. The bardic voice, the survivor of a vanished regime who remains to tell its story—a role which Page ascribed to the blacks—has been a post of honor in Western literature from time immemorial. The virtues of Page's white Virginians are not imaginable or possible without the context of black Virginians.

Further, a bit of historical perspective might remind us that Page's attitude toward the black people, if paternalistic, was admirable and moral given the parameters of his time. For the choice in late nineteenth century America, as unpalatable as the historical truth may be, was not between old Virginia paternalism and social and political equality. It was between old Virginia paternalism and the hard racism that can be seen, for instance, in the works of Thomas Dixon.

If it is true that race relations are today better in the South than in other parts of the United States, and many would agree that they are, then surely it has something to do with the world that Page portrayed and the realities that lay behind it. For Southerners white and black the South has been a place they have to live in, and a place that is on the whole worth preserving—not a political abstraction to divert attention from the contradictions and hypocrisies of American society at large.

Given the long record of the crimes, follies, and misfortunes of

mankind, and the realities of his era, Page's position is eminently
moral and constructive. He reconciled the South to a failed sacrifice that was as great as any ever undergone by a large group of
Americans. (The war killed a quarter of the white men in the
Southeastern States and set the South back three generations
economically.) And he also provided some of the grounds for
future incorporation of black and white in a once-more viable
Southern society.

The South had to come to terms with the greatest bloodletting
in American history and the defeat of cherished hopes. And with
potential for racial conflict such as was unknown in the Northern
and Western States until the 1960's. Page in response created an
ideal fictional world, but faced with the circumstances of despair
and insoluble conflict, idealism was a heroic and constructive
response.

In a literary sense he kept alive the reality of black characters in
mainstream American literature, and therefore kept open a vital
line that stretches on to William Faulkner's Lucas Beauchamp in
Intruder in the Dust and Dilsey in *The Sound and the Fury.*
Faulkner's characters were created in a literary age that was
"realistic" rather than "sentimental" like Page's, but the line of
descent is real, nonetheless.

The voices that Page creates in his work, black and white, are
authentic Southern voices. Public voices, perhaps, that do not say
everything they know and feel, that tactfully treat some trouble-
some subjects, and that consciously dramatize themselves—all of
which are things that Southerners, black and white, are wont to
do in real life. But they are authentic voices, in their own terms.

No writer can entirely escape his age. Page's age was one of
sentimentality, something which his audience and editors expected. As Jay B. Hubbell, one of the leading students of Southern
literature, has put it, Page's picture of Ole Virginia is a painting,
not a photograph. If he did not escape sentimentality, he did at
times surmount it. Often his effects are not so much sentimental
as truly poignant. How skillfully he surmounted the cheaper
forms of sentiment can be proved by a comparison with some of
the now-forgotten popular literature of the time, and by the fact

that he created a painting that, though unmistakably of a certain period, will endure in its interest to later generations.

Southern writers that followed him inevitably rebelled against Page. One thinks, for instance, of his fellow Richmonders, James Branch Cabell and Ellen Glasgow. But the next generation rediscovered the path.

The plantation society presented by such twentieth century writers as William Faulkner in *The Unvanquished*, Caroline Gordon in *Penhally*, or Shelby Foote in *Jordan County*, is a tougher and more realistic and earthy and ambiguous world than Page's. But like Page, these writers surmount the limitations of their own period ("realism") to redeem rather than reject Southern history. They create a world that is essentially admirable, that offers us in place of cynicism and despair a glimpse of heroism and honor that is a model for later generations of Southerners. This, surely, owes something to the trails blazed by Page.

It is difficult to judge Page fairly because it is difficult to recover a clear view of the plantation, which has been subjected to so much positive (*Gone with the Wind*) and negative (*Roots*) romanticism, and which has become politicized as the abode of the ultimate horror of American history, slavery.

The plantation already had a long literary tradition when Page began to write, developed by such writers as John P. Kennedy and William Gilmore Simms in the antebellum era. The literary convention of the plantation was as old as American literature, because the plantation was as old as American history.

Despite the tendency of scholars to mistake literary traditions for life, the plantation was far more than a scene for fiction—it was a historical reality of immense importance, central to American history and a characteristically American institution. It was not a remote quaintness or peculiar evil on the fringes of society. It is quite safe to say that without the institution of the plantation, the whole first two centuries of American development would have been retarded and the course of American history would have been quite different. And not necessarily better if we eliminate all the positive benefits that accrued to American society from the class that produced Washington and Jefferson.

Strictly speaking, the plantation is defined as a large agricultural unit with a dependent labor force, engaged at least in part in the production of staple crops, such as tobacco, cotton, or sugar, for the world market. The plantation was already well established in Latin America and the Caribbean before it appeared in seventeenth century Virginia and Carolina. In North America it took on Anglo-Saxon and Protestant features and existed in the midst of a largely yeoman society, which gave it distinguishing characteristics.

The amount of attention historians have paid to the plantation and the moral and ideological passions that it has aroused belie their frequent tendency to minimize its importance or deny its centrality. For some modern historians, like Kenneth Stampp, the plantation was only a particularly ugly form of capitalism. Here we find a failure of historical imagination, an inability to conceive of a different society in its own terms or to understand any other way of life except as a defective form of Americanism.

Most historians, however, whatever their value judgments, understand that the plantation world was a unique form of society. One convincing formulation is given by the Italian historian Raimondo Luraghi in *The Rise and Fall of the Plantation South*. The South was a seignurial society, neither feudal nor capitalist, with its own social reality and its own ethics—and not merely a debased form of bourgeois society. It is this world that is the locale of Page's fiction.

Antebellum Southern writers who used the plantation as a scene for fiction had been romantics to a degree, but had never lost a certain earthy realism. In keeping with his era and the elegaic nature of his mission, Page progressed further along the road to sentiment. We should remember that this was what the Northern audience wanted. (Southerners were too poor to buy enough books to make any writer a success.) Even so, Page, like his predecessors, never quite loses touch with the reality that the plantation is first and foremost a working farm. We always know that crops have to be planted, flooded creeks crossed, provisions put up for the winter, horses cared for. In real life the ending does not always work out so happily as in "Meh Lady," but the hardships portrayed in that story were very real and intimately known.

There is no need to over-emphasize Page's sentimentality. The seemingly improbable plot of "Marse Chan," for instance, is, as Page explained in his introduction to the Plantation Edition, based on the real story of a soldier whose sweetheart had told him to come home only with honor, and who was killed shortly after. The real story involved a Georgia private and not an FFV, however.

Readers who want to read more of Page after *In Ole Virginia* might look at the story collection *The Burial of the Guns*, where they will find deft and realistic treatments of social issues. The title story concerns the war—heroism and pride in defeat. But the other stories are more contemporary: social hypocrisy and triumphant spinsterhood in "My Cousin Fanny"; alcoholism and postwar demoralization in "The Gray Jacket of No. 4"; deception and disappointed love in "Miss Dangerlie's Roses"; and the sufferings and courage of the poorest class of white Southerners in "Little Darby." None of these stories would satisfy an exponent of French naturalism, but given the standards and tastes of the time, they deal with social issues in an unflinching way.

Superficially, Page fits perfectly the prevailing historical stereotype of the Southern Bourbon. As misleadingly described in the works of C. Vann Woodward, the Bourbon was a member of the antebellum gentry who made his peace with Northern capital, uniting with the most exploitive elements of American society for his own profit, while diverting the South from its real problems by sentimentalizing its past.

Though this historical interpretation is widely accepted, it is not strictly true, in regard either to Page or to the politics of the leading class in the South after the war. Rather than aiding and abetting the vested interests of the age, Southerners quite often provided a leavening influence of old-fashioned liberalism in a rapacious, utilitarian society—which was a heritage of the plantation class and its preference for honor over profit, its distaste for ruthless individualism, and its purchase on the ethics of an earlier American republicanism that had been forgotten in the North.

Page's novel *Gordon Keith* (1903), though it is not a successful work of fiction, deals with the shallowness and vanity of modern New York society and its pursuit of wealth. And in *John Marvel, Assistant* (1909), he exhibits sympathetic interest in the plights of labor and of Jews. In the larger sense, he is a critic, not an abettor, of the abuses of the Gilded Age. Indeed, the planter class had always been the seat of American liberalism, ever since Mr. Jefferson had stood up to General Hamilton and his schemes.

The idea of the plantation rests most uneasily in the American consciousness. On the one hand, it has been determined to be the seat of all horror. On the other, it is inextricably tied to some of the highest moments and grandest personalities of American history. One suspects that most of the thousands of tourists who throng Mount Vernon and Monticello imagine them to be something like Ohio farms. But, of course, they are nothing of the kind; they are plantations, examples of the very society with which Page is concerned.

Americans are unable to deal with the plain fact that eight of our first twelve Presidents were the masters of plantations, not marginally but in their primary social identity, and resort to all sorts of subterfuges to thrust the fact from mind. But the essence of American nationality and American institutions lies in the plantation quite as much as in the New England town meeting, or more so. How do we reconcile this to the images that appear in *Roots* and a host of other less celebrated works?

It may be true that the plantation is something of another age and that it embodied evils that have now been happily surpassed; but that is not the whole story. Is it not better and truer to view the society that produced Washington and Jefferson and Lee in the light provided by Page than in the lurid colors of neoabolitionist melodrama?

And why is it, if the plantation is a place of horror, that even today its relics give us a sense of peace and order, of communion with the roots of our society and a better past, while the vast expanses of modern urban democracy and egalitarianism give us only a sense of unease? We approach here some profound regions of the American soul, however strenuously denied, of which Page is the artistic medium.

Page's world is indeed an idealistic world, not likely to satisfy such modern types as the pragmatist, the utilitarian, the ideologue, or the cynic. And it is true that at times in his work such qualities as honor, duty, courage, and sacrifice approach an unpersuasive abstraction. But not always.

For Page does present human qualities and aspirations and behaviors that really did exist at one time. We know that people with the virtues he portrays did live. The heroism in adversity, the tragic deaths by battle and fever, the extravagant chivalric gestures, the sensitive pride, the aristocratic ethics, the unswerving loyalty, the affections between masters and servants, all really did exist, no matter how much moderns may choose to disbelieve them. They can be abundantly documented, to the satisfaction of any honest observer, in the hard documentary record of thousands of Southern families. It is just that now historians prefer to emphasize other things.

For us Page has made, in fiction, a number of satisfying human characters, characters who give us hope in the potential of our nature and who are models that we badly need of grace, courage, and honor. They are far more persuasive and useful than any number of politicians' and social scientists' paeans to democracy and progress. In that sense, Page is not so outdated as some think, and in fact will never be outdated. And, as well, *In Ole Virginia* is full of just plain good tales, well told, which is what a book of stories should be.

CLYDE N. WILSON

In Ole Virginia

MARSE CHAN.

A TALE OF OLD VIRGINIA.

ONE afternoon, in the autumn of 1872, I was riding leisurely down the sandy road that winds
along the top of the water-shed between two of the
smaller rivers of eastern Virginia. The road I was
travelling, following " the ridge " for miles, had just
struck me as most significant of the character of the
race whose only avenue of communication with the
outside world it had formerly been. Their once
splendid mansions, now fast falling to decay, appeared to view from time to time, set back far from
the road, in proud seclusion, among groves of oak
and hickory, now scarlet and gold with the early
frost. Distance was nothing to this people ; time
was of no consequence to them. They desired but
a level path in life, and that they had, though the
way was longer, and the outer world strode by them
as they dreamed.

I was aroused from my reflections by hearing some
one ahead of me calling, " Heah !—heah—whoo-oop,
heah ! "

Turning the curve in the road, I saw just before
me a negro standing. with a hoe and a watering-pot

in his hand.　He had evidently just gotten over the
" worm-fence " into the road, out of the path which
led zigzag across the " old field " and was lost to
sight in the dense growth of sassafras.　When I rode
up, he was looking anxiously back down this path
for his dog.　So engrossed was he that he did not
even hear my horse, and I reined in to wait until he
should turn around and satisfy my curiosity as to
the handsome old place half a mile off from the
road.

The numerous out-buildings and the large barns
and stables told that it had once been the seat of
wealth, and the wild waste of sassafras that covered the broad fields gave it an air of desolation
that greatly excited my interest.　Entirely oblivi-
ous of my proximity, the negro went on calling
" Whoo-oop, heah ! " until along the path, walking
very slowly and with great dignity, appeared a
noble-looking old orange and white setter, gray
with age, and corpulent with excessive feeding.
As soon as he came in sight, his master began:

" Yes, dat you !　You gittin' deaf as well as bline,
I s'pose !　Kyarnt heah me callin', I reckon ?
Whyn't yo' come on, dawg ? "

The setter sauntered slowly up to the fence and
stopped, without even deigning a look at the speaker, who immediately proceeded to take the rails
down, talking meanwhile :

" Now, I got to pull down de gap, I s'pose !　Yo'

so sp'ilt yo' kyahn hardly walk. Jes' ez able to git over it as I is! Jes' like white folks—think 'cuz you's white and I's black, I got to wait on yo' all de time. Ne'm mine, I ain' gwi' do it!"

The fence having been pulled down sufficiently low to suit his dogship, he marched sedately through, and, with a hardly perceptible lateral movement of his tail, walked on down the road. Putting up the rails carefully, the negro turned and saw me.

"Sarvent, marster," he said, taking his hat off. Then, as if apologetically for having permitted a stranger to witness what was merely a family affair, he added : " He know I don' mean nothin' by what I sez. He's Marse Chan's dawg, an' he's so ole he kyahn git long no pearter. He know I'se jes' prod-jickin' wid 'im."

"Who is Marse Chan?" I asked; "and whose place is that over there, and the one a mile or two back—the place with the big gate and the carved stone pillars?"

"Marse Chan," said the darky, "he's Marse Channin'—my young marster; an' dem places—dis one's Weall's, an' de one back dyar wid de rock gate-pos's is ole Cun'l Chahmb'lin's. Dey don' nobody live dyar now, 'cep' niggers. Arfter de war some one or nurr bought our place, but his name done kind o' slipped me. I nuver hearn on 'im befo'; I think dey's half-strainers. I don' ax none on 'em no odds. I lives down de road heah, a little piece, an' I jes' steps down of a evenin' and looks arfter de graves."

"Well, where is Marse Chan?" I asked.

"Hi! don' you know? Marse Chan, he went in de army. I was wid im. Yo' know he warn' gwine an' lef' Sam."

"Will you tell me all about it?" I said, dismounting.

Instantly, and as if by instinct, the darky stepped forward and took my bridle. I demurred a little; but with a bow that would have honored old Sir Roger, he shortened the reins, and taking my horse from me, led him along.

"Now tell me about Marse Chan," I said.

"Lawd, marster, hit's so long ago, I'd a'most forgit all about it, ef I hedn' been wid him ever sence he wuz born. Ez 'tis, I remembers it jes' like 'twuz yistiddy. Yo' know Marse Chan an' me—we wuz boys togerr. I wuz older'n he wuz, jes' de same ez he wuz whiter'n me. I wuz born plantin' corn time, de spring arfter big Jim an' de six steers got washed away at de upper ford right down dyar b'low de quarters ez he wuz a bringin' de Chris'mas things home; an' Marse Chan, he warn' born tell mos' to de harves' arfter my sister Nancy married Cun'l Chahmb'lin's Torm, 'bout eight years arfterwoods.

"Well, when Marse Chan wuz born, dey wuz de grettes' doin's at home you ever did see. De folks

all hed holiday, jes' like in de Chris'mas. Ole
marster (we didn' call 'im *ole* marster tell arfter
Marse Chan wuz born—befo' dat he wuz jes' de
marster, so)—well, ole marster, his face fyar shine
wid pleasure, an' all de folks wuz mighty glad, too,
'cause dey all loved ole marster, and aldo' dey did
step aroun' right peart when ole marster was lookin'
at 'em, dyar warn' nyar han' on de place but what,
ef he wanted anythin', would walk up to de back
poach, an' say he warn' to see de marster. An'
ev'ybody wuz talkin' 'bout de young marster, an'
de maids an' de wimmens 'bout de kitchen wuz
sayin' how 'twuz de purties' chile dey ever see ; an'
at dinner-time de mens (all on 'em hed holiday)
come roun' de poach an' ax how de missis an' de
young marster wuz, an' ole marster come out on de
poach an' smile wus'n a 'possum, an' sez, ' Thankee!
Bofe doin' fust rate, boys ; ' an' den he stepped
back in de house, sort o' laughin' to hisse'f, an' in
a minute he come out ag'in wid de baby in he
arms, all wrapped up in flannens an' things, an' sez,
' Heah he is, boys.' All de folks den, dey went up
on de poach to look at 'im, drappin' dey hats on de
steps, an' scrapin' dey feets ez dey went up. An'
pres'n'y ole marster, lookin' down at we all chil'en
all packed togerr down dyah like a parecel o' sheep-
burrs, cotch sight o' *me* (he knowed my name,
'cause I use' to hole he hoss fur 'im sometimes ; but
he didn' know all de chil'en by name, dey wuz so

many on 'em), an' he sez, 'Come up heah.' So up
I goes tippin', skeered like, an' old marster sez,
'Ain' you Mymie's son?' 'Yass, seh,' sez I. 'Well,'
sez he, 'I'm gwine to give you to yo' young Marse
Channin' to be his body-servant,' an' he put de
baby right in my arms (it's de truth I'm tellin'
yo'!), an' yo' jes' ought to a-heard de folks sayin',
'Lawd! marster, dat boy'll drap dat chile!' 'Naw,
he won't,' sez marster; 'I kin trust 'im.' And den
he sez: 'Now, Sam, from dis time you belong to
yo' young Marse Channin'; I wan' you to tek keer
on 'im ez long ez he lives. You are to be his boy
from dis time. An' now,' he sez, 'carry 'im in de
house.' An' he walks arfter me an' opens de do's
fur me, an' I kyars 'im in my arms, an' lays 'im
down on de bed. An from dat time I was tooken
in de house to be Marse Channin's body-servant.

"Well, you nuver see a chile grow so. Pres'n'y
he growed up right big, an' ole marster sez he must
have some edication. So he sont 'im to school
to ole Miss Lawry down dyar, dis side o' Cun'l
Chahmb'lin's, an' I use' to go 'long wid 'im an' tote
he books an' we all's snacks; an' when he larnt to
read an' spell right good, an' got 'bout so-o big,
ole Miss Lawry she died, an' ole marster said he
mus' have a man to teach 'im an' trounce 'im. So
we all went to Mr. Hall, whar kep' de school-house
beyant de creek, an' dyar we went ev'y day, 'cep

Sat'd'ys of co'se, an' sich days ez Marse Chan din' warn' go, an' ole missis begged 'im off.

"Hit wuz down dyar Marse Chan fust took no-tice o' Miss Anne. Mr. Hall, he taught gals ez well ez boys, an' Cun'l Chahmb'lin he sont his daughter (dat's Miss Anne I'm talkin' about). She wuz a leetle bit o' gal when she fust come. Yo' see, her ma wuz dead, an' ole Miss Lucy Chahmb'lin, she lived wid her brurr an' kep' house for 'im; an' he wuz so busy wid politics, he didn' have much time to spyar, so he sont Miss Anne to Mr. Hall's by a 'ooman wid a note. When she come dat day in de school-house, an' all de chil'en looked at her so hard, she tu'n right red, an' tried to pull her long curls over her eyes, an' den put bofe de backs of her little han's in her two eyes, an' begin to cry to herse'f. Marse Chan he was settin' on de een' o' de bench nigh de do', an' he jes' reached out an' put he arm roun' her an' drawed her up to 'im. An' he kep' whisperin' to her, an' callin' her name, an' coddlin' her; an' pres'n'y she took her han's down an' begin to laugh.

"Well, dey 'peared to tek' a gre't fancy to each urr from dat time. Miss Anne she warn' nuthin' but a baby hardly, an' Marse Chan he wuz a good big boy 'bout mos' thirteen years ole, I reckon. Hows'ever, dey sut'n'y wuz sot on each urr an' (yo' heah me!) ole marster an' Cun'l Chahmb'lin dey 'peared to like it 'bout well ez de chil'en. Yo' see, Cun'l Chahmb'lin's place j'ined ourn, an' it looked jes' ez natural fur dem two chil'en to marry an' mek it one plantation, ez it did fur de creek to run down de bottom from our place into Cun'l Chahmb'lin's. I don' rightly think de chil'en thought 'bout gittin' *married,* not den, no mo'n I thought 'bout marryin' Judy when she wuz a little gal at Cun'l Chahmb'lin's, runnin' 'bout de house, huntin' fur Miss Lucy's spectacles; but dey wuz good frien's from de start. Marse Chan he use' to kyar Miss Anne's books fur her ev'y day, an' ef de road wuz muddy or she wuz tired, he use' to tote her; an' 'twarn' hardly a day passed dat he didn' kyar her some'n' to school—apples or hick'y nuts, or some'n. He wouldn' let none o' de chil'en tease her, nurr. Heh! One day, one o' de boys poked he finger at Miss Anne, and arfter school Marse Chan he axed 'im 'roun' hine de school-house out o' sight, an' ef he didn' whop 'im!

"Marse Chan, he wuz de peartes' scholar ole Mr. Hall hed, an' Mr. Hall he wuz mighty proud o' 'im. I don' think he use' to beat 'im ez much ez he did de urrs, aldo' he wuz de head in all debilment dat went on, jes' ez he wuz in sayin' he lessons.

"Heh! one day in summer, jes' fo' de school broke up, dyah come up a storm right sudden, an' riz de creek (dat one yo' cross' back yonder), an Marse Chan he toted Miss Anne home on he back. He ve'y off'n did dat when de parf wuz muddy

But dis day when dey come to de creek, it had done washed all de logs 'way. 'Twuz still mighty high, so Marse Chan he put Miss Anne down, an' he took a pole an' waded right in. Hit took 'im long up to de shoulders. Den he waded back, an' took Miss Anne up on his head an' kyared her right over. At fust she wuz skeered; but he tol' her he could swim an' wouldn' let her git hu't, an' den she let 'im kyar her 'cross, she hol'in' his han's. I warn' 'long dat day, but he sut'n'y did dat thing.

"Ole marster he wuz so pleased 'bout it, he giv' Marse Chan a pony; an' Marse Chan rode 'im to school de day arfter he come, so proud, an' sayin' how he wuz gwine to let Anne ride behine 'im; an' when he come home dat evenin' he wuz walkin'. 'Hi! where's yo' pony?' said ole marster. 'I give 'im to Anne,' says Marse Chan. 'She liked 'im, an' —I kin walk.' 'Yes,' sez ole marster, laughin', 'I s'pose you's already done giv' her yo'se'f, an' nex' thing I know you'll be givin' her this plantation and all my niggers.'

"Well, about a fortnight or sich a matter arfter dat, Cun'l Chahmb'lin sont over an' invited all o' we all over to dinner, an' Marse Chan wuz 'spressly named in de note whar Ned brought; an' arfter dinner he made ole Phil, whar wuz his ker'ige-driver, bring roun' Marse Chan's pony wid a little side-saddle on 'im, an' a beautiful little hoss wid a bran'-new saddle an' bridle on 'im; an' he gits up

an' meks Marse Chan a gre't speech, an' presents
'im de little hoss; an' den he calls Miss Anne, an'
she comes out on de poach in a little ridin' frock,
an' dey puts her on her pony, an' Marse Chan
mounts his hoss, an' dey goes to ride, while de
grown folks is a-laughin' an' chattin' an' smokin'
dey cigars.

"Dem wuz good ole times, marster—de bes' Sam
ever see! Dey wuz, in fac'! Niggers didn' hed
nothin' 't all to do—jes' hed to 'ten' to de feedin'
an' cleanin' de hosses, an' doin' what de marster tell
'em to do; an' when dey wuz sick, dey had things
sont 'em out de house, an' de same doctor come to
see 'em whar 'ten' to de white folks when dey wuz
po'ly. Dyar warn' no trouble nor nothin'.

"Well, things tuk a change arfter dat. Marse
Chan he went to de bo'din' school, whar he use' to
write to me constant. Ole missis use' to read me
de letters, an' den I'd git Miss Anne to read 'em
ag'in to me when I'd see her. He use' to write to
her too, an' she use' to write to him too. Den Miss
Anne she wuz sont off to school too. An' in de
summer time dey'd bofe come home, an' yo' hardly
knowed whether Marse Chan lived at home or over
at Cun'l Chahmb'lin's. He wuz over dyah constant.
'Twuz always ridin' or fishin' down dyah in de
river; or sometimes he' go over dyah, an' 'im an'
she'd go out an' set in de yard onder de trees; she
settin' up mekin' out she wuz knittin' some sort o'

bright-cullored some'n', wid de grarss growin all up
'g'inst her, an' her hat th'owed back on her neck,
an' he readin' to her out books; an' sometimes
dey'd bofe read out de same book, fust one an' den
todder. I use' to see 'em! Dat wuz when dey wuz
growin' up like.

"Den ole marster he run for Congress, an' ole
Cun'l Chahmb'lin he wuz put up to run 'g'inst ole
marster by de Dimicrats; but ole marster he beat
'im. Yo' know he wuz gwine do dat! Co'se he
wuz! Dat made ole Cun'l Chahmb'lin mighty
mad, and dey stopt visitin' each urr reg'lar, like dey
had been doin' all 'long. Den Cun'l Chahmb'lin he
sort o' got in debt, an' sell some o' he niggers, an'
dat's de way de fuss begun. Dat's whar de lawsuit
cum from. Ole marster he didn' like nobody to sell
niggers, an' knowin' dat Cun'l Chahmb'lin wuz sell-
in' o' his, he writ an' offered to buy his M'ria an' all
her chil'en, 'cause she hed married our Zeek'yel.
An' don' yo' think, Cun'l Chahmb'lin axed ole marster mo' 'n th'ee niggers wuz wuth fur M'ria! Befo'
old marster bought her, dough, de sheriff cum an'
levelled on M'ria an' a whole parecel o' urr niggers. Ole marster he went to de sale, an' bid for
'em; but Cun'l Chahmb'lin he got some one to bid
'g'inst ole marster. Dey wuz knocked out to ole
marster dough, an' den dey hed a big lawsuit, an'
ole marster wuz agwine to co't, off an' on, fur some
years, till at lars' de co't decided dat M'ria belonged

to ole marster. Ole Cun'l Chahmb'lin den wuz so
mad he sued ole marster for a little strip o' lan'
down dyah on de line fence, whar he said belonged
to 'im. Evy'body knowed hit belonged to ole marster. Ef yo' go down dyah now, I kin show it to yo',
inside de line fence, whar it hed done bin ever
since long befo' Cun'l Chahmb'lin wuz born. But
Cun'l Chahmb'lin wuz a mons'us perseverin' man,
an' ole marster he wouldn' let nobody run over im.
No, dat he wouldn'! So dey wuz agwine down to
co't about dat, fur I don' know how long, till ole
marster beat 'im.

"All dis time, yo' know, Marse Chan wuz agoin'
back'ads an' for'ads to college, an' wuz growed up a
ve'y fine young man. He wuz a ve'y likely gent'-
man! Miss Anne she hed done mos' growed up
too—wuz puttin' her hyar up like ole missis use' to
put hers up, an' 't wuz jes' ez bright ez de sorrel's
mane when de sun cotch on it, an' her eyes wuz
gre't big dark eyes, like her pa's, on'y bigger an' not
so fierce, an' 'twarn' none o' de young ladies ez
purty ez she wuz. She an' Marse Chan still set a
heap o' sto' by one 'nurr, but I don' think dey
wuz easy wid each urr ez when he used to tote
her home from school on his back. Marse Chan he
use' to love de ve'y groun' she walked on, dough,
in my 'pinion. Heh! His face 'twould light up
whenever she come into chu'ch, or anywhere, jes'
like de sun hed come th'oo a chink on it suddenly.

"Den ole marster lost he eyes. D' yo' ever heah
'bout dat? Heish! Didn' yo'? Well, one night
de big barn cotch fire. De stables, yo' know, wuz
under de big barn, an' all de hosses wuz in dyah.
Hit 'peared to me like 'twarn' no time befo' all de
folks an' de neighbors dey come, an' dey wuz a-totin'
water, an' a-tryin' to save de po' critters, and dey
got a heap on 'em out; but de ker'ige-hosses dey
wouldn' come out, an' dey wuz a-runnin' back'ads
an' for'ads inside de stalls, a-nikerin' an' a-screamin',
like dey knowed dey time hed come. Yo' could
heah 'em so pitiful, an' pres'n'y old marster said to
Ham Fisher (he wuz de ker'ige-driver), ' Go in dyah
an' try to save 'em; don' let 'em bu'n to death.'
An' Ham he went right in. An' jest arfter he got
in, de shed whar it hed fus' cotch fell in, an' de
sparks shot 'way up in de air; an' Ham didn' come
back, an' de fire begun to lick out under de eaves
over whar de ker'ige hosses' stalls wuz, an' all of a
sudden ole marster tu'ned an' kissed ole missis, who
wuz standin' nigh him, wid her face jes' ez white ez
a sperit's, an', befo' anybody knowed what he wuz
gwine do, jumped right in de do', an' de smoke
come po'in' out behine 'im. Well, seh, I nuver
'spects to heah tell Judgment sich a soun' ez de
folks set up! Ole missis she jes' drapt down on her
knees in de mud an' prayed out loud. Hit 'peared
like her pra'r wuz heard; for in a minit, right out
de same do', kyarin' Ham Fisher in his arms, come

ole marster, wid his clo's all blazin . Dey flung
water on 'im, an' put 'im out ; an', ef you b'lieve
me, yo' wouldn' a-knowed 'twuz ole marster. Yo'
see, he hed find Ham Fisher done fall down in de
smoke right by the ker'ige-hoss' stalls, whar he sont
him, an' he hed to tote 'im back in his arms th'oo
de fire what hed done cotch de front part o' de
stable, and to keep de flame from gittin' down
Ham Fisher's th'ote he hed tuk off his own hat and
mashed it all over Ham Fisher's face, an' he hed
kep' Ham Fisher from bein' so much bu'nt ; but *he*
wuz bu'nt dreadful! His beard an' hyar wuz all
nyawed off, an' his face an' han's an' ı.eck wuz scor-
ified terrible. Well, he jes' laid Ham Fisher down,
an' then he kind o' staggered for'ad, an' ole missis
ketch' 'im in her arms. Ham Fisher, he warn'
bu'nt so bad, an' he got out in a month or two ; an'
arfter a long time, ole marster he got well, too ; but
he wuz always stone blind arfter thaı. He nuver
could see none from dat night.

"Marse Chan he comed home from college toreckly, an' he sut'n'y did nuss ole marster faithful—
jes' like a 'ooman. Den he took charge of de plantation arfter dat ; an' I use' to wait on 'im jes' like
when we wuz boys togedder ; an' sometimes we'd slip
off an' have a fox-hunt, an' he'd be jes' like he wuz
in ole times, befo' ole marster got bline, an' Miss
Anne Chahmb'lin stopt comin' over to our house,
an' settin' onder de trees, readin' out de same book.

"He sut'n'y wuz good to me. Nothin' nuver made no diffunce 'bout dat. He nuver hit me a lick in his life—an' nuver let nobody else do it, nurr.

"I 'members one day, when he wuz a leetle bit o' boy, ole marster hed done tole we all chil'en not to slide on de straw-stacks; an' one day me an' Marse Chan thought ole marster hed done gone 'way from home. We watched him git on he hoss an' ride up de road out o' sight, an' we wuz out in de field a-slidin' an a-slidin', when up comes ole marster. We started to run; but he hed done see us, an' he called us to come back; an' sich a whuppin' ez he did gi' us!

"Fust he took Marse Chan, an' den he teched me up. He nuver hu't me, but in co'se I wuz a-hollerin' ez hard ez I could stave it, 'cause I knowed dat wuz gwine mek him stop. Marse Chan he hed'n open he mouf long ez ole marster wuz tunin' 'im; but soon ez he commence warmin' me an' I begin to holler, Marse Chan he bu'st out cryin', an' stept right in befo' ole marster, an' ketchin' de whup, sed:

"'Stop, seh! Yo' sha'n't whup 'im; he b'longs to me, an' ef you hit 'im another lick I'll set 'im free!'

"I wish yo' hed see ole marster. Marse Chan he warn' mo'n eight years ole, an' dyah dey wuz—old marster stan'in' wid he whup raised up, an' Marse

Chan red an' cryin', hol'in' on to it, an' sayin' I b'longst to 'im.

"Ole marster, he raise' de whup, an' den he drapt it, an' broke out in a smile over he face, an' he chuck' Marse Chan onder de chin, an' tu'n right roun' an' went away, laughin' to hisse'f, an' I heah' 'im tellin' ole missis dat evenin', an' laughin' 'bout it.

"'Twan' so mighty long arfter dat when dey fust got to talkin' 'bout de war. Dey wuz a-dictatin' back'ads an' for'ds 'bout it fur two or th'ee years 'fo' it come sho' nuff, you know. Ole marster, he was a Whig, an' of co'se Marse Chan he tuk after he pa. Cun'l Chahmb'lin, he wuz a Dimicrat. He wuz in favor of de war, an' ole marster and Marse Chan dey wuz agin' it. Dey wuz a-talkin' 'bout it all de time, an' purty soon Cun'l Chahmb'lin he went about ev'vywhar speakin' an' noratin' 'bout Ferginia ought to secede; an' Marse Chan he wuz picked up to talk agin' 'im. Dat wuz de way dey come to fight de duil. I sut'n'y wuz skeered fur Marse Chan dat mawnin', an' he was jes' ez cool! Yo' see, it hap- pen so: Marse Chan he wuz a-speakin' down at de Deep Creek Tavern, an' he kind o' got de bes' of ole Cun'l Chahmb'lin. All de white folks laughed an' hoorawed, an' ole Cun'l Chahmb'lin—my Lawd! I t'ought he'd 'a' bu'st, he was so mad. Well, when it come to his time to speak, he jes' light into Marse Chan. He call 'im a traitor, an' a ab'litionis', an' I don' know what all. Marse Chan, he jes' kep' cool till de ole Cun'l light into he pa. Ez soon ez he name ole marster, I seen Marse Chan sort o' lif' up he head. D' yo' ever see a hoss rar he head up right sudden at night when he see somethin' comin' to'ds 'im from de side an' he don' know what 'tis? Ole Cun'l Chahmb'lin he went right on. He said ole marster hed taught Marse Chan; dat ole marstei wuz a wuss ab'litionis' dan he son. I looked at Marse Chan, an' sez to myse'f: 'Fo' Gord! old Cun'l Chahmb'lin better min', an' I hedn' got de wuds out, when ole Cun'l Chahmb'lin 'cuse' old marster o' cheatin' 'im out o' he niggers, an' stealin' piece o' he lan'—dat's de lan' I tole you 'bout. Well, seh, nex' thing I knowed, I heahed Marse Chan—hit all happen right 'long togerr, like lightnin' and thunder when they hit right at you—I heah 'im say:

"'Cun'l Chahmb'lin, what you say is false, an' yo' know it to be so. You have wilfully slandered one of de pures' an' nobles' men Gord ever made, an' nothin' but yo' gray hyars protects you.'

"Well, ole Cun'l Chahmb'lin, he ra'ed an' he pitch'd. He said he wan' too ole, an' he'd show 'im so.

"'Ve'y well,' says Marse Chan.

"De meetin broke up den. I wuz hol'in' de hosses out dyar in de road by de een' o' de poach, an' I see Marse Chan talkin' an' talkin' to Mr. Gordon an' anudder gent'man, and den he come out an' got on de sorrel an' galloped off. Soon ez he got

out o' sight he pulled up, an' we walked along tell
we come to de road whar leads off to'ds Mr. Barbour's. He wuz de big lawyer o' de country. Dar
he tu'ned off. All dis time he hedn' sed a wud, 'cep'
to kind o' mumble to hisse'f now and den. When
we got to Mr. Barbour's, he got down an' went in.
Dat wuz in de late winter; de folks wuz jes' be-
ginnin' to plough fur corn. He stayed dyar 'bout
two hours, an' when he come out Mr. Barbour come
out to de gate wid 'im an' shake han's arfter he got
up in de saddle. Den we all rode off. 'Twuz late
den—good dark; an' we rid ez hard ez we could,
tell we come to de ole school-house at ole Cun'l
Chahmb'lin's gate. When we got dar, Marse Chan
got down an' walked right slow 'roun' de house.
Arfter lookin' roun' a little while an' tryin' de do' to
see ef it wuz shet, he walked down de road tell he
got to de creek. He stop' dyar a little while an'
picked up two or three little rocks an' frowed 'em
in, an' pres'n'y he got up an' we come on home. Ez
he got down, he tu'ned to me an', rubbin' de sorrel's
nose, said : ' Have 'em well fed, Sam ; I'll want 'em
early in de mawnin'.'

"Dat night at supper he laugh an' talk, an' he set
at de table a long time. Arfter ole marster went to
bed, he went in de charmber an' set on de bed by 'im
talkin' to 'im an' tellin' 'im 'bout de meetin' an' e'vy-
thing ; but he nuver mention ole Cun'l Chahmb'lin's
name. When he got up to come out to de office in

de yard, whar he slept, he stooped down an' kissed
'im jes' like he wuz a baby layin' dyar in de bed, an'
he'd hardly let ole missis go at all. I knowed some'n
wuz up, an' nex mawnin' I called 'im early befo' light,
like he tole me, an' he dressed an' come out pres'n'y
jes' like he wuz goin' to church. I had de hosses ready,
an' we went out de back way to'ds de river. Ez we
rode along, he said :

"'Sam, you an' I wuz boys togedder, wa'n't we?'

"'Yes,' sez I, 'Marse Chan, dat we wuz.'

"'You have been ve'y faithful to me,' sez he, 'an'
I have seen to it that you are well provided fur.
You want to marry Judy, I know, an' you'll be able
to buy her ef you want to.'

"Den he tole me he wuz goin' to fight a duil, an'
in case he should git shot, he had set me free an'
giv' me nuff to tek keer o' me an' my wife ez long ez
we lived. He said he'd like me to stay an' tek keer
o' ole marster an' ole missis ez long ez dey lived, an'
he said it wouldn' be very long, he reckoned. Dat
wuz de on'y time he voice broke—when he said
dat ; an' I couldn' speak a wud, my th'oat choked
me so.

"When we come to de river, we tu'ned right up
de bank, an' arfter ridin' 'bout a mile or sich a matter, we stopped whar dey wuz a little clearin' wid
elder bushes on one side an' two big gum-trees on
de urr, an' de sky wuz all red, an' de water down
to'ds whar the sun wuz comin' wuz jes' like de sky.

"Pres'n'y Mr. Gordon he come, wid a 'hogany box 'bout so big 'fore 'im, an' he got down, an' Marse Chan tole me to tek all de hosses an' go 'roun' behine de bushes whar I tell you 'bout—off to one side; an' 'fore I got 'roun' dar, ole Cun'l Chahmb'lin an' Mr. Hennin an' Dr. Call come ridin' from t'urr way, to'ds ole Cun'l Chahmb'lin's. When dey hed tied dey hosses, de urr gent'mens went up to whar Mr. Gordon wuz, an' arfter some chattin' Mr. Hennin step' off 'bout fur ez 'cross dis road, or mebbe it mout be a little furder; an' den I seed 'em th'oo de bushes loadin' de pistils, an' talk a little while; an' den Marse Chan an' ole Cun'l Chahmb'lin walked up wid de pistils in dey han's, an' Marse Chan he stood wid his face right to'ds de sun. I seen it shine on him ies' ez it come up over de low groun's, an' he look like he did sometimes when he come out of church. I wuz so skeered I couldn' say nothin'. Ole Cun'l Chahmb'lin could shoot fust rate, an' Marse Chan he never missed.

"Den I heared Mr. Gordon say, 'Gent'mens, is yo' ready?' and bofe of 'em sez, 'Ready,' jes' so.

"An' he sez, 'Fire, one, two'—an' ez he said 'one,' ole Cun'l Chahmb'lin raised he pistil an' shot right at Marse Chan. De ball went th'oo nis hat. I seen he hat sort o' settle on he head ez de bullit hit it, an' *he* jes' tilted his pistil up in de a'r an'

shot—*bang;* an' ez de pistil went *bang,* he sez to
Cun'l Chahmb'lin, 'I mek you a present to yo'
fam'ly, seh!'

"Well, dey had some talkin' arfter dat. I didn't
git rightly what it wuz; but it 'peared like Cun'l
Chahmb'lin he warn't satisfied, an' wanted to have
anurr shot. De seconds dey wuz talkin', an'
pres'n'y dey put de pistils up, an' Marse Chan an'
Mr. Gordon shook han's wid Mr. Hennin an' Dr.
Call, an' come an' got on dey hosses. An' Cun'l
Chahmb'lin he got on his horse an' rode away wid
de urr gent'mens, lookin' like he did de day befo'
when all de people laughed at 'im.

"I b'lieve ole Cun'l Chahmb'lin wan' to shoot
Marse Chan, anyway!

"We come on home to breakfast, I totin' de box
wid de pistils befo' me on de roan. Would you
b'lieve me, seh, Marse Chan he nuver said a wud
'bout it to ole marster or nobody. Ole missis didn'
fin' out 'bout it for mo'n a month, an' den, Lawd!
how she did cry and kiss Marse Chan ; an' ole marster, aldo' he never say much, he wuz jes' ez please'
ez ole missis. He call' me in de room an' made me
tole 'im all 'bout it, an' when I got th'oo he gi' me
five dollars an' a pyar of breeches.

"But ole Cun'l Chahmb'lin he nuver did furgive
Marse Chan, an' Miss Anne she got mad too. Wimmens is mons'us onreasonable nohow. Dey's jes'
like a catfish: you can n' tek hole on 'em like

udder folks, an' when you gits 'm yo' can n' always hole 'em.

" What meks me think so ? Heaps o' things— dis : Marse Chan he done gi' Miss Anne her pa jes' ez good ez I gi' Marse Chan's dawg sweet 'taters, an' she git mad wid 'im ez if he hed kill 'im 'stid o' sen'in' 'im back to her dat mawnin' whole an' soun'. B'lieve me! she wouldn' even speak to him arfter dat !

" Don' I 'member dat mawnin' !

" We wuz gwine fox-huntin', 'bout six weeks or sich a matter arfter de duil, an' we met Miss Anne ridin' 'long wid anurr lady an' two gent'mens whar wuz stayin' at her house. Dyar wuz always some one or nurr dyar co'ting her. Well, dat mawnin' we meet 'em right in de road. 'Twuz de fust time Marse Chan had see her sence de duil, an' he raises he hat ez he pahss, an' she looks right at 'im wid her head up in de yair like she nuver see 'im befo' in her born days ; an' when she comes by me, she sez, ' Good-mawnin', Sam ! ' Gord ! I nuver see nuthin' like de look dat come on Marse Chan's face when she pahss 'im like dat. He gi' de sorrel a pull dat fotch 'im back settin' down in de san' on he hanches. He ve'y lips wuz white. I tried to keep up wid 'im, but 'twarn' no use. He sont me back home pres'n'y, an' he rid on. I sez to myself, ' Cun'l Chahmb'lin, don' yo' meet Marse Chan dis mawnin'. He ain' bin lookin' 'roun' de ole school-house, whar he an' Miss Anne use' to go to school to ole Mr. Hall together, fur nuffin'. He won' stan' no prodjickin' to-day.'

" He nuver come home dat night tell 'way late, an' ef he'd been fox-huntin' it mus' ha' been de ole red whar lives down in de greenscum mashes he'd been chasin'. De way de sorrel wuz gormed up wid sweat an' mire sut'n'y did hu't me. He walked up to de stable wid he head down all de way, an' I'se seen 'im go eighty miles of a winter day, an' prance into de stable at night ez fresh ez ef he hed jes' cantered over to ole Cun'l Chahmb'lin's to supper. I nuver seen a hoss beat so sence I knowed de fetlock from de fo'lock, an' bad ez he wuz he wan' ez bad ez Marse Chan.

" Whew! he didn' git over dat thing, seh—he nuver did git over it.

" De war come on jes' den, an Marse Chan wuz elected cap'n ; but he wouldn' tek it. He said Firginia hadn' seceded, an' he wuz gwine stan' by her. Den dey 'lected Mr. Gordon cap'n.

" I sut'n'y did wan' Marse Chan to tek de place, cuz I knowed he wuz gwine tek me wid 'im. He wan' gwine widout Sam. An' beside, he look so po' an' thin, I thought he wuz gwine die.

" Of co'se, ole missis she heared 'bout it, an' she met Miss Anne in de road, an' cut her jes' like Miss Anne cut Marse Chan.

" Ole missis, she wuz proud ez anybody ! So we

wuz mo' strangers dan ef we hadn' live' in a hunderd miles of each urr. An' Marse Chan he wuz
gittin' thinner an' thinner, an' Firginia she come out,
an' den Marse Chan he went to Richmond an' listed,
an' come back an' sey he wuz a private, an' he didn'
know whe'r he could tek me or not. He writ to
Mr. Gordon, hows'ever, an' 'twuz 'cided dat when he
went I wuz to go 'long an' wait on him an' de cap'n
too. I didn' min' dat, yo' know, long ez I could go
wid Marse Chan, an' I like' Mr. Gordon, anyways.

"Well, one night Marse Chan come back from
de offis wid a telegram dat say, 'Come at once,' so
he wuz to start nex' mawnin'. He uniform wuz all
ready, gray wid yaller trimmin's, an' mine wuz
ready too, an' he had ole marster's sword, whar de
State gi' 'im in de Mexikin war ; an' he trunks wuz
all packed wid ev'rything in 'em, an' my chist was
packed too, an' Jim Rasher he druv 'em over to de
depo' in de waggin, an' we wuz to start nex' mawnin'
'bout light. Dis wuz 'bout de las' o' spring, you
know. Dat night ole missis made Marse Chan
dress up in he uniform, an' he sut'n'y did look
splendid, wid he long mustache an' he wavin' hyar
an' he tall figger.

"Arfter supper he come down an' sez : 'Sam, I
wan' you to tek dis note an' kyar it over to Cun'l
Chahmb'lin's, an' gi' it to Miss Anne wid yo' own
han's, an' bring me wud what she sez. Don' let

any one know 'bout it, or know why you've gone.'
'Yes, seh,' sez I.

"Yo' see, I knowed Miss Anne's maid over at ole
Cun'l Chahmb'lin's—dat wuz Judy whar is my wife
now—an' I knowed I could wuk it. So I tuk de
roan an' rid over, an' tied 'im down de hill in de
cedars, an' I wen' 'roun' to de back yard. 'Twuz a
right blowy sort ɔ' night ; de moon wuz jes' risin',
but de clouds wuz so big it didn' shine 'cep' th'oo a
crack now an' den. I soon foun' my gal, an' arfter
tellin' her two or three lies 'bout herse'f, I got her
to go in an' ax Miss Anne to come to de do'. When
she come, I gi' her de note, an' arfter a little while
she bro't me anurr, an' I tole her good-by, an'
she gi' me a dollar, an' I come home an' gi' de letter
to Marse Chan. He read it, an' tole me to have de
hosses ready at twenty minits to twelve at de corner
of de garden. An' jes' befo' dat he come out ez ef
he wuz gwine to bed, but instid he come, an' we all
struck out to'ds Cun'l Chahmb'lin's. When we got
mos' to de gate, de hosses got sort o' skeered, an' I
see dey wuz some'n or somebody standin' jes' inside ; an' Marse Chan he jumpt off de sorrel an'
flung me de bridle and he walked up.

"She spoke fust ('twuz Miss Anne had done come
out dyar to meet Marse Chan), an' she sez, jes' ez
cold ez a chill, ' Well, seh, I granted your favor. I
wished to relieve myse'f of de obligations you placed
me under a few months ago, when you made me a

present of my father, whom you fust insulted an
then prevented from gittin' satisfaction.'

" Marse Chan he didn' speak fur a minit, an' den
he said: 'Who is with you?' (Dat wuz ev'y wud.)

"'No one,' sez she; 'I came alone.'

"' My God!' sez he, 'you didn' come all through
those woods by yourse'f at this time o' night?'

"'Yes, I'm not afraid,' sez she. (An' heah dis
nigger! I don' b'lieve she wuz.)

" De moon come out, an' I cotch sight o' her
stan'in' dyar in her white dress, wid de cloak she
had wrapped herse'f up in drapped off on de groun',
an' she didn' look like she wuz 'feared o' nuthin'.
She wuz mons'us purty ez she stood dyar wid de
green bushes behine her, an' she hed jes' a few
flowers in her breas'—right hyah—and some leaves
in her sorrel hyar; an' de moon come out an' shined
down on her hyar an' her frock, an' 'peared like de
light wuz jes' stan'in' off it ez she stood dyar lookin'
at Marse Chan wid her head tho'd back, jes' like dat
mawnin' when she pahss Marse Chan in de road
widout speakin' to 'im, an' sez to me, ' Good mawnin', Sam.'

" Marse Chan, he den tole her he hed come to
say good-by to her, ez he wuz gwine 'way to de war
nex' mawnin'. I wuz watchin' on her, an' I tho't,
when Marse Chan tole her dat, she sort o' started
an' looked up at 'im like she wuz mighty sorry, an'
'peared like she didn' stan' quite so straight arfter

dat. Den Marse Chan he went on talkin' right fars
to her; an' he tole her how he had loved her ever
sence she wuz a little bit o' baby mos', an' how he
nuver 'membered de time when he hedn' 'spected
to marry her. He tole her it wuz his love for her
dat hed made 'im stan' fust at school an' collige,
an' hed kep' 'im good an' pure; an' now he wuz
gwine 'way, wouldn' she let it be like 'twuz in ole
times, an' ef he come back from de war wouldn' she
try to think on him ez she use' to do when she wuz
a little guirl?

"Marse Chan he had done been talkin' so serious,
he hed done tuk Miss Anne's han', an' wuz lookin'
down in her face like he wuz list'nin' wid his eyes.

"Arfter a minit Miss Anne she said somethin',
an' Marse Chan he cotch her urr han' an' sez:

"'But if you love me, Anne?'

"When he said dat, she tu'ned her head 'way
from 'im, an' wait' a minit, an' den she said—right
clear:

"'But I don' love yo'.' (Jes' dem th'ee wuds!)
De wuds fall right slow—like dirt falls out a spade
on a coffin when yo's buryin' anybody, an' seys,
'Uth to uth.' Marse Chan he jes' let her hand
drap, an' he stiddy hisse'f 'g'inst de gate-pos', an' he
didn' speak torekly. When he did speak, all he sez
wuz:

"'I mus' see you home safe.'

"I 'clar, marster, I didn' know 'twuz Marse

Chan's voice tell I look at 'im right good. Well,
she wouldn' let 'im go wid her. She jes' wrap' her
cloak 'roun' her shoulders, an' wen' 'long back by
herse'f, widout doin' more'n jes' look up once at
Marse Chan leanin' dyah 'g'inst de gate-pos' in he
sodger clo's, wid he eyes on de groun'. She said
'Good-by' sort o' sorf, an' Marse Chan, widout
lookin' up, shake han's wid her, an' she wuz done
gone down de road. Soon ez she got 'mos' 'roun'
de curve, Marse Chan he followed her, keepin' under
de trees so ez not to be seen, an' I led de hosses on
down de road behine 'im. He kep' 'long behine her
tell she wuz safe in de house, an' den he come an'
got on he hoss, an' we all come home.

"Nex' mawnin' we all come off to j'ine de army.
An' dey wuz a-drillin' an' a-drillin' all 'bout for a
while an' dey went 'long wid all de res' o' de army,
an' I went wid Marse Chan an' clean he boots, an'
look arfter de tent, an' tek keer o' him an' de hosses.
An' Marse Chan, he wan' a bit like he use' to be.
He wuz so solum an' moanful all de time, at leas'
'cep' when dyah wuz gwine to be a fight. Den he'd
peartin' up, an' he alwuz rode at de head o' de company, 'cause he wuz tall; an' hit wan' on'y in battles
whar all his company wuz dat *he* went, but he use'
to volunteer whenever de cun'l wanted anybody to
fine out anythin', an' 'twuz so dangersome he didn'
like to mek one man go no sooner'n anurr, yo'
know, an' ax'd who'd volunteer. *He* 'peared to like

to go prowlin' aroun' 'mong dem Yankees, an' he use' to tek me wid 'im whenever he could. Yes, seh, he sut'n'y wuz a good sodger! He didn' mine bullets no more'n he did so many draps o' rain. But I use' to be pow'ful skeered sometimes. It jes' use' to 'pear like fun to 'im. In camp he use' to be so sorrerful he'd hardly open he mouf. You'd 'a' tho't he wuz seekin', he used to look so moanful; but jes' le' 'im git into danger, an' he use' to be like ole times—jolly an' laughin' like when he wuz a boy.

"When Cap'n Gordon got he leg shot off, dey mek Marse Chan cap'n on de spot, 'cause one o' de lieutenants got kilt de same day, an' turr one (named Mr. Ronny) wan' no 'count, an' all de company said Marse Chan wuz de man.

"An' Marse Chan he wuz jes' de same. He didn' never mention Miss Anne's name, but I knowed he wuz thinkin' on her constant. One night he wuz settin' by de fire in camp, an' Mr. Ronny—he wuz de secon' lieutenant—got to talkin' 'bout ladies, an' he say all sorts o' things 'bout 'em, an' I see Marse Chan kinder lookin' mad; an' de lieutenant mention Miss Anne's name. He hed been courtin' Miss Anne 'bout de time Marse Chan fit de duil wid her pa, an' Miss Anne hed kicked 'im, dough he wuz mighty rich, 'cause he warn' nuthin' but a half-strainer, an' 'cause she like Marse Chan, I believe dough she didn' speak to 'im; an' Mr. Ronny he got

drunk, an' 'cause Cun'l Chahmb'lin tole 'im not to
come dyah no more, he got mighty mad. An' dat
evenin' I'se tellin' yo' 'bout, he wuz talkin', an' he
mention' Miss Anne's name. I see Marse Chan tu'n
he eye 'roun' on 'im an' keep it on he face, and
pres'n'y Mr. Ronny said he wuz gwine hev some fun
dyah yit. He didn' mention her name dat time;
but he said dey wuz all on 'em a parecel of stuck-
up 'risticrats, an' her pa wan' no gent'man anyway,
an'—— I don' know what he wuz gwine say (he
nuver said it), fur ez he got dat far Marse Chan riz
up an' hit 'im a crack, an' ne fall like he hed been
hit wid a fence-rail. He challenged Marse Chan to
fight a duil, an' Marse Chan he excepted de challenge, an' dey wuz gwine fight; but some on 'em
tole 'im Marse Chan wan' gwine mek a present o'
him to his fam'ly, an' he got somebody to bre'k up
de duil; twan' nuthin' dough, but he wuz 'fred to
fight Marse Chan. An' purty soon he lef' de com-
p'ny.

"Well, I got one o' de gent'mens to write Judy a
letter for me, an' I tole her all 'bout de fight, an'
how Marse Chan knock Mr. Ronny over fur speakin'
discontemptuous o' Cun'l Chahmb'lin, an' I tole her
how Marse Chan wuz a-dyin' fur love o' Miss Anne.
An' Judy she gits Miss Anne to read de letter fur
her. Den Miss Anne she tells her pa, an'—you
mind, Judy tells me all dis arfterwards, an' she say
when Cun'l Chahmb'lin hear 'bout it, he wuz set-

tin' on de poach, an' he set still a good while, an'
den he sey to hisse'f :

" ' Well, he carn' he'p bein' a Whig.'

" An' den he gits up an' walks up to Miss Anne
an' looks at her right hard ; an' Miss Anne she hed
done tu'n away her haid an' wuz makin' out she wuz
fixin' a rose-bush 'g'inst de poach ; an' when her pa
kep' lookin' at her, her face got jes' de color o' de
roses on de bush, and pres'n'y her pa sez :

" ' Anne! '

" An' she tu'ned roun', an' he sez :

" ' Do yo' want 'im ? '

" An' she sez, ' Yes,' an' put her head on he shoulder an' begin to cry ; an' he sez :

" ' Well, I won' stan' between yo' no longer.
Write to 'im an' say so.'

" We didn' know nuthin' 'bout dis den. We wuz
a-fightin' an' a-fightin' all dat time ; an' come one
day a letter to Marse Chan, an' I see 'im start to
read it in his tent, an' he face hit look so cu'ious, an
he han's trembled so I couldn' mek out what wuz
de matter wid 'im. An' he fol' de letter up an' wen'
out an' wen' way down 'hine de camp, an' stayed
dyah 'bout nigh an hour. Well, seh, I wuz on de
lookout for 'im when he come back, an', fo' Gord, ef
he face didn' shine like a angel's ! I say to myse'f,
' Um'm! ef de glory o' Gord ain' done shine on
'im! ' An' what yo' 'spose 'twuz ?

" He tuk me wid 'im dat evenin', an' he tell me

he hed done git a letter from Miss Anne, an' Marse Chan he eyes look like gre't big stars, an' he face wuz jes' like 'twuz dat mawnin' when de sun riz up over de low groun', an' I see 'im stan'in' dyah wid de pistil in he han', lookin' at it, an' not knowin' but what it mout be de lars' time, an' he done mek up he mine not to shoot ole Cun'l Chahmb'lin fur Miss Anne's sake, what writ 'im de letter.

"He fol' de letter wha' was in his han' up, an' put it in he inside pocket—right dyar on de lef' side; an' den he tole me he tho't mebbe we wuz gwine hev some warm wuk in de nex' two or th'ee days, an' arfter dat ef Gord speared 'im he'd git a leave o' absence fur a few days, an' we'd go home.

"Well, dat night de orders come, an' we all hed to git over to'ds Romney; an' we rid all night till 'bout light; an' we halted right on a little creek, an' we stayed dyah till mos' breakfas' time, an' I see Marse Chan set down on de groun' 'hine a bush an' read dat letter over an' over. I watch 'im, an' de battle wuz a-goin' on, but we had orders to stay 'hine de hill, an' ev'y now an' den de bullets would cut de limbs o' de trees right over us, an' one o' dem big shells what goes '*Awhar—awhar—awhar!*' would fall right 'mong us; but Marse Chan he didn' mine it no mo'n nuthin'! Den it 'peared to git closer an' thicker, and Marse Chan he calls me, an' I crep' up, an' he sez:

"'Sam, we'se goin' to win in dis battle, an' den

we'll go home an' git married; an' I'se goin' home
wid a star on my collar.' An' den he sez, 'Ef I'm
wounded, kyar me home, yo' hear?' An' I sez,
'Yes, Marse Chan.'

"Well, jes' den dey blowed boots an' saddles, 'an
we mounted; an' de orders come to ride 'roun' de
slope, an' Marse Chan's comp'ny wuz de secon', an'
when we got 'roun' dyah, we wuz right in it. Hit
wuz de wust place ever dis nigger got in. An' dey
said, 'Charge 'em!' an' my king! ef ever you see
bullets fly, dey did dat day. Hit wuz jes' like hail;
an' we wen' down de slope (I long wid de res') an'
up de hill right to'ds de cannons, an' de fire wuz so
strong dyar (dey hed a whole rigiment o' infintrys
layin' down dyar onder de cannons) our lines sort o'
broke an' stop; de cun'l was kilt, an' I b'lieve dey
wuz jes' 'bout to bre'k all to pieces, when Marse
Chan rid up an' cotch hol' de fleg an' hollers, 'Foller me!' an' rid strainin' up de hill 'mong de cannons. I seen 'im when he went, de sorrel four good
lengths ahead o' ev'y urr hoss, jes' like he use' to
be in a fox-hunt, an' de whole rigiment right arfter
'im. Yo' ain' nuver hear thunder! Fust thing I
knowed, de roan roll' head over heels an' flung me
up 'g'inst de bank, like yo' chuck a nubbin over
'g'inst de foot o' de corn pile. An dat's what kep'
me from bein' kilt, I 'spects. Judy she say she
think 'twuz Providence, but I think 'twuz de bank.
O' co'se, Providence put de bank dyah, but how

come Providence nuver saved Marse Chan? When I look' 'roun', de roan wuz layin' dyah by me, stone dead, wid a cannon-ball gone 'mos' th'oo him, an our men hed done swep' dem on t'urr side from de top o' de hill. 'Twan' mo'n a minit, de sorrel come gallupin' back wid his mane flyin', an' de rein hangin' down on one side to his knee. 'Dyar!' says I, 'fo' Gord! I 'specks dey done kill Marse Chan, an' I promised to tek care on him.'

" I jumped up an' run over de bank, an' dyar, wid a whole lot o' dead men, an' some not dead yit, onder one o' de guns wid de fleg still in he han', an' a bullet right th'oo he body, lay Marse Chan. I tu'n 'im over an' call 'im, 'Marse Chan!' but 'twan' no use, he wuz done gone home, sho' 'nuff. I pick' 'im up in my arms wid de fleg still in he han's, an' toted 'im back jes' like I did dat day when he wuz a baby, an' ole marster gin 'im to me in my arms, an' sez he could trus' me, an' tell me to tek keer on 'im long ez he lived. I kyar'd 'im 'way off de battlefiel' out de way o' de balls, an' I laid 'im down onder a big tree till I could git somebody to ketch de sorrel for me. He wuz cotched arfter a while, an' I hed some money, so I got some pine plank an' made a coffin dat evenin', an' wrapt Marse Chan's body up in de fleg, an' put 'im in de coffin; but I didn' nail de top on strong, 'cause I knowed ole missis wan' see 'im; an' I got a' ambulance an' set out for home dat night. We reached dyar de nex

evein', arfter travellin' all dat night an' all nex'
day.

" Hit 'peared like somethin' hed tole ole missis
we wuz comin' so; for when we got home she wuz
waitin' for us—done drest up in her best Sunday-
clo'es, an' stan'n' at de head o' de big steps, an' ole
marster settin' in his big cheer—ez we druv up de
hill to'ds de house, I drivin' de ambulance an' de
sorrel leadin' 'long behine wid de stirrups crost over
de saddle.

" She come down to de gate to meet us. We took
de coffin out de ambulance an' kyar'd it right into de
big parlor wid de pictures in it, whar dey use' to
dance in ole times when Marse Chan wuz a school-
boy, an' Miss Anne Chahmb'lin use' to come over,
an' go wid ole missis into her chamber an' tek her
things off. In dyar we laid de coffin on two o' de
cheers, an' ole missis nuver said a wud; she jes'
looked so ole an' white.

" When I had tell 'em all 'bout it, I tu'ned right
'roun' an' rid over to Cun'l Chahmb'lin's, 'cause I
knowed dat wuz what Marse Chan he'd 'a' wanted
me to do. I didn' tell nobody whar I wuz gwine,
'cause yo' know none on 'em hadn' nuver speak to
Miss Anne, not sence de duil, an' dey didn' know
'bout de letter.

" When I rid up in de yard, dyar wuz Miss Anne
a-stan'in' on de poach watchin' me ez I rid up. I
tied my hoss to de fence, an' walked up de parf.

She knowed by de way I walked dyar wuz some
thin' de motter, an' she wuz mighty pale. I drapt
my cap down on de een' o' de steps an' went up.
She nuver opened her mouf ; jes' stan' right still
an' keep her eyes on my face. Fust, I couldn'
speak ; den I cotch my voice, an' I say, ' Marse Chan,
he done got he furlough.'

   " Her face was mighty ashy, an' she sort o' shook,
but she didn' fall. She tu'ned roun' an' said, ' Git
me de ker'ige ! ' Dat wuz all.

   " When de ker'ige come 'roun', she hed put on
her bonnet, an' wuz ready. Ez she got in, she sey
to me, ' Hev yo' brought him home ? ' an' we drove
'long, I ridin' behine.

   " When we got home, she got out, an' walked up
de big walk—up to de poach by herse'f. Ole missis
hed done fin' de letter in Marse Chan's pocket, wid
de love in it, while I wuz 'way, an' she wuz a-waitin'
on de poach. Dey sey dat wuz de fust time ole
missis cry when she find de letter, an' dat she
sut'n'y did cry over it, pintedly.

   " Well, seh, Miss Anne she walks right up de
steps, mos' up to ole missis stan'in' dyar on de
poach, an' jes' falls right down mos' to her, on her
knees fust, an' den flat on her face right on de flo',
ketchin' at ole missis' dress wid her two han's—so.

   " Ole missis stood for 'bout a minit lookin' down
at her, an' den she drapt down on de flo' by her, an'
took her in bofe her arms.

" I couldn' see, I wuz cryin' so myse'f, an' ev'y-body wuz cryin'. But dey went in arfter a while in de parlor, an' shet de do'; an' I heahd 'em say, Miss Anne she tuk de coffin in her arms an' kissed it, an' kissed Marse Chan, an' call 'im by his name, an' her darlin', an' ole missis lef' her cryin' in dyar tell some on 'em went in, an' found her done faint on de flo'.

" Judy (she's my wife) she tell me she heah Miss Anne when she axed ole missis mout she wear mo'nin' fur 'im. I don' know how dat is ; but when we buried 'im nex' day, she wuz de one whar walked arfter de coffin, holdin' ole marster, an' ole missis she walked next to 'em.

" Well, we buried Marse Chan dyar in de ole grabeyard, wid de fleg wrapped roun' 'im, an' he face lookin' like it did dat mawnin' down in de low groun's, wid de new sun shinin' on it so peaceful.

" Miss Anne she nuver went home to stay arfter dat ; she stay wid ole marster an' ole missis ez long ez dey lived. Dat warn' so mighty long, 'cause ole marster he died dat fall, when dey wuz fallerin' fur wheat—I had jes' married Judy den—an' ole missis she warn' long behine him. We buried her by him next summer. Miss Anne she went in de hospitals toreckly arfter ole missis died ; an' jes' fo' Richmond fell she come home sick wid de fever. Yo' nuver would 'a' knowed her fur de same ole Miss Anne. She wuz light ez a piece o' peth, an' so white, 'cep her eyes an' her sorrel hyar, an' she kep' on gittin'

whiter an' weaker. Judy she sut'n'y did nuss her
faithful. But she nuver got no betterment! De
fever an' Marse Chan's bein' kilt hed done strain
her, an' she died jes' fo' de folks wuz sot free.

"So we buried Miss Anne right by Marse Chan,
in a place whar ole missis hed tole us to leave, an'
dey's bofe on 'em sleep side by side over in de ole
grabeyard at home.

"An' will yo' please tell me, marster? Dey tells
me dat de Bible sey dyar won' be marryin' nor
givin' in marriage in heaven, but I don' b'lieve it
signifies dat—does you?"

I gave him the comfort of my earnest belief in
some other interpretation, together with several
spare "eighteen-pences," as he called them, for
which he seemed humbly grateful. And as I rode
away I heard him calling across the fence to his wife,
who was standing in the door of a small white-
washed cabin, near which we had been standing for
some time:

"Judy, have Marse Chan's dawg got home?"

"UNC' EDINBURG'S DROWNDIN'."

A PLANTATION ECHO.

"WELL, suh, dat's a fac—dat's what Marse George al'ays said. 'Tis hard to spile Christmas anyways."

The speaker was "Unc' Edinburg," the driver from Werrowcoke, where I was going to spend Christmas; the time was Christmas Eve, and the place the muddiest road in eastern Virginia—a measure which, I feel sure, will, to those who have any experience, establish its claim to distinction.

A half-hour before he had met me at the station, the queerest-looking, raggedest old darky conceivable, brandishing a cedar-staffed whip of enormous proportions in one hand, and clutching a calico letter-bag with a twisted string in the other; and with the exception of a brief interval of temporary suspicion on his part, due to the unfortunate fact that my luggage consisted of only a hand-satchel instead of a trunk, we had been steadily progressing in mutual esteem.

"Dee's a boy standin' by my mules; I got de ker'idge heah for you" had been his first remark on my making myself known to him. "Mistis say as how you might bring a trunk."

I at once saw my danger, and muttered something about "a short visit," but this only made matters worse.

"Dee don' nobody nuver pay short visits dyah," he said, decisively, and I fell to other tactics.

"You couldn' spile Christmas den noways," he repeated, reflectingly, while his little mules trudged knee-deep through the mud. "'Twuz Christmas den, sho' 'nough," he added, the fires of memory smouldering, and then, as they blazed into sudden flame, he asserted, positively : "Dese heah free-issue niggers don' know what Christmas is. Hawg meat an' pop crackers don' meck Christmas. Hit tecks ole times to meck a sho'-'nough, tyahin'-down Christmas. Gord! I's seen 'em! But de wuss Christmas I ever seen tunned out de best in de een," he added, with sudden warmth, "an' dat wuz de Christmas me an' Marse George an' Reveller all got drownded down at Braxton's Creek. You's hearn 'bout dat ?"

As he was sitting beside me in solid flesh and blood, and looked as little ethereal in his old hat and patched clothes as an old oak stump would have done, and as Colonel Staunton had made a world-wide reputation when he led his regiment through the Chickahominy thickets against McClellan's intrenchments, I was forced to confess that I had never been so favored, but would like to hear about it now; and with a hitch of the lap blanket under his outside knee, and a supererogatory jerk of the reins, he began:

" Well, you know, Marse George was jes' eighteen when he went to college. I went wid him, 'cause me an' him wuz de same age ; I was born like on a Sat'day in de Christmas, an' he wuz born in de new year on a Chuesday, an' my mammy nussed us bofe at one breast. Dat's de reason maybe huccome we took so to one nurr. He sutney set a heap o' sto' by me ; an' I 'ain' nuver see nobody yit wuz good to me as Marse George."

The old fellow, after a short reverie, went on :

" Well, we growed up togerr, jes as to say two stalks in one hill. We cotch ole hyahs togerr, an' we hunted 'possums togerr, an' 'coons. Lord! he wuz a climber! I 'member a fight he had one night up in de ve'y top of a big poplar tree wid a 'coon, whar he done gone up after, an' he flung he hat over he head ; an' do' de varmint leetle mo' tyah him all to pieces, he fotch him down dat tree 'live ; an' me an' him had him at Christmas. 'Coon meat mighty good when dee fat, you know ? "

As this was a direct request for my judgment, I did not have the moral courage to raise an issue, although my views on the subject of 'coon meat are well known to my family ; so I grunted something which I doubt not he took for assent, and he proceeded :

"Dee warn' nuttin he didn' lead de row in ; he wuz de bes' swimmer I ever see, an' he handled a skiff same as a fish handle heself. An' I wuz wid him constant ; wharever you see Marse George, dyah Edinburg sho', jes' like he shadow. So twuz, when he went to de university ; 'twarn' nuttin would do but I got to go too. Marster he didn' teck much to de notion, but Marse George wouldn' have it no urr way, an' co'se mistis she teck he side. So I went 'long as he body-servant to teck keer on him an' help meck him a gent'man. An' he wuz, too. From time he got dyah tell he cum 'way he wuz de head man.

"Dee warn' but one man dyah didn' compliment him, an' dat wuz Mr. Darker. But he warn' nuttin! not dat he didn' come o' right good fambly— 'cep' dee politics ; but he wuz sutney pitted, jes' like sometimes you see a weevly runty pig in a right good litter. Well, Mr. Darker he al'ays 'ginst Marse George ; he hate me an him bofe, an' he sutney act mischeevous todes us ; 'cause he know he warn' as we all. De Stauntons dee wuz de popularitiest folks in Virginia ; an' dee wuz high-larnt besides. So when Marse George run for de medal, an' wuz to meck he gret speech, Mr. Darker he speak 'ginst him. Dat's what Marse George whip him 'bout. 'Ain' nobody nuver told you 'bout dat?"

I again avowed my misfortune ; and although it manifestly aroused new doubts, he worked it off on the mules, and once more took up his story :

"Well, you know, dee had been speakin' 'ginst one nurr ev'y Sat'dy night ; and ev'ybody knowed Marse George wuz de bes' speaker, but dee give him one mo' sho', an' dee was bofe gwine spread dee. selves, an' dee wuz two urr gent'mens also gwine speak. An' dat night when Mr. Darker got up he meck sich a fine speech ev'ybody wuz s'prised ; an' some on 'em say Mr. Darker done beat Marse George. But shuh ! I know better'n dat ; an' Marse George face look so curious ; but, suh, when he riz I knowed der wuz somen gwine happen—I wuz leanin' in de winder. He jes step out in front an' throwed up he head like a horse wid a rank kyurb on him, and den he begin ; an' twuz jes like de river when hit gits out he bank. He swep' ev'ything. When he fust open he mouf I knowed twuz comin' ; he face wuz pale, an' he wuds tremble like a fiddle-string, but he eyes wuz blazin', an' in a minute he wuz jes reshin'. He voice soun' like a bell ; an' he jes wallered dat turr man, an' wared him out ; an' when he set down dee all yelled an' hollered so you couldn' heah you' ears. Gent'mans, twuz royal !

" Den dee tuck de vote, an' Marse George got it munanimous, an' dee all hollered agin, all 'cep' a few o' Mr. Darker's friends. An' Mr. Darker he wuz de second. An' den dee broke up. An' jes den Marse George walked thoo de crowd straight up to him.

an' lookin' him right in de eyes, says to him, 'You stole dat speech you made to-night.' Well, suh, you ought to 'a hearn 'em; hit soun' like a mill-dam. You couldn' heah nuttin 'cep' roarin', an' you couldn' see nuttin 'cep' shovin'; but, big as he wuz, Marse George beat him; an' when dee pull him off, do' he face wuz mighty pale, he stan' out befo' 'em all, dem whar wuz 'ginst him, an' all, an' as straight as an arrow, an' say: 'Dat speech wuz written an' printed years ago by somebody or nurr in Congress, an' this man stole it; had he beat me only, I should not have said one word; but as he has beaten others, I shall show him up!' Gord, suh, he voice wuz clear as a game rooster. I sutney wuz proud on him.

"He did show him up, too, but Mr. Darker ain' wait to see it; he lef' dat night. An' Marse George he wuz de popularest gent'man at dat university. He could handle dem students dyah same as a man handle a hoe.

"Well, twuz de next Christmas we meet Miss Charlotte an' Nancy. Mr. Braxton invite we all to go down to spen' Christmas wid him at he home. An' sich a time as we had!

"We got dyah Christmas Eve night—dis very night—jes befo' supper, an' jes natchelly froze to death," he pursued, dealing in his wonted hyperbole, "an' we jes had time to git a apple toddy or two when supper was ready, an' wud come dat dee

wuz waitin' in de hall. I had done fix Marse
George up gorgeousome, I tell you; and when he
walk down dem stairs in dat swaller-tail coat, an'
dem paten'-leather pumps on, dee warn nay one
dyah could tetch him; he looked like he own 'em
all. I jes rest my mind. I seen him when he shake
hands wid 'em all roun', an' I say, ' Um-m-m ! he
got 'em.'

"But he ain' teck noticement o' none much tell
Miss Charlotte come. She didn' live dyah, had jes
come over de river dat evenin' from her home, 'bout
ten miles off, to spen' Christmas like we all, an' she
come down de stairs jes as Marse George finish
shakin' hands. I seen he eye light on her as she
come down de steps smilin', wid her dim blue dress
trainin' behind her, an' her little blue foots peepin'
out so pretty, an' holdin' a little hankcher, lookin'
like a spider-web, in one hand, an' a gret blue fan in
turr, spread out like a peacock tail, an' jes her
roun' arms an' th'oat white, an' her gret dark eyes
lightin' up her face. I say, ' Dyah 'tis !' and when
de ole Cun'l stan' aside an' interduce 'em, an' Marse
George step for'ard an' meck he grand bow, an' she
sort o' swing back an' gin her curtchy, wid her dress
sort o' dammed up 'ginst her, an' her arms so white,
an' her face sort o' sunsetty, I say, ' Yes, Lord ! Edinburg, dyah you mistis.' Marse George look like he
think she done come down right from de top o' de
blue sky an' bring piece on it wid her. He ain'

nuver took he eyes from her dat night. Dee glued
to her, mun! an' she—well, do' she mighty rosy, an'
look mighty unconsarned, she sutney ain' hender
him. Hit look like kyarn nobody else tote dat fan
an' pick up dat hankcher skusin o' him; an' after
supper, when dee all playin' blindman's-buff in de
hall—I don' know how twuz—but do' she jes as
nimble as a filly, an' her ankle jes as clean, an' she
kin git up her dress an' dodge out de way o' ev'y-
body else, somehow or nurr she kyarn help him
ketchin' her to save her life; he al'ays got her corndered; an' when dee'd git fur apart, dat ain' nuttin,
dee jes as sure to come togerr agin as water is whar
you done run you hand thoo. An' do' he kiss ev'y-
body else under de mistletow, 'cause dee be sort o'
cousins, he ain' nuver kiss her, nor nobody else
nurr, 'cep' de ole Cun'l. I wuz standin' down at
de een de hall wid de black folks, an' I notice it
'tic'lar, 'cause I done meck de 'quaintance o' Nancy;
she wuz Miss Charlotte's maid; a mighty likely
young gal she wuz den, an' jes as impident as a fly.
She see it too, do' she ain' 'low it.

"Fust thing I know I seen a mighty likely light-
skinned gal standin' dyah by me, wid her hyah mos'
straight as white folks, an' a mighty good frock on,
an' a clean apron, an' her hand mos' like a lady, only
it brown, an' she keep on 'vidin' her eyes twix me
an' Miss Charlotte; when I watchin' Miss Charlotte
she watchin' me, an' when I steal my eye 'roun' on

her she noticin' Miss Charlotte; an' presney I sort
o' sidle longside her, an' I say, ' Lady, you mighty
sprightly to-night.' An' she say she 'bleeged to be
sprightly, her mistis look so good; an' I ax her
which one twuz, an' she tell me, ' Dat queen one
over dyah,' an' I tell her dee's a king dyah too, she
got her eye set for; an' when I say her mistis tryin'
to set her cap for Marse George, she fly up, an' say
she an' her mistis don' have to set dee cap for nobody; *dee* got to set dee cap an' all dee clo'es for
dem, an' den dee ain' gwine cotch 'em, 'cause dee
ain' studyin' 'bout no up-country folks whar dee
ain' nobody know nuttin 'bout.

" Well, dat oudaciousness so aggrivate me, I lite
into dat nigger right dyah. I tell her she ain' been
nowhar 'tall ef she don' know we all; dat we wuz
de bes' of quality, de ve'y top de pot; an' den I tell
her 'bout how gret we wuz; how de ker'idges wuz
al'ays hitched up night an' day, an' niggers jes thick
as weeds; an' how Unc' Torm he wared he swaller-
tail ev'y day when he wait on de table; and Marse
George he won' wyah a coat mo'n once or twice
anyways, to save you life. Oh! I sutney 'stonish
dat nigger, 'cause I wuz teckin up for de fambly, an'
I meck out like dee use gold up home like urr folks
use wood, an' sow silver like urr folks sow wheat;
an' when I got thoo dee wuz all on 'em listenin', an'
she 'lowed dat Marse George he were ve'y good,
sho 'nough, ef twarn for he nigger; but I ain' tarri-

fyin' myself none 'bout dat, 'cause I know she jes projickin, an' she couldn' help bein' impident ef you wuz to whup de frock off her back.

"Jes den dee struck up de dance. Dee had wheel de pianer out in de hall, and somebody say Jack Forester had come cross de river, an' all on 'em say dee mus' git Jack; an' presney he come in wid he fiddle, grinnin' and scrapin', 'cause he wuz a notable fiddler, do' I don' think he wuz equal to we all's Tubal, an' I know he couldn' tech Marse George, 'cause Marse George wuz a natchel fiddler, jes like 'coons is natchel pacers, an' mules is natchel kickers. Howsomever, he sutney jucked a jig sweet, an' when he shake dat bow you couldn' help you foot switchin' a leetle—not ef you wuz a member of de chutch. He wuz a mighty sinful man, Jack wuz, an' dat fiddle had done drawed many souls to torment.

"Well, in a minute dee wuz all flyin', an' Jack he wuz rockin' like boat rockin' on de water, an' he face right shiny, an' he teef look like ear o' corn he got in he mouf, an' he big foot set 'way out keepin' time, an' Marse George he was in de lead row dyah too; ev'y chance he git he tunned Miss Charlotte— 'petchel motion, right hand across, an' cauliflower, an' croquette—dee croquette plenty o' urrs, but I notice dee ain' nuver fail to tun one nurr, an' ev'y tun he gin she wrappin' de chain roun' him; once when dee wuz 'prominadin-all' down we all's een

o' de hall, as he tunned her somebody step on her
dress an' to' it. I heah de screech o' de silk, an'
Nancy say, 'O Lord!' den she say, 'Nem mine!
now I'll git it!' an' dee stop for a minute for Marse
George to pin it up, while turrers went on, an'
Marse George wuz down on he knee, an' she look
down on him mighty sweet out her eyes, an' say,
'Hit don' meck no difference,' an' he glance up an'
cotch her eye, an', jes 'dout a wud, he tyah a gret
piece right out de silk an' slipt it in he bosom, an'
when he got up, he say, right low, lookin' in her
eyes right deep, 'I gwine wyah dis at my weddin','
an' she jes look sweet as candy; an ef Nancy ever
wyah dat frock I ain' see it.

"Den presney dee wuz talkin' 'bout stoppin'. De
ole Cun'l say hit time to have prars, an' dee wuz
beggin' him to wait a leetle while; an' Jack Forester lay he fiddle down nigh Marse George, an' he
picked 't up an' drawed de bow 'cross it jes to try
it, an' den jes projickin' he struck dat chune 'bout
'You'll ermember me.' He hadn' mo'n tech de
string when you could heah a pin drap. Marse
George he warn noticin', an' he jes lay he face on de
fiddle, wid he eyes sort o' half shet, an' drawed her
out like he'd do some nights at home in dee moonlight on de gret porch, tell on a sudden he looked
up an' cotch Miss Charlotte eye leanin' for'ards so
earnest, an' all on 'em list'nin', an' he stopt, an' dee
all clapt dee hands, an' he sudney drapt into a jig

Jack Forester ain' had to play no mo' dat night
even de ole Cun'l ketched de fever, an' he stept out
in de flo', in he long-tail coat an' high collar, an'
knocked 'em off de ' Snow-bud on de Ash-bank,' an'
' Chicken in de Bread-tray,' right natchel.

"Oh, he could jes plank 'em down!

"Oh, dat wuz a Christmas like you been read
'bout! An' twuz hard to tell which gittin cotch
most, Marse George or me; 'cause dat nigger she jes
as confusin' as Miss Charlotte. An' she sutney wuz
sp'ilt dem days; ev'y nigger on dat place got he eye
on her, an' she jes az oudacious an' aggrivatin as jes
womens kin be.

"Dees monsus 'ceivin' critters, womens is, jes as
onreliable as de hind-leg of a mule; a man got to
watch 'em all de time; you kyarn break 'em like
you kin horses.

"Now dat off mule dyah" (indicating, by a lazy
but not light lash of his whip the one selected for his
illustration), "dee ain' no countin' on her at all; she
go 'long all day, or maybe a week, jes dat easy an'
sociable, an' fust thing you know you ain' know
nuttin, she done knock you brains out; dee ain' no
pendence to be placed in 'em 'tall, suh; she jes as
sweet as a kiss one minute, an' next time she come
out de house she got her head up in de air, an' her
ears backed, an' goin' 'long switchin' herself like I
ain' good 'nough for her to walk on.

"' Fox-huntin's?' oh, yes, suh, ev'y day mos'; an'

when Marse George didn' git de tail, twuz 'cause
twuz a bob-tail fox—you heah me! He play de
fiddle for he pastime, but he fotched up in de saddle
—dat he cradle!

" De fust day dee went out I heah Nancy quoilin
'bout de tail layin' on Miss Charlotte dressin'-table
gittin' hyahs over ev'ything.

" One day de ladies went out too, Miss Charlotte
'mongst 'em, on Miss Lucy gray myah Switchity,
an' Marse George he rid Mr. Braxton's chestnut
Willful.

" Well, suh, he stick so close to dat gray myah,
he leetle mo' los' dat fox; but, Lord! he know what
he 'bout—he monsus 'ceivin' 'bout dat—he know de
way de fox gwine jes as well as he know heself ; an'
all de time he leadin' Miss Charlotte whar she kin
heah de music, but he watchin' him too, jes as narrow as a ole hound.   So, when de fox tun de head
o' de creek, Marse George had Miss Charlotte on de
aidge o' de flat, an' he de fust man see de fox tun
down on turr side wid de hounds right rank after
him.   Dat sort o' set him back, 'cause by rights de
fox ought to 'a double an' come back dis side : he
kyarn git out dat way ; an' two or three gent'mens
dee had see it too, an' wuz jes layin de horses to de
groun to git roun' fust, 'cause de creek wuz heap
too wide to jump, an' wuz 'way over you head, an
hit cold as Christmas, sho 'nough ; well, suh, when
dee tunned, Mr. Clarke he wuz in de lead (he wuz

ridin' for Miss Charlotte too), an' hit fyah set **Marse**
George on fire; he ain' said but one wud, ' Wait,'
an' jes set de chestnut's head straight for de creek,
whar de fox comin' wid he hyah up on he back, an'
de dogs ravlin mos' on him.

" De ladies screamed, an' some de gent'mens hollered for him to come back, but he ain' mind; he
went 'cross dat flat like a wild-duck; an' when he
retch de water he horse try to flinch, but dat hand
on de bridle, an' dem rowels in he side, an' he
'bleeged to teck it.

" Lord! suh, sich a screech as dee set up! But he
wuz swimmin' for life, an' he wuz up de bank an' in
de middle o' de dogs time dee tetched ole **Gray**
Jacket ; an' when Mr. Clarke got dyah Marse George
wuz stan'in' holdin' up de tail for Miss Charlotte to
see, turr side de creek, an' de hounds wuz wallerin'
all over de body, an' I don' think Mr. Clarke done
got up wid 'em yit.

" He cotch de fox, an' he cotch some'n' else besides, in my 'pinion, 'cause when de ladies went upstairs dat night Miss Charlotte had to wait on de
steps for a glass o' water, an' couldn' nobody git it
but Marse George; an' den when she tell him good-
night over de banisters, he couldn' say it good
enough; he got to kiss her hand; an' she ain' do
nuttin but jes peep upstairs ef anybody dyah lookin';
an' when I come thoo de do' she juck her hand 'way
an' ran upstairs jes as farst as she could. Marse

George look at me sort o' laughin', an' say : ' Con-
found you ! Nancy couldn' been very good to you.'
An' I say, ' She le' me squench my thirst kissin' her
hand ;' an' he sort o' laugh an' tell me to keep my
mouf shet.

"But dat ain' de on'y time I come on 'em. Dee
al'ays gittin' corndered ; an' de evenin' befo' we come
'way I wuz gwine in thoo de conservity, an' dyah
dee wuz sort o' hide 'way. Miss Charlotte she wuz
settin' down, an' Marse George he wuz leanin' over
her, got her hand to he face, talkin' right low an'
lookin' right sweet, an' she ain' say nuttin ; an' presney he drapt on one knee by her, an' slip he arm
roun' her, an' try to look in her eyes, an' she so
'shamed to look at him she got to hide her face on
he shoulder, an' I slipt out.

"We come 'way next mornin'. When marster
heah 'bout it he didn' teck to de notion at all, 'cause
her pa—dat is, he warn' her own pa, 'cause he had
married her ma when she wuz a widder after Miss
Charlotte pa died—an' he politics warn' same as
ourn. ' Why, you kin never stand him, suh,' he said
to Marse George. ' We won't mix any mo'n fire and
water ; you ought to have found that out at college ;
dat fellow Darker is his son.'

" Marse George he say he know dat ; but he on'y
de step-brurr of de young lady, an' ain' got a drap
o' her blood in he veins, an' he didn' know it when
he meet her, an' anyhow hit wouldn' meck any dif-

fence; an' when de mistis see how sot Marse George is on it she teck he side, an' dat fix it ; 'cause when ole mistis warn marster to do a thing, hit jes good as done.   I don' keer how much he rar roun' an' say he ain' gwine do it, you jes well go 'long an' put on you hat ; you gwine see him presney doin' it jes peaceable as a lamb.   She tun him jes like she got bline-bridle on him, an' he ain' nuver know it.

"So she got him jes straight as a string.   An' when de time come for Marse George to go, marster he mo' consarned 'bout it 'n Marse George; he ain' say nuttin 'bout it befo' ; but now he walkin' roun' an' roun' axin mistis mo' questions 'bout he cloes an' he horse an' all ; an' dat mornin' he gi' him he two Sunday razors, an' gi' me a pyah o' boots an' a beaver hat, 'cause I wuz gwine wid him to kyar he portmanteau, an' git he shavin' water, sence marster say ef he wuz gwine marry a Locofoco, he at least must go like a gent'man ; an' me an' Marse George had done settle it 'twixt us, cause we al'ays set bofe we traps on de same hyah parf.

"Well, we got 'em, an' when I ax dat gal out on de wood-pile dat night, she say bein' as her mistis gwine own me, an' we bofe got to be in de same estate, she reckon she ain' nuver gwine to be able to git shet o' me ; an' den I clamp her.   Oh, she wuz a beauty !"

A gesture and guffaw completed the recital of his conquest.

"Yes, suh, we got 'em sho!" he said, presently, " Dee couldn' persist us; we crowd 'em into de fence an' run 'em off dee foots.

" Den come de 'gagement; an' ev'ything wuz smooth as silk. Marse George an' me wuz ridin' over dyah constant, on'y we nuver did git over bein' skeered when we wuz ridin' up dat turpentine road facin' all dem winders. Hit 'pear like ev'ybody in de wull 'mos' wuz lookin' at us.

" One evenin' Marse George say   Edinburg, d'you ever see as many winders p'intin' one way in you' life? When I git a house,' he say, ' I gwine have all de winders lookin' turr way.'

" But dat evenin', when I see Miss Charlotte come walkin' out de gret parlor wid her hyah sort o' rumpled over her face, an' some yaller roses on her bres, an' her gret eyes so soft an' sweet, an' Marse George walkin' 'long hinst her, so peaceable, like she got chain roun' him, I say, ' Winders ain' nuttin.'

" Oh, twuz jes like holiday all de time! An' den Miss Charlotte come over to see mistis, an' of co'se she bring her maid wid her, 'cause she 'bleeged to have her maid, you know, an' dat wuz de bes' of all.

" Dat evenin', 'bout sunset, dee come drivin' up in de big ker'idge, wid de gret hyah trunk stropped on de seat behind, an' Nancy she settin' by Billy, an' Marse George settin' inside by he rose-bud, 'cause he had done gone down to bring her up; an' marster

he done been drest in he blue coat an' yallow west-
ket ever sence dinner, an' walkin' roun', watchin' up
de road all de time, an' tellin' de mistis he reckon
dee ain' comin', an ole mistis she try to pacify him,
an' she come out presney drest, an' rustlin' in her
stiff black silk an' all; an' when de ker'idge come in
sight, ev'ybody wuz runnin'; an' when dee draw up
to de do', Marse George he help her out an' 'duce
her to marster an' ole mistis; an' marster he start
to meck her a gret bow, an' she jes put up her mouf
like a little gal to be kissed, an' dat got him. An'
mistis teck her right in her arms an' kiss her twice,
an' de servants dee wuz all peepin' an' grinnin'.

" Ev'ywhar you tun you see a nigger teef, 'cause
dee all warn see de young mistis whar good 'nough
for Marse George. Dee ain' gwine be married tell
de next fall, 'count o' Miss Charlotte bein' so young;
but she jes good as b'longst to we all now ; an' ole
marster an' mistis dee jes as much in love wid her
as Marse George. Hi! dee warn pull de house
down an' buil' it over for her! An' ev'y han' on de
place he peepin' to try to git a look at he young
mistis whar he gwine b'longst to. One evenin' dee
all on 'em come roun' de porch an' send for Marse
George, an' when he come out, Charley Brown (he
al'ays de speaker, 'cause he got so much mouf, kin'
talk pretty as white folks), he say dee warn interduce
to de young mistis, an' pay dee bespects to her; an'
presney Marse George lead her out on de porch

laughin' at her, wid her face jes rosy as a wine-sap
apple, an' she meck 'em a beautiful bow, an' speak
to 'em ev'y one, Marse George namin' de names;
an' Charley Brown he meck her a pretty speech, an'
tell her we mighty proud to own her; an' one o'
dem impident gals ax her to gin her dat white frock
when she git married; an' when she say, 'Well,
what am I goin' wear?' Sally say, 'Lord, honey,
Marse George gwine dress you in pure gol'!' an'
she look up at him wid sparks flashin' out her eyes,
while he look like dat ain' good 'nough for her.
An' so twuz, when she went 'way, Sally Marshall
got dat frock, an' proud on it I tell you.

"Oh, yes; he sutney mindin' her tender. Hi!
when she go to ride in evenin' wid him, de ain' no
horse-block good 'nough for her! Marse George
got to have her step in he hand; an' when dee out
walkin' he got de umbreller holdin' 't over her all
de time, he so feared de sun 'll kiss her; an' dee
walk so slow down dem walks in de shade you got
to sight 'em by a tree to tell ef dee movin' 'tall.
She use' to look like she used to it too, I tell you,
'cause she wuz quality, one de white-skinned ones;
an' she'd set in dem big cheers, wid her little foots
on de cricket whar Marse George al'ays set for her,
he so feared dee'd tetch de groun', jes like she on
her throne; an' ole marster he'd watch her 'mos'
edmirin as Marse George; an' when she went 'way
hit sutney was lonesome. Hit look like daylight

gone wid her. I don' know which I miss mos', Miss Charlotte or Nancy.

" Den Marse George was 'lected to de Legislature, an' ole Jedge Darker run for de Senator, an' Marse George vote gin him and beat him. An' dat com-mence de fuss ; an' den dat man gi' me de whuppin, an' dat breck 'tup an' breck he heart.

" You see, after Marse George wuz 'lected ('lec-tions wuz 'lections dem days; dee warn' no bait-gode 'lections, wid ev'y sort o' worms squirmin' up 'ginst one nurr, wid piece o' paper d' ain' know what on, drappin' in a chink; didn' nuttin but gent'mens vote den, an' dee took dee dram, an' vote out loud, like gent'mens)—well, arter Marse George wuz 'lected, de parties wuz jes as even balanced as stil-yuds, an' wen dee ax Marse George who wuz to be de Senator, he vote for de Whig, 'ginst de old jedge, an' dat beat him, of co'se. An' dee ain' got sense to know he 'bleeged to vote wid he politics. Dat he sprinciple ; he kyarn vote for Locofoco, I don' keer ef he is Miss Charlotte pa, much less her step-pa. Of co'se de ole jedge ain' speak to him arter dat, nur is Marse George ax him to. But who dat gwine s'pose women-folks got to put dee mouf in too ? Miss Charlotte she write Marse George a let-ter dat pester him mightily ; he set up all night answerin' dat letter, an' he mighty solemn, I tell you. An' I wuz gittin' right grewsome myself, cause I studyin' 'bout dat gal down dyah whar '

done gi' my wud to, an' when dee ain' no letters
come torectly hit hard to tell which one de anx-
iouser, me or Marse George. Den presney I so
'straughted 'long o' it I ax Aunt Haly 'bouten it;
she know all sich things, 'cause she 'mos' a hunderd
years ole, an' seed evil sperits, an' got skoripins up
her chimley, an' knowed conjure ; an' she ax me
what wuz de signication, an' I tell her I ain' able
nuther to eat nor to sleep, an' dat gal come foolin'
'long me when I sleep jes like as natche' as er I see
her sho 'nough. An' she say I done conjured ; dat
de gal done tricked me.

"Oh, Gord ! dat skeered me !

"You white folks, marster, don' b'lieve nuttin like
dat ; y' all got too much sense, 'cause y' all kin read ;
but niggers dee ain' know no better, an' I sutney
wuz skeered, 'cause Aunt Haly say my coffin done
seasoned, de planks up de chimley.

"Well, I got so bad Marse George ax me 'bout it,
an' he sort o' laugh an' sort o' cuss, an' he tell Aunt
Haly ef she don' stop dat foolishness skeerin' me
he'll sell her an' tyah her ole skoripin house down.
Well, co'se he jes talkin', an' he ax me next day
how'd I like to go an' see my sweetheart. Gord !
suh, I got well torectly. So I set off next evenin',
feelin' jes big as ole marster, wid my pass in my
pocket, which I warn' to show nobody 'douten I
'bleeged to, 'cause Marse George didn't warn nobody to know he le' me go. An' den dat rascallion

teck de shut off my back. But ef Marse George
didn' pay him de wuth o' it !

" I done git 'long so good, too.

"When Nancy see me she sutney was 'stonished.
She come roun' de cornder in de back yard whar I
settin' in Nat's do' (he wuz de gardener), wid her
hyah all done untwist, an' breshed out mighty fine,
an' a clean ap'on wid fringe on it, meckin' out she
so s'prised to see me (whar wuz all a lie, 'cause some
on 'em done notify her I dyah), an' she say, ' Hi !
what dis black nigger doin' heah ? '

" An' I say, ' Who you callin' nigger, you impident, kercumber-faced thing you ? ' Den we shake
hands, an' I tell her Marse George done set me free
—dat I done buy myself ; dat's de lie I done lay off
to tell her.

" An' when I tole her dat, she bust out laughin',
an' say, well, I better go 'long 'way, den, dat she
don' warn no free nigger to be comp'ny for her.
Dat sort o' set me back, an' I tell her she kickin' 'fo'
she spurred, dat I ain' got her in my mine ; I got a
nurr gal at home whar grievin' 'bout me dat ve'y
minute. An' after I tell her all sich lies as dat
presney she ax me ain' I hongry ; an' ef dat nigger
didn' git her mammy to gi' me de bes' supter !
Umm-m ! I kin mos' tas'e it now. Wheat bread
off de table, an' zerves, an' fat bacon, tell I couldn'
put a nurr moufful nowhar sep'n I'd teck my hat.
Dat night I tote Nancy water for her, an' I tell her

all 'bout ev'ything, an' she jes sweet as honey. Next
mornin', do', she done sort o' tunned some, an' ain'
so sweet. You know how milk gits sort o' bonny-
clabberish? An' when she see me she 'gin to 'buse
me—say I jes tryin' to fool her, an' all de time got
nurr wife at home, or gittin' ready to git one, for all
she know, an' she ain' know wherr Marse George
ain' jes 'ceivin' as I is ; an' nem mine, she got plenty
warn marry her ; an' as to Miss Charlotte, she got
de whole wull ; Mr. Darker he ain' got nobody in
he way now, dat he deah all de time, an' ain' gwine
West no mo'. Well, dat aggrivate me so I tell her
ef she say dat 'bout Marse George I gwine knock
her ; an' wid dat she got so oudacious I meck out I
gwine 'way, an' lef' her, an' went up todes de barn ;
an' up dyah, fust thing I know, I come across dat
ar man Mr. Darker. Soon as he see me he begin to
cuss me, an' he ax me what I doin' on dat land, an' I
tell him nuttin. An' he say, well, he gwine gi' me
some'n ; he gwine teach me to come prowlin' round
gent'men's houses. An' he meck me go in de barn
an' teck off my shut, an' he beat me wid he whup
tell de blood run out my back. He sutney did beat
me scandalous, 'cause he done hate me an' Marse
George ever since we wuz at college togurr. An'
den he say : 'Now you git right off dis land. Ef
either you or you marster ever put you foot on
it, you'll git de same thing agin.' An' I tell you,
Edinburg he come way, 'cause he sutney had worry

me. I ain' stop to see Nancy or nobody; I jes come
'long, shakin' de dust, I tell you. An' as I come 'long
de road I pass Miss Charlotte walkin' on de lawn
by herself, an' she call me: 'Why, hi! ain' dat Edinburg?'

"She look so sweet, an' her voice soun' so cool, I
say, 'Yes'm; how you do, missis?' An' she say,
she ve'y well, an' how I 'been, an' whar I gwine? I
tell her I ain' feelin' so well, dat I gwine home.
'Hi!' she say, 'is anybody treat you bad?' An' I
tell her, 'Yes'm.' An' she say, 'Oh! Nancy don'
mean nuttin by dat; dat you mus'n mine what
womens say, an' do, 'cause dee feel sorry for it next
minute; an' sometimes dee kyarn help it, or maybe
hit you fault; an' anyhow, you ought to be willin'
to overlook it; an' I better go back an' wait till to-
morrow—ef—ef I ain' 'bleeged to git home to-day.'

"She got mighty mixed up in de een part o' dat,
an' she looked mighty anxious 'bout me an' Nancy;
an' I tell her, 'No'm, I 'bleeged to git home.'

"Well, when I got home Marse George he warn
know all dat gwine on; but I mighty sick—dat man
done beat me so; an' he ax me what de marter, an'
I upped an' tell him.

"Gord! I nuver see a man in sich a rage. He
call me in de office an' meck me teck off my shut,
an' he fyah bust out cryin'. He walked up an' down
dat office like a caged lion. Ef he had got he hand
on Mr. Darker den, he'd 'a kilt him, sho!

He wuz most 'stracted. I don't know what he'd been ef I'd tell him what Nancy tell me. He call for Peter to git he horse torectly, an' he tell me to go an' git some'n' from mammy to put on my back, an' to go to bed torectly, an' not to say nuttin to nobody, but to tell he pa he'd be away for two days, maybe; an' den he got on Reveller an' galloped 'way hard as he could, wid he jaw set farst, an' he heaviest whup clamped in he hand. Gord! I wuz most hopin' he wouldn' meet dat man, 'cause I feared ef he did he'd kill him; an' he would, sho, ef he had meet him right den; dee say he leetle mo' did when he fine him next day, an' he had done been ridin' den all night; he cotch him at a sto' on de road, an' dee say he leetle mo' cut him all to pieces; he drawed a weepin on Marse George, but Marse George wrench it out he hand an' flung it over de fence; an' when dee got him 'way he had weared he whup out on him; an' he got dem whelps on him now, ef he ain' dead. Yes, suh, he ain' let nobody else do dat he ain' do heself, sho!

" Dat done de business!

" He sont Marse George a challenge, but Marse George sont him wud he'll cowhide him agin ef he ever heah any mo' from him, an' he 'ain't. Dat perrify him, so he shet he mouf. Den come he ring an' all he pictures an' things back—a gret box on 'em, and not a wud wid 'em. Marse George, I think he know'd dee wuz comin', but dat ain' keep it from

huttin him, 'cause he done been 'gaged to Miss
Charlotte, an' got he mine riveted to her; an' do'
befo' dat dee had stop writin', an' a riff done git
'twixt 'em, he ain' satisfied in he mine dat she ain't
gwine 'pologizee—I know by Nancy; but now he
got de confirmation dat he done for good, an' dat
de gret gulf fixed 'twix him an' Aberham bosom.
An,' Gord, suh, twuz torment, sho 'nough! He ain'
say nuttin 'bout it, but I see de light done pass from
him, an' de darkness done wrap him up in it. In a
leetle while you wouldn' 'a knowed him. Den ole
mistis died.

" B'lieve me, ole marster he 'most much hut by
Miss Charlotte as Marse George. He meck a 'tempt
to buy Nancy for me, so I find out arterward, an'
write Jedge Darker he'll pay him anything he'll ax
for her. but he letter wuz sont back 'dout any answer. He sutney was mad 'bout it—he say he'd
horsewhip him as Marse George did dat urr young
puppy, but ole mistis wouldn' le' him do nuttin, and
den he grieve heself to death. You see he mighty
ole, anyways. He nuver got over ole mistis' death.
She had been failin' a long time, an' he ain tarry
long 'hinst her; hit sort o' like breckin up a holler
—de ole 'coon goes 'way soon arter dat; an' marster nuver could pin he own collar or buckle he
own stock—mistis she al'ays do dat; an' do' Marse
George do de bes' he kin, an' mighty willin', he
kyarn handle pin like a woman; he hand tremble

like a p'inter dog; an' anyways he ain' ole mistis.
So ole marster foller her dat next fall, when dee
wuz gittin in de corn, an' Marse George he ain' got
nobody in de wull left; he all alone in dat gret
house, an' I wonder sometimes he ain' die too, 'cause
he sutney wuz fond o' ole marster.

"When ole mistis wuz dyin', she tell him to be
good to ole marster, an' patient wid him, 'cause he
ain' got nobody but him now (ole marster he had jes
step out de room to cry); an' Marse George he lean
over her an' kiss her an' promise her faithful he
would. An' he sutney wuz tender wid him as a
woman; an' when ole marster die, he set by him
an' hol' he hand an' kiss him sorf, like he wuz ole
mistis.

"But, Gord! twuz lonesome arter dat, an' Marse
George eyes look wistful, like he al'ays lookin' far
'way; an' Aunt Haly say he see harnts whar walk
'bout in de gret house. She say dee walk dyah constant of nights sence ole marster done alterate de
rooms from what dee wuz when he gran'pa buil'
'em, an' dat dee huntin' for dee ole chambers an'
kyarn git no rest 'cause dee kyarn fine 'em. I don't
know how dat wuz. I know Marse George *he* used
to walk about heself mightily of nights. All night
long, all night long, I'd heah him tell de chickens
crowin' dee second crow, an' some mornin's I'd go
dyah an' he ain' even rumple de bed. I thought sho
he wuz gwine die, but I suppose he done 'arn he

5

days to be long in de land, an' dat save him. But hit sutney wuz lonesome, an' he nuver went off de plantation, an' he got older an' older, tell we all thought he wuz gwine die.

"An' one day come jes befo' Christmas, 'bout nigh two year after marster die, Mr. Braxton ride up to de do'. He had done come to teck Marse George home to spen' Christmas wid him. Marse George warn git out it, but Mr. Braxton won' teck no disapp'intment; he say he gwine baptize he boy, an' he done name him after Marse George (he had marry Marse George cousin, Miss Peggy Carter, an' he vite Marse George to de weddin', but he wouldn' go, do' I sutney did want him to go, 'cause I heah Miss Charlotte was nominated to marry Mr. Darker, an' I warn know what done 'come o' dat bright-skinned nigger gal whar I used to know down dyah); an' he say Marse George got to come an' stan' for him, an' gi' him a silver cup an' a gol' rattle. So Marse George he finally promise to come an' spend Christmas Day, an' Mr. Braxton went 'way next mornin', an den hit tun in an' rain so I feared we couldn' go, but hit cler off de day befo' Christmas Eve an' tun cold. Well, suh, we ain' been nowhar for so long I wuz skittish as a young filly; an' den you know twuz de same ole place.

"We didn' git dyah till supper-time, an' twuz a good one too, 'cause seventy miles dat cold a weather hit whet a man's honger jes like a whetstone.

" Dee sutney wuz glad to see we all. We rid roun' by de back yard to gi' Billy de horses, an' we see dee wuz havin' gret fixin's; an' den we went to de house, jest as some o' de folks run in an' tell 'em we wuz come. When Marse George stept in de hall, dee all clustered roun' him like dee gwine hug him, dee faces fyah dimplin' wid pleasure, an' Miss Peggy she jes reched up an' teck him in her arms an' hug him.

" Dee tell me in de kitchen dat dee wuz been 'spectin' of Miss Charlotte over to spend Christmas too, but de river wuz so high dee s'pose dee couldn' git 'cross. Chile, dat sutney disapp'int me!

" Well, after supper de niggers had a dance. Hit wuz down in de wash-house, an' de table wuz set in de carpenter shop jes' by. Oh, hit sutney wuz beautiful! Miss Lucy an' Miss Ailsy dee had superintend ev'ything wid dee own hands. So dee wuz down dyah wid dee ap'ons up to dee chins, an' dee had de big silver strandeliers out de house, two on each table, an' some o' ole mistis's best damas' table-clothes, an' ole marster's gret bowl full o' egg-nog; hit look big as a mill-pond settin' dyah in de cornder; an' dee had flowers out de greenhouse on de table, an' some o' de chany out de gret house, an' de dinin'-room cheers set roun' de room. Oh! oh! nuttin warn too good for niggers dem times; an' de little niggers wuz runnin' roun' right 'stracted, squealin' an' peepin' an' gittin in de way onder you foots; an' de mens dee wuz totin' in de wood—gret hickory logs, look like stock whar you gwine saw—an' de fire so big hit look like you gwine kill hawgs, 'cause hit sutney wuz cold dat night. Dis nigger ain' nuver gwine forgit it! Jack Forester he had come 'cross de river to lead de fiddlers, an' he say he had to put he fiddle onder he coat an' poke he bow in he breeches leg to keep de strings from poppin', an' dat de river would freeze over sho ef twarn so high; but twuz jes snortin', an' he had hard wuck to git over in he skiff, an' Unc' Jeems say he ain' gwine come out he boat-house no mo' dat night—he done tempt Providence often 'nough dat day.

"Den ev'ything wuz ready, an' de fiddlers got dee dram an' chuned up, an' twuz lively, I tell you! Twuz jes as thick in dyah as blackberries on de blackberry bush, 'cause ev'y gal on de plantation wuz dyah shakin' her foot for some young buck, an' back-steppin' for to go 'long. Dem ole sleepers wuz jes a-rockin', an' Jack Forester he wuz callin' de figgers for to wake 'em up. I warn' dancin', 'cause I done got 'ligion an' longst to de chutch since de trouble done tetch us up so rank; but I tell you my foots wuz pintedly eechchin for a leetle sop on it, an' I had to come out to keep from crossin' 'em onst, anyways. Den, too, I had a tetch o' misery in my back, an' I lay off to git a tas'e o' dat egg-nog out dat big bowl, wid snow-drift on it, from Miss Lucy—she al'ays mighty fond o' Marse George; so

I slip into de carpenter shop, an' ax her kyarn I do
nuttin for her, an' she laugh an' say, yes, I kin drink
her health, an' gi' me a gret gobletful, an' jes den de
white folks come in to 'spec' de tables, Marse George
in de lead, an' dee all fill up dee glasses an' pledge
dee health, an' all de servants', an' a merry Christmas; an' den dee went in de wash-house to see de
dancin', an' maybe to teck a hand deeself, 'cause
white folks' 'ligion ain' like niggers', you know; dee
got so much larnin dee kin dance, an' fool de devil
too.   An' I stay roun' a little while, an' den went in
de kitchen to see how supper gittin on, 'cause I wuz
so hongry when I got dyah I ain' able to eat 'nough
at one time to 'commodate it, an' de smell o' de tuc-
keys an' de gret saddlers o' mutton in de tin-kit-
chens wuz mos' 'nough by deeself to feed a right
hongry man; an' dyah wuz a whole parcel o' niggers
cookin' an' tunnin 'bout for life, an' dee faces jes as
shiny as ef dee done bas'e 'em wid gravy; an' dyah,
settin' back in a cheer out de way, wid her clean
frock up off de flo', wuz dat gal!   I sutney did feel
curious.

"I say, 'Hi! name o' Gord! whar'd you come
from?' She say, 'Oh, Marster! ef heah ain' dat free
nigger agin!' An' ev'ybody laughed.

"Well, presny we come out, cause Nancy warn see
de dancin', an' we stop a leetle while 'hind de cornder
out de wind while she tell me 'bout ev'ything.   An'
she say dat's all a lie she tell me dat day 'bout Mr.

Darker an' Miss Charlotte; an' he done gone 'way
now for good 'cause he so low down an' wuthless dee
kyarn nobody stand him; an' all he warn marry Miss
Charlotte for is to git her niggers. But Nancy say
Miss Charlotte nuver could abide him; he so 'sateful,
spressly sence she fine out what a lie he told 'bout
Marse George. You know, Mr. Darker he done meck
'em think Marse George sont me dyah to fine out ef
he done come home, an' den dat he fall on him wid
he weepin when he ain' noticin' him, an' sort o' out
de way too, an' git two urr mens to hold him while
he beat him, all 'cause he in love wid Miss Charlotte.
D'you ever, ever heah sich a lie? An' Nancy say,
do' Miss Charlotte ain' b'lieve it all togerr, hit look
so reasonable she done le' de ole jedge an' her ma,
who wuz 'pending on what she heah, 'duce her to
send back he things; an' dee ain' know no better not
tell after de ole jedge die; den dee fine out 'bout de
whuppin me, an' all; an' den Miss Charlotte know
huccome I ain' gwine stay dat day; an' she say dee
wuz sutney outdone 'bout it, but it too late den; an'
Miss Charlotte kyarn do nuttin but cry 'bout it, an'
dat she did, pintedly, 'cause she done lost Marse
George, an' done 'stroy he life; an' she nuver keer
'bout nobody else sep Marse George, Nancy say.
Mr. Clarke he hangin' on, but Miss Charlotte she
done tell him pintedly she ain' nuver gwine marry
nobody. An' dee jes done come, she say, 'cause dee
had to go 'way round by de rope ferry 'long o' de

river bein' so high, an' dee ain' know tell dee done
git out de ker'idge an' in de house dat we all wuz
heah; an' Nancy say she glad dee ain', 'cause she
'feared ef dee had, Miss Charlotte wouldn' 'a come.

"Den I tell her all 'bout Marse George, cause I know
she 'bleeged to tell Miss Charlotte. Twuz powerful
cold out dyah, but I ain' mine dat, chile. Nancy she
done had to wrop her arms up in her ap'on an' she
kyarn meck no zistance 'tall, an' dis nigger ain' keer-
in nuttin 'bout cold den.

"An' jes den two ladies come out de carpenter
shop an' went 'long to de wash-house, an' Nancy say,
'Dyah Miss Charlotte now;' an' twuz Miss Lucy
an' Miss Charlotte; an' we heah Miss Lucy coaxin'
Miss Charlotte to go, tellin' her she kin come right
out; an' jes den dee wuz a gret shout, an' we went
in hinst 'em. Twuz Marse George had done teck
de fiddle, an' ef he warn' natchelly layin' hit down!
he wuz up at de urr een o' de room, 'way from we
all, 'cause we wuz at de do', nigh Miss Charlotte
whar she wuz standin' 'hind some on 'em, wid her
eyes on him mighty timid, like she hidin' from him,
an' ev'y nigger in de room wuz on dat flo'. Gord!
suh, dee wuz grinnin' so dee warn' a toof in dat
room you couldn' git you tweezers on; an' you
couldn' heah a wud, dee so proud o' Marse George
playin' for 'em.

"Well, dee danced tell you couldn' tell which wuz
de clappers an' which de back-steppers; de whole

house look like it wuz rockin'; an' presney somebody say supper, an' dat stop 'em, an' dee wuz a
spell for a minute, an' Marse George standin' dyah
wid de fiddle in he hand. He face wuz tunned
away, an' he wuz studyin'—studyin' 'bout dat urr
Christmas so long ago—an' sudney he face drapt
down on de fiddle, an' he drawed he bow 'cross de
strings, an' dat chune begin to whisper right sorf.
Hit begin so low ev'ybody had to stop talkin' an'
hold dee mouf to heah it; an' Marse George he ain'
know nuttin 'bout it, he done gone back, an' standin'
dyah in de gret hall playin' it for Miss Charlotte,
whar done come down de steps wid her little blue
foots an' gret fan, an' standin' dyah in her dim blue
dress an' her fyah arms, an' her gret eyes lookin' in
he face so earnest, whar he ain' gwine nuver speak
to no mo'. I see it by de way he look—an' de fiddle
wuz jes pleadin'. He drawed it out jes as fine as a
stran' o' Miss Charlotte's hyah.

"Hit so sweet, Miss Charlotte, mun, she couldn'
stan' it; she made to de do'; an' jes while she
watchin' Marse George to keep him from seein' her
he look dat way, an' he eyes fall right into hern.

"Well, suh, de fiddle drapt down on de flo'—per-
lang!—an' he face wuz white as a sycamore limb.

"Dee say twuz a swimmin' in de head he had; an'
Jack say de whole fiddle warn' wuff de five dollars.

"Me an' Nancy followed 'em tell dee went in de
house, an' den we come back to de shop whar de

supper wuz gwine on, an' got we all supper an' a
leetle sop o' dat yaller gravy out dat big bowl, an'
den we all rejourned to de wash-house agin, an' got
onder de big bush o' misseltow whar hangin' from
de jice, an' ef you ever see scufflin' dat's de time.

" Well, me an' she had jes done lay off de whole
Christmas, when wud come dat Marse George want
he horses.

" I went, but it sutney breck me up ; an' I wonder
whar de name o' Gord Marse George gwine sen' me
dat cold night, an' jes as I got to de do' Marse
George an' Mr. Braxton come out, an' I know torectly Marse George wuz gwine home. I seen he
face by de light o' de lantern, an' twuz set jes rigid
as a rock.

" Mr. Braxton he wuz beggin' him to stay; he tell
him he ruinin' he life, dat he sho dee's some mistake,
an' twill be all right. An' all de answer Marse George
meck wuz to swing heself up in de saddle, an' Reveller he look like he gwine fyah 'stracted. He al'ays
mighty fool anyways when he git cold, dat horse wuz.

" Well, we come 'long 'way, an' Mr. Braxton an'
two mens come down to de river wid lanterns to see
us cross, 'cause twuz dark as pitch, sho 'nough.

" An' jes 'fo' I started I got one o' de mens to hol'
my horses, an' I went in de kitchen to git warm, an'
dyah Nancy wuz. An' she say Miss Charlotte upsteairs cryin' right now, 'cause she think Marse
George gwine cross de river 'count o' her, an' she

whimper a little herself when I tell her good-by.
But twuz too late den.

"Well, de river wuz jes natchelly b'ilin', an' hit
soun' like a mill-dam roarin' by; an' when we got
dyah Marse George tunned to me an' tell me he
reckon I better go back. I ax him whar he gwine,
an' he say, 'Home.' 'Den I gwine wid you,' I says.
I wuz mighty skeered, but me an' Marse George wuz
boys togerr; an' he plunged right in, an' I after him.

"Gord! twuz cold as ice; an' we hadn' got in befo'
bofe horses wuz swimmin' for life. He holler to me
to byah de myah head up de stream; an' I did try,
but what's a nigger to dat water! Hit jes pick me
up an' dash me down like I ain' no mo'n a chip, an'
de fust thing I know I gwine down de stream like a
piece of bark, an' water washin' all over me. I
knowed den I gone, an' I hollered for Marse George
for help. I heah him answer me not to git skeered,
but to hold on; but de myah wuz lungin' an' de
water wuz all over me like ice, an' den I washed off
de myah back, an' got drownded.

"I 'member comin' up an' hollerin' agin for help,
but I know den 'tain' no use, dee ain' no help den,
an' I got to pray to Gord, an' den some'n hit me an'
I went down agin, an'—de next thing I know I wuz
in de bed, an' I heah 'em talkin' 'bout wherr I dead
or not, an' I ain' know myself tell I taste de whiskey
dee po'rin' down my jugular.

"An' den dee tell me 'bout how when I hollered

Marse George tun back an' struck out for me for
life, an' how jes as I went down de last time he
cotch me an' helt on to me tell we wash down to
whar de bank curve, an' dyah de current wuz so
rapid hit yuck him off Reveller back, but he helt on
to de reins tell de horse lunge so he hit him wid he
fo' foot an' breck he collar-bone, an' den he had to
let him go, an' jes helt on to me; an' jes den we
wash up agin de bank an' cotch in a tree, an' de
mens got dyah quick as dee could, an' when dee
retched us Marse George wuz holdin' on to me, an'
had he arm wropped roun' a limb, an' we wuz lodged
in de crotch, an' bofe jes as dead as a nail : an' de
myah she got out, but Reveller he wuz drownded,
wid his foot cotch in de rein an' de saddle tunned
onder he side ; an' dee ain' know wherr Marse
George ain' dead too, 'cause he not only drownded,
but he lef' arm broke up nigh de shoulder.

"An' dee say Miss Charlotte she 'mos' 'stracted ;
dat de fust thing anybody know 'bout it wuz when
some de servants bust in de hall an' holler, an' say
Marse George an' me done bofe washed 'way an'
drownded, an' dat she drapt down dead on de flo',
an' when dee bring her to she 'low to Miss Lucy dat
she de 'casion on he death; an' dee say dat when de
mens wuz totin' him in de house, an' wuz shufflin'
de feets not to meck no noige, an' a little piece o'
blue silk drapt out he breast whar somebody picked
up an' gin Miss Lucy, Miss Charlotte breck right

down agin; an' some on 'em say she sutney did keei
for him; an' now when he layin' upstairs dyah dead,
hit too late for him ever to know it.

"Well, suh, I couldn' teck it in dat Marse George
and Reveller wuz dead, an' jes den somebody say
Marse George done comin' to an' dee gi' me so
much whiskey I went to sleep.

"An' next mornin' I got up an' went to Marse
George room, an' see him layin' dyah in de bed, wid
he face so white an' he eyes so tired-lookin', an' he
ain' know me no mo' 'n ef he nuver see me, an' I
couldn' stan' it; I jes drap down on de flo' an' bust
out cryin'. Gord! suh, I couldn' help it, 'cause
Reveller wuz drownded, an' Marse George he wuz
mos' gone.

"An' he came nigher goin' yit, 'cause he had sich
a strain, an' been so long in de water, he heart done
got numbed, an' he got 'lirium, an' all de time he
thought he tryin' to git 'cross de river to see Miss
Charlotte, an' hit so high he kyarn git dyah.

"Hit sutney wuz pitiful to see him layin' dyah
tossin' an' pitchin', not knowin' whar he wuz, tell
it teck all Mr. Braxton an' me could do to keep
him in de bed, an' de doctors say he kyarn hol' out
much longer.

"An' all dis time Miss Charlotte she wuz gwine
'bout de house wid her face right white, an' Nancy
say she don' do nuttin all day long in her room but
cry an' say her pra'rs, prayin' for Marse George, whai

dyin' upsteairs by 'count o' not knowin' she love him,
an' I tell Nancy how he honin' all de time to see her,
an' how he constant callin' her name.

"Well, so twuz, tell he mos' done wyah heself out;
an' jes lay dyah wid his face white as de pillow, an'
he gret pitiful eyes rollin' 'bout so restless, like he
still lookin' for her whar he all de time callin' her
name, an' kyarn git 'cross dat river to see.

" An' one evenin 'bout sunset he 'peared to be
gwine; he weaker 'n he been at all, he ain' able to
scuffle no mo', an' jes layin' dyah so quiet, an'
presney he say, lookin' mighty wistful,

" 'Edinburg, I'm goin' to-night; ef I don' git 'cross
dis time, I'll gin't up.'

"Mr. Braxton wuz standin' nigh de head o' de
bed, an' he say, 'Well, by Gord! he *shall* see her!'
—jes so. An' he went out de room, an' to Miss
Charlotte do', an' call her, an' tell her she got to
come, ef she don't, he'll die dat night; an' fust thing
I know, Miss Lucy bring Miss Charlotte in, wid her
face right white, but jes as tender as a angel's, an'
she come an' stan' by de side de bed, an' lean down
over him, an' call he name, 'George!'—jes so.

" An' Marse George he ain' answer; he jes look
at her study for a minute, an' den he forehead
got smooth, an' he tun he eyes to me, an say
'Edinburg, I'm 'cross.' "

MEH LADY : A STORY OF THE WAR.

"WON' dat Phil go 'stracted when he gits a pike on de een o' dis feller!"

The speaker was standing in the dogwood bushes just below me, for I was on the embankment, where the little foot-path through the straggling pines and underbrush ran over it. He was holding in his hand a newly peeled cedar fishing-pole, while a number more lay in the path at the foot of the old redoubt.

I watched for a moment in silence, and then said:

" Hello! Uncle, what are you doing? "

" Gittin' fishin'-poles for de boys, suh," he answered promptly and definitely. " We's 'spectin' 'em soon." Then he added confidentially:

" Dee won' have none from nowhar else, suh; dee done heah dee ma tell how Marse Phil used to git poles right heah on dis ridge, an' dee oon' fling a line wid nay urr sort o' poles at all. Dat Phil he mo' like Marse Phil 'n he like he pa; sometimes I think he Marse Phil done come back—he's he ve'y spit an' image."

" Who are the boys? " I asked, taking a seat on the moss-covered breastwork.

" Hi! we all's boys—Meh Lady's. De fish run

nin' good now, an' dee'll be heah toreckly. Dee up
in New York now, but me an' Hannah got a lettet
from 'em yistidy. You cyarn' keep 'em dyah long
after de fish 'gins to run ; no suh, dat you cyarn'.
Dat Phil, I boun' studyin' 'bout his pole right now."
And a short laugh of delight followed the reflection.

" How many are there ? "

" Fo' on 'em, suh, wid de little gal, an' she jes'
like Meh Lady wuz at her age, tryin' to keep up wid
her brurrs, an' do ev'ything dee do. Lord ! suh, hit
cyars me back so sometimes, I mos' furgit de ain'
nuver been no war nor nuttin'. Yes, suh, dee tu'ns
de house upside down when dee comes, jes' like
Marse Phil an' Meh Lady. Um—m ! [making that
peculiar sound so indescribably suggestive], *dee* used
to jes' teoh de wull to pieces. You see, after Marse
Jeems die' an' lef' Mistis heah wid jes' dem two, she
used to gi' 'em dee head, an' dee all over de plantation. Meh Lady (de little white mistis). in her little
white apron wid her curls all down in her eyes, used
to look white 'mong dem urr chil'ns as a clump
o' blackberry blossoms 'mong de blackberries. I
don' keer what Hannah do wid dat hyah it wouldn'
lay smoove. An' her eyes ! I do b'lieve she laugh
mo' wid 'em 'n wid her mouf. She wuz de 'light o'
dis plantation ! When she'd come in you' house
'twuz like you'd shove back de winder an' let piece
o' de sun in on de flo'—you could almos' see by her !
An' Marse Phil, he used to wyah her ! I don' keer

whar you see one, dyah turr, she lookin' up at him, pushin' her hyah back out her big brown eyes, an' tryin' to do jes' what he do. When Marse Phil went byah-footed, she had to go byah-footed too, an' she'd foller him down to de mill-pond th'oo briers an' ev'ywhar, wid her little white foots scratchin' an' gittin' briers in 'em ; but she ain' mine dat so he ain' lef' her. Dat's de way 'twuz, spang tell Marse Phil went to college, or you jes' as well say, tell he went in de army, cause he home ev'y Christmas an' holiday all de time he at de univusity, an' al'ays got somebody or nurr wid him. You cyarn' keep bees 'way after dee fine de honeysuckle bush, an' dem young bucks dee used to be roun' her constant. Hit look like ef she drap her hankcher hit teck all on em' to pick 't up. Dee so perseverin' (Mr. Watkins spressly), I tell Hannah I specks one on 'em gwine be Mistis' son-in-law ; but Hannah say de chile jes' 'joyin' herself an' projeckin' wid 'em, an' ain' love none on 'em hard as Marse Phil. An' so 'twuz! Hannah know. Her cap'n ain' come yit ! When dee cap'n come dee know it, an' ef dee don' know it when he come, dee know it p'intedly when he go 'way.

"We wuz rich den, quarters on ev'y hill, an' niggers mo' 'n you could tell dee names ; dee used to be thirty cradlers in de harves'-fiel' an' binders mo' 'n you kin count.

"Den Marse Phil went in de war. You wuz too

young to know 'bout dat, marster?   Say you wuz?
Dat's so!" (This in ready acquiescence to my reply
that every Southerner knew of the war.)   "Well,
hit 'peared like when it start de ladies wuz ambi-
tiouser for it mos' 'n de mens.   Um! dee wuz rank
sho' 'nough.   At fust dee didn' know what 'twuz,
hit come so sudden.   One mornin' I was standin'
right by de po'ch, an' Marse Phil ride up in de yard.
I see him time he tunned de curve o' de avenue; I
know he seat, 'cause I larn him to ride; dese hands
set him up on de horse fust time he ever tetch ᴅe
saddle, when he little fat legs couldn' retch to de
little skeurts.   Well, I call Mistis an' Meh Lady, an'
dee come out jes' as he gallop up in de yard.   He
speak to me, an' run up de gre't steps, an' Mistis
teck him right in her arms, an' helt him farst, an'
when she le' him go her face look mighty cu'yus;
an' when dee went into de house I notice Marse
Phil taller'n he wuz at Christmas, an' he han' 'em in
stately like he pa.

"'Twuz he done come home to go in de army, an'
he done stop in Richmon' to git he permission,
'cause he feared he ma oon' let him go bedout it;
an' he say, Mr. Watkins an' heap o' de boys done
lef' an' gone home to raise companies.   Mistis—
Hannah say—grieve might'ly when tain' nobody see
her, an' she got her do' locked heap, sayin' her prars
for him; but she ain' say a wud 'bout he goin', she
nor Meh Lady nurr—dee jes' dat ambitious 'bout it.

De thorybreds goes wid dee heads up till dee drap,
you know.

"After dat you ain' see nuttin' but gittin' ready;
cuttin' an' sewin', an' meckin' tents, an' bandages, an' uniforms, an' lint—'twuz wuss'n when
dee meckin' up de folks' winter clo'es! an' when
Marse Phil fetch he s'o'de home an' put on he boots
an' spurs whar I done black, an' git he seat on Paladin, twarn' nay han' on de place but what say Marse
Phil 'bleeged to whup 'em ef dee come close enough.
Well, so he went off to de war, an' Left-hand Torm
went wid him to wait on him an' ten' to de horses,
and Mistis an' Meh Lady ain' had time to cry tell dee
rid roun' de curve, an' Marse Phil tu'n an' wave he
hat to 'em stan'in dyah on de po'ch ; an' den Mistis
tu'n roun' an' walk in de house right quick wid her
mouf wuckin', an' lock herse'f in her chamber, an'
Meh Lady set down on de steps an' cry by herse'f.

"Dat wuz de een o' de ole times, an' dem whar
ain' nuver had dee foots to git 'quainted wid de
ground wuz stomped down in de dut.

"Oh! yes, suh, he come back," said he presently,
in answer to a question from me, "but de war had
been gwine on for mo' 'n a year befo' he did.   Heaps
o' urr soldiers used to come ; dee'd kiver up de gre't
road an' de plantation sometimes, an' eat up ev'y-
thing on de place.   But Marse Phil he ain' nuver git
home ; he 'bleeged to stay to keep de Yankeys back;
he wid Gener'l Jackson, an' he fightin' all de time·

he git two or th'ee balls th'oo he clo'es an' he cap—he
write we all 'bout it ; two bring de blood, but not
much, he say, dee jes' sort o' bark him.   Oh ! dee
wuz jes' p'intedly notifyin' him ; ev'y chance dee'd
git dee'd plump at him same as when you'd
plump at de middle man.   But dat ain' pester him,
chile !

"But one mornin' when we ain' heah from him in
long time an' think he up in de valley, Marse Phil
ride right up in de yard, an' Mistis' face light up to
see him tell she look mos' like a young ooman.   He
say he ain' got long to stay, dat de army gwine
down de big road an' he 'bleeged to git right back
to he bat'ry—he jes' ride 'cross to see he ma an' Meh
Lady an' all on us, he say, an' he mighty hongry,
'cause he ain' had nuttin' to eat sence early de
day befo', an' he want me to feed Paladin at de rack ;
an' Meh Lady, chile ! she lef' him walkin' 'bout in
de house wid he ma, wid he arm roun' her, an'
twis'in' he mustache, whar showin' leetle sence he
sich a man, an' axin' he ma don't she think it a fine
mustache, dat all de girls say' tis, an' axin' 'bout
ev'ybody ; an' she come cut an' 'tend to gittin' him
some'n' to eat wid her own hands, an' he sut'n'y did
eat hearty ; an' den he come 'way, an' he stoop down
an' kiss he ma an' Meh Lady, an' tell 'em he gwine
to be a cun'l one dese days ; an' Mistis she ain' able
to say nuttin', but jes' look at him wistful as he
went down de steps, den she run down after him an'

ketch him after he git on de groun' an' kiss him an'
breck out cryin' ; she say she ain' begrudge him, but
she love him so much. He kiss her mighty sorf'
two or th'ee times, an' den she let him go, an' he
come an git on he horse an' rid 'way at a gallop out
de back gate wid he cap on de side he head, an'
dee went in de house, an' dat horse warn' go up de
stable right den.

" De nex' day we hear de cannons 'way down de
country jes' like thunder right study, an' Mistis and
Meh Lady dee set on de po'ch an' listen to 'em wid
dee face mighty solemn all day long. An' dat night
'bout de fust rooster-crow Left-hand Torm come
home on de gray, an' knock at Mistis' winder, an'
say Marse Phil done shoot in de breast, an' he don't
know wherr he dead or not ; he say he warn' dead
when he come 'way, but de doctor wuz wid him, an'
he had sent him after he ma to come to him at once,
an' he had been ridin' hard all night long ever sence
jes' befo' sunset ; an' Torm say he bat'ry wuz de
fust on de groun', an' he post it on de aidge o' de
woods in a oat-fiel', jes' like cradlers, you know, an'
he drive de enemy out dee breas'wucks, an' he see
him when he lead he bat'ry 'cross de oat-fiel', he
guns all six in a strainin' gallop, an' he and Paladin
in de lead cheerin', wid bullits an' shells hailin' all
roun' him ; an' he wuz de fust man in de redoubt, he
say, an' he fall jes' as he jump he horse over, an'
den he lay dyah an' fight he guns tell he faint. An'

Torm say de gener'l say he'd ruther been Marse Phil fightn' he bat'ry dat day den 'a' been President de Confederate States.

"Well, suh, Mistis she had jump out o' bed de fust step o' Torm in de yard; she hadn' even teck off her clo'es, an' she jes' stand still like she ain' heah good, wid her face lookin' like she done dead. Meh Lady she tell Torm to tell me to git de kerridge as soon as I kin, an' to tell her mammy please to come dyah quick.

"An' when day broke I wuz standin' at de gate wid de kerridge; done feed my horses an' a good bag o' clean oats in de boot. Mistis she come out wid Meh Lady an' Hannah, an' her face sut'n'y wuz grievious. I ain' know tell I see de way she look how it hu't her, but I been see dead folks look better'n she look den. All she say wuz :

"'Try an' git me dyah, Billy;' an' I say, 'Yes'm, I'm gwine to ef Gord'll le' me.' I did git her dyah, too; ef I didn' meck dem horses flinder !

"But dead mens ! I nuver see as many in my life as I see dat evenin'. Amb'lances an' waggins full on 'em, an dem whar jes' good as dead; de road wuz chocked up wid 'em ! Dee all know Marse Phil bat'ry; dee say hit de fust in de fight yistidy an' it cut all to pieces; an' pres'n'y a gent'man whar I ax as he gallop past me rein up he horse an' say he know him well, an' he wuz shot yistidy an' left on de fiel' ; he done teck off he cap when he see Mistis an' Meh Lady in de kerridge, an' he voice drapt mighty low, an' he say Marse Phil wuz shot 'bout fo' o'clock leadin' he bat'ry, an' he did splendid wuck.

"He voice sort o' 'passionate, an' he face so pitiful when he say dat, I know 'tain' no hope to save him, an' ef I git Mistis dyah in time, dat's all.

"'Drive on quick,' says Mistis, an' I druv on. I done meck up my mine to git she an' Meh Lady to Marse Phil, whar I 'sponsible for dat night, ef Gord'll le' me. An' I did, too, mon! I see de soldiers all 'long de road look at me, an some on 'em holler to me dat I cyarn' go dat way ; but I ain' pay no 'tention to 'em, I jes' push on ; an' pres'n'y risin' a little ridge I see de house de gent'man done tell me 'bout, settin' in de oat-fiel' 'bout a half a mile ahead, an' I jes' pushin' for it, when th'ee or fo' mens standin' dyah in de road 'yant de ridge, a little piece befo' me, say 'Halt.' I ain' pay no 'tention to 'em, jes' drive on so, an' dee holler 'Halt' ag'in ; an' when I ain' stop den nuther, jes' drive on right study, a spreckle-face feller run up an' ketch Remus' head, an' anurr one done p'int he gun right at me. I say, 'Whyn' you le' go de horse, mon ! ain' you got no better sense 'n to ketch holt Mistis' horses, juckin' dat horse' mouf dat way ? Le' go de horse' head, don' you heah me ?'

"I clar! ef I warn' dat outdone, I wuz jes' 'bout
to wrap my whip 'roun' him, when Mistis open de
do' an' step out. She say she wan' go on ; dee say
she cyarn' do it ; den she say she gwine, dat her son
dyin' dyah in de house an' she gwine to him. She
talk mighty sorf' but mighty 'termined like. Dee
sort o' reason wid her, but she jes' walk on by wid
her head up, an' tell me to foller her, an' dat I did,
mon! an' lef' 'em dyah in de road holdin' dee gun.
De whole army couldn' 'a' keep her fum Marse Phil
den.

"I got to de house toreckly an' drive up nigh as
I could fur de gre't trenches 'cross de yard, whar
look like folks been ditchin'. A gent'man come to
de do', an' Mistis ax, 'Is he 'live yet?' He say,
'Yes, still alive ;' an' she say 'Where?' an' went
right in an' Meh Lady wid her ; an' I heah say he
open he eyes as she went in an' sort o' smile, an'
when she kneel down an' kiss him he whisper he
ready to go den, an' he wuz too.

" He went dat night in he mother's arms, an' Meh
Lady an' Hannah at he side, like I tole 'em I
was gwine do when I start fum home dat mornin',
an' he wuz jes' as peaceful as a baby. He tole he
ma when he wuz dyin' dat he had try to do he
duty, an' dat 'twuz jes' like ole times, when he
used to go to sleep in her lap in he own room,
wid her arms 'roun' him. Mistis sen' me fur a
amb'lance dat night, an' we put him in de coffin

next mornin' an' start, 'cause Mistis she gwine cyar
Marse Phil home an' lay him in de gyardin, whar she
kin watch him.

"We travel all day an' all night, an' retch home
'bout sunrise, and den we had to dig de grave.

"An' when we got home Mistis she had de coffin
brought in, and cyared him in he own room
while we waitin', and she set in dyah all day long
wid him, and he look like a boy sleepin' dyah so
young, in he little gray jacket wid he s'o'de 'cross he
breas'. We bury him in de gyardin dat evenin', and
dyar warn' 'nough gent'mens in de county to be he
pall-bearers, so de hands on de place toted him, and
it ease' me might'ly to git meh arm onder him right
good, like when he wuz a little chap runnin' 'roun'
callin' me ' Unc' Billy,' and pesterin' me to go fishin'.
And de gener'l write Mistis a letter and say de Con-
fede'cy moan he loss, and he meck him a cun'l in de
oat-fiel' de day he wuz shot, and hit's dat on he
tombstone now ; you kin go dyah in de gyardin an'
read it.

"And we hang he s'o'de on de wall in he own
room over de fireplace, and dyah it hang now for
to show to de boys what a soldier he wuz.

"Well, after dat, things sut'n'y went bad. De
house looked dat lonesome I couldn' byah to look at
it ; ev'ything I see look' like Marse Phil jes' done
put it down, or jes' comin' after it. Mistis and Meh
Lady dee wuz in deep mo'nin', of co'se, and it look

like de house in mo'nin' too. And Mistis her hyah
got whiter and whiter. De on'y thing 'peared to gi'
her any peace o' mine wuz settin' in Marse Phil'
room. She used to set dyah all day, sewin' for de
soldiers. She ain' nuver let nobody tetch dat room,
hit al'ays sort o' secret to her after dat. And Meh
Lady she took holt de plantation, an' ole Billy wuz
her head man.

"Dat's de way 'twuz for two years tell mos' in de
summer. Den—

"Hit happen one day. I wuz jes' come out meh
house after dinner, gwine to de stable. I warn'
studyin' 'bout Yankeys, I wuz jes' studyin' 'bout
how peaceable ev'ything wuz, when I heah somebody hollerin', and heah come two womens 'cross de
hill from de quarters, hard as dee could tyah, wid dee
frocks jes' flying. One o' de maids in de yard de first
to ketch de wud, and she say, ' De Yankeys!' And
'fo' Gord! de wuds warn' out her mouf befo' de
whole top o' de hill wuz black wid 'em. Yo' could
see 'em gallopin' and heah de s'o'des rattlin' spang
at de house. Meh heart jump right up in meh mouf.
But I step back in meh house and got meh axe.
And when I come out, de black folks wuz all run out
dee houses in de back yard, talkin' and predictifyin';
and some say dee gwine in de house and stan' behin'
Meh Lady; and some dee gwine git onder de beds;
and some wuz pacifyin' 'em, and sayin', *dee* ain' gwi'
do nuttin'. I jes' parse long by 'em right quick, and

went 'cross de yard to de house, and I put meh head in and say :

"'De Yankeys yander comin' down de hill.'

"You ought to 'a' seen dee face. Meh Lady hands drapt in her lap, and she looked at Mistis so anxious, she skeer' me. But do' her face tu'n mighty white, 't warn' mo' 'n a minute. She riz right quiet, and her head wuz jes' as straight as Meh Lady. She says to her :

"'Hadn' you better stay here?'

"'No,' says she, 'I will go with you.'

"'Come on,' says she, and dee walked out de do', and locked it behine her, and Mistis put de key in her pocket.

"Jes' as she got dyah, dee rid into de yard, an' in a minute it wuz jes' as full of 'em as a bait-go'd is o' wums, ridin' 'g'inst one anurr, an' hollerin' an' laughin' an' cussin'; an' outside de yard, an' todes de stables, dee wuz jes' swarmin'. Dee ain' ax nobody no odds 'bout nuttin', an' as to key, dee ain' got no use fur dat ; jes' bu'st a do' down quicker 'n you kin onlock it. Dee wuz in de smoke-house an' de store-room quicker 'n I been tellin' you 'bout it. But dat ain' 'sturb Mistis, nor Meh Lady nurr. Dee wuz standin' in de front do' jes' as study as ef dee wuz waitin' fur somebody whar come to dinner. Dee come pourin' up de steps an' say dee gwine th'oo de house.

"'There is no one in there,' said Mistis.

" ' What are you doin' on de po'ch?' says one, sort
o' impident like, wid a thing on he shoulder.

" ' I always receive my visitors at my front do','
says Mistis.

" ' Don't you invite 'em in?' says he, sort o' laughin' an' pushin' by her. Jes' den I heah a noige, an'
we tu'n roun', an' de hall wuz right full on 'em—had
come in de back do'. Mistis tunned right roun' an'
walk into de house right quick, puttin' Meh Lady
'long befo' her. Right straight th'oo 'em all she
walk, an' up to Marse Phil' room do', whar she stan'
wid her back 'g'inst it, holdin' de side. Dee wuz
squandered all over de house by dis time an' teckin'
ev'ything dee want an' didn' want, an' what dee
didn' teck dee wuz cuttin' up. But soon as dee
see Mistis at Marse Phil' do', dee come right up to
her.

" ' I want to go in dyah,' says one—de same one
whar had spoke so discontemptious to de Mistis on
de po'ch.

" ' You cyarn' do it,' says Mistis.

" ' Well, I'm goin' to,' says he.

" ' You are not,' says Mistis, lookin' at him right
study, wid her head up an' her eyes blazin'. I had
my axe in my han', an' I wuz mighty skeered, but I
know ef he had lay his han' on de Mistis I was gwine
split him wide open. He know better 'n to tetch
her, do'. He sort o' parly, like he warn' swade her,
an' all de urrs stop an' listen.

"'Who's in dyah?' says he.

"'No one,' says Mistis.

"'Well, what's in dyah?' says he.

"'The memory of my blessed dead,' says Mistis. She speak so solemn, hit 'peared to kind o' stall him, an' he give back an' mumble some'n'. Pres'n'y do anurr one come up fum nigh de do', an' say to Mistis :

"'Where is you' son? We want him.'

"'Beyond your reach,' says Mistis, her voice kine o' breakin', an' Meh Lady bu'st out cryin'.

"'His grave is in de gyardin', she says, wid her hankcher to her eyes.

"Gord! suh! I couldn' stan' no mo'. I jes' cotch a grip on my axe, an' I ain' know what mout 'a' happen', but he took off he hat an' tu'n 'way. An' jes' den sich a racket riz nigh de do', I thought must be some on 'em got to killin' one 'nurr. I heah somebody's voice rahin' an' pitchin' and callin' 'em thieves an' hounds, an' in a minute, whack, whack, thump, thump, I heah de licks soun' like he hittin' on barrel-head, an' I see a s'o'de flyin' like wheel-spokes, an' de men in de hall dee jes' squander; an' as de larst one jump off de po'ch, a young gent'man tunned an' walked in de do', puttin' he s'o'de back in he scabbard. When he got 't in, he teck off he cap, an' walkin' 'bout half-way up to we all, he say :

"'I kinnot 'pologize 'nough, madam, for dese outages; dee officers ought to be shot for toleratin' it. It is against all orders.'

"'I don't know; it is our first sperience,' says Mistis. 'We are much ondebted to you, though, suh.'

"'Mayn't I interduce myself?' says he, comin' up a little closer to we all, an' meckin' anurr bow very grand. 'I think I may claim to be a kinsman at least of my young Southern cousin here' (meckin' a bow to Meh Lady whar wuz standin' lookin' at him); 'I'm half Virginian myself. I am Captain Wilton, the son of Colonel Churchill Wilton, of de ole army,' says he.

"'It is impossible,' says Mistis, bowin' low'n him. 'Churchill Wilton was a Virginian, do' he lived at de Norf; he wuz my husband's cousin an' my dear friend.' (He come from New York or somewhar, an' he had been co'tin' Mistis same time Marster co't her. I know him well: he gi' me a yaller satin weskit; a likely gent'man too, but Marster beat him. You know he gwine do dat.) 'But you cannot be his son, nor a Virginian; Virginians never invade Virginia.'

"'But I am, neverdeless,' says he, sort o' smilin'; 'an' I have, as a boy, often hear' him speak of you.'

"'We claim no kinsmen among Virginia's enemies,' says Meh Lady, speakin' fur de fust time, wid her eyes flashin', an' teckin' holt of Mistis' han', an'

raisin' herse'f up mighty straight. She wuz standin
by her ma, I tell you ; dee bofe had de same sperit
—de chip don' fly fur fum de stump. But he wuz
so likely-lookin', standin' dyah in de gre't hall meckin' he bow, an' sayin' he Cap'n Wilton, I mos' think
she'd 'a' gi'n in ef it hadn' been fur dat blue uniform
an' dat s'o'de by he side. De wud seemed to hut
him mons'ous do', an' he raise he head up mighty
like we all folks when dee gittin' outdone. Mistis,
she add on to Meh Lady, an' answer he 'quest 'bout
dinner. Ez he had come to teck possession, says
she, de whole place wuz his, an' he could give what
orders he please, on'y she an' Meh Lady would
'quest to be excused ; an' wid dat she took Meh
Lady' han', an' wid a gre't bow start to sweep by
him. But dee ain' git ahead o' him ; befo' dee git
de wuds out dee mouf, he meck a low bow hisse'f
an' say he beg dee pardin, he cyarn' intrude on ladies,
an' wid dat he sort o' back right stately to de front
do', an' wid anurr bow done gone, he saber clam'rin
down de steps. I 'clar', I wuz right sorry fur him,
an' I b'lieve Mistis an' Meh Lady dee wuz too,
'cause he sut'n'y did favor Marse Phil when he r'ar
he head up so tall, an' back out dat do' so gran'.
Meh Lady mine smite her good, 'cause she tu'n to
me an' tell me to go and tell 'Lijah to see ef he
couldn' get him some'n', an' call him, an' pres'n'y
she come in de dinin'-room lookin' herse'f. After
'Lijah set de place do', an' went out to look fur him.

dyah wuz a soldier standin' at ev'y po'ch right solum,
an' anurr one at de kitchin; an' when we come to
fine out, dee wuz guards Cap'n Wilton done pos'
dyah to p'teck de house, but *he* done gone 'long, so
I give he snack to de guards.

"Well, dee took mos' all de corn dat our folks
done lef' out de corn-house, an' after a while mos'
on 'em bridle up an' went 'long, an' den at larst de
guards dee went 'long 'hind de turrs; an' de larst
one hadn' hardly got to de een de avenue when heah
come over de hill some o' our men ridin' 'long de
road fum turr way. Meh Lady wuz standin in de
yard looking mighty 'strustid at de way dee done do
de place, 'cause dee had done teoh it all to pieces;
an' her eyes light up at de sight o' our men, an' she
sort o' wave her hankcher at 'em, an' dee wuz comin'
down de hill turr side de creek right study, when, as
Gord would have it, we heah a horse foot flyin', an'
right fum turr way right down de avenue, he horse
in a lather, come dat same young gent'man, Cap'n
Wilton. Our mens see him at de same time, an'
start to gallopin' down de hill to git him. He ain'
mine 'em do'; he gallop up to de gate an' pull a letter
out he pocket. Meh Lady she wuz so consarned 'bout
him, she sort o' went todes him, callin' to him to do
pray go 'way. He ain' mine dat; he jes' set still
on he nick-tail bay, an' hole he paper todes her right
patient, tell she run down de walk close up to him,
beggin' him to go 'way. Den he teck off he cap an'

ben' over, an' present her de paper he got, an' tell
her hit a letter he got fum Gen'l McClenan, he come
back to gi' her.   Meh Lady, chile! she so busy beggin' him to go 'way an' save hisse'f, she forgit to
thank him.   She jes' pleadin' fur him to go, an' hit
'pear like de mo' she beg, de mo' partic'ler he settin'
dyah at de gate lookin' at her, not noticin' our mens,
wid a sort o' cu'yus smile on he face, tell jes' as our
mens gallop up in one side de yard, an' call to him
to s'render, he say ' Good-by, an' tu'nned an' lay he
gre't big bay horse' foot to de groun'.   Dee shoot at
him an' ride after him, an' Meh Lady she holler to
'em not to shoot him ; but she needn' fluster herse'f,
dee jes' as well try to shoot de win', or ride to ketch
a bud, de way dat horse run.   He wuz a flyer!   He
run like he jes' start, an' de Cap'n done ride him
thirty miles sence dinner to git dat paper fum Gen'l
McClenan fur Meh Lady.

   " Well, suh, dat night de plantation wuz fyah 'live
wid soldiers—our mens ; dee wuz movin' all night
long, jes' like ants, an' all over todes de gre't road
de camp-fires look like stars ; an' nex' mornin' dee
wuz movin' 'fo' daylight, gwine 'long down de road,
an' 'bout dinner-time hit begin, an' from dat time
tell in de night, right down yander way, de whole
uth wuz rockin'.   You'd a-thought de wull wuz split-
tin open, an' sometimes ef you'd listen right good
you could heah 'em yellin', like folks in de harves'
fiel' hollerin' after a ole hyah.

" De nex' day we know we all done scotch 'em,
an' dee begin to bring de wounded an' put 'em in
folks' houses. Dee bring 'em in amb'lances an'
stretchers, tell ev'y room in de house wuz full up,
'sep' on'y Mistis' chahmber an' Meh Lady' room an'
Marse Phil' room. An' dyah wuz de grettest cuttin
up o' sheets an' linen an' things fur bandages an'
lint you ever see. Mistis an' Meh Lady even cut up
dee under-clo'es fur lint, 'cause you know dee wuz
'bleeged to have linen, an' Mistis an' Meh Lady teoh
up dee under-clo'es tell dee got smack out. Hannah
had to go 'long afterwards an' gi' 'em some dee done
done gi' her. Well, so 'twuz, de house wuz full like
a hospittle, an' doctors gwine in an' out, an' ridin'
back'ards an' for'ards, an' cuttin' off legs an' arms,
an' hardly got time to tu'n 'roun'. 'Twuz mighty
hard on Meh Lady, but she had grit to stan' it. Hi!
de ve'y mornin' after de battle a doctor come out de
room whar a wounded gent'man wuz, an' ketch sight
o' Meh Lady parsin' th'oo de hall, an' say, ' I want
you to help me,' an' she say, ' What you want me to
do ? ' an' he say, ' You've got to hold a man's arm,'
an' she say, ' To bandage it ? ' an' he say, ' No, to
cut it off ; ' an' she say she cyarn' do it, an' he say
she kin an' she must. Den she say she'll faint, an'
he say ef she do he'll die, an' he ain' got a minute to
spyah now. Den ef she ain' walk right in an' hole
he arm, tell de doctor cut 't off an' dress it, an' den
widout a wud she say, ' Is you done ? ' an' he say,

' Yes ; ' an' she walk out an' cross de yard to her
mammy' house right quick, an' fall right dead down
on de flo'. I wan' dyah, but Hannah sut'n'y wuz
outdone 'bout dat thing, an', you know, she ain'
nuver let Mistis know a wud 'bout it, not nuver—
she so feared she'd 'sturb her! Dat's de blood she
wuz ; an' dem wuz times folks wa'n't dem kind!
Well, dat same evenin'—de day after de battle—Meh
Lady she ax one de doctors ef many o' de cav'lry
wuz into de fight, an' he say she'd think so ef she'd
been dyah ; dat de cav'lry had meck some splendid
charges bofe sides ; dat de Yankey cav'lry had charge
th'oo a bresh o' pines on de 'streme left spang up
'g'inst our breas'wucks, an' a young Yankey cap'n in
de front o' all, wid he cap on he s'o'de, on a nick-tail
bay, had led 'em, an' had spur he horse jam up to
our line, an' bofe had fall up 'g'inst de breas'wucks.
I tell you he sut'n'y wuz pleased wid him ; he say
he nuver see a braver feller ; he had made a p'int to
try an' save him (an' he'd like to 'a' had dat horse
too), but he was shot so bad he fear'd 'tain' much
show fur him, as he sort o' knocked out he senses
when he fall as well as shot. An' he say, ' He sich
a likely young feller, an' meck sich a splendid charge,
I teck a letter out he pocket to 'dentify him, an'
heah 'tis now,' he says ; ' Cap'n Shelly Wilton,' he
says, handin' it to Meh Lady.

"When he say dat, Meh Lady ain' say nuttin
an Mistis she tu'n 'roun' an' walk in Marse Phil'

room right quick an' shet de do' easy. Den pres'n'y
she come out an' ax Meh Lady to have de kerridge
gitten, an' den she walk up to de doctor, an' ax him
won' he go down wid her to de place whar he lef'
dat young Yankey cap'n an' bring him dyah to her
house. An' she say he her husband' cousin, an' she
onder obligations to him. So dee went, honey, down
to de battle-fiel' all roun' de road, an' 'twuz mos'
wuss 'n when we all went down to de Peninsular
after Marse Phil, de road wuz so full of wounded
mens; an' when we fine him 'twuz right dyah at dat
gap—he fall right dyah, an' dee had cyar'ed him
over de hill; an' do' all say he 'bleeged to die, Mistis
she had him tecken up an' brung right to her house,
an' when we got home she lead de way an' went
straight long th'oo de hall, an', befo' Gord! she
opened de do' herse'f an' cyar him right in an' lay
him right down into Marse Phil' baid. Some say
hit 'cause he marster's kinfolk; but Hannah, she
know, an' she say hit 'cause Mistis grievin' 'bout
Marse Phil. I ain' know huccome 'tis; but dyah *into*
Marse Phil' baid dee put him, an' dyah he stay good,
an' Mistis an' Meh Lady to nuss him same like he
wuz Marse Phil hisse'f. 'Twuz a spell do', I tell
you! Dyah wuz all de turrs well an' gone befo' he
know wherr he dead or 'live. Mistis, after de battle,
an' all de 'citement sort o' let down ag'in, had to
keep her room right constant, and all de nussin'
an' waitin' fall on Meh Lady an' Hannah, an' dee

sut'n'y did do dee part faithful by all on 'em, till
fust one an' den anurr went away ; 'cause, you know,
we couldn' tell when de Yankeys wuz gwine to come
an' drive our mens back, an' our soldiers didn' want
to be tecken pris'ners, an' moved 'way. An' pres'n'y
dyah warn' none lef' but jes' Cap'n Wilton, an' he
still layin' dyah in de baid, tossin' an' talkin', wid he
eyes wide open an' ain' know nuttin'. De doctor
say he wound better, but he got fever, an' he cyarn'
hole out much longer ; say he'd been dead long ago
but he so strong. An' one night he went to sleep,
an' de doctor come over fum camp an' say he wan'
nuver gwine wake no mo' he reckon, jes' a byah
chance ef he ain' 'sturbed. An' he ax Meh Lady
kin she keep him 'sleep she reckon, an' she say she'll
try, an' she did, mon. Mistis she wuz sick in baid
an' dyah ain' nobody to nuss him, skusin' Meh Lady,
an' she set by dat baid all dat night an' fan him right
easy all night long ; all night long she fan him, an'
jes' befo' sun up he open he eyes an' look at her.
Hannah she jes' gone in dyah, thinkin' de chile tire'
to death, an' she say jes' as she tip in he open he
eyes an' he look at Meh Lady so cu'yus, settin' dyah
by him watchin' ; den he shet he eyes a little while
an' sleep a little mo' ; den he open 'em an' look
ag'in an' sort o' smile like he know her ; an' den he
went to sleep good, an' Hannah she tuck de fan an'
sont de chile to her own room to baid. Yes, suh,
she did dat thing, she did! An' I heah him say

afterwards, when he wake up, all he could think 'bout wuz he done git to heaven.

" Well, after dat, Meh Lady she lef' him to Mistis an' Hannah, an' pres'n'y he git able to be holped out on de big po'ch an' kivered up wid a shawl an' things in a big arm-cheer. An' 'cause Mistis she mos' took to her baid, an' keep her room right constant, Meh Lady she got to entertain him. Oh! she sut'n'y did pomper him, readin' to him out o' books, an' settin by him on de po'ch. You see, he done git he pay-role, an' she 'bleeged to teck keer on him den, 'cause she kind o' 'sponsible for him, an' he sut'n'y wuz satisfied, layin' dyah wid he gray eyes followin' her study ev'ywhar she tu'n, jes' like some dem pictures hangin' up in de parlor.

" I 'members de fust day he walked. He done notify her, and she try to 'swade him, but he monsus sot in he mind when he done meck it up, and she got to gi' in, like women-folks after dee done 'spressify some ; and he git up and walk down de steps, and 'cross de yard to a rose-bush nigh de gate wid red roses on it, she walkin' by he side lookin' sort o' anxious. When he git dyah, dee talk a little while, den he breck one and gi' 't to her, and dee come back. Well, he hadn' git back to he cheer befo' heah come two or th'ee gent'mens ridin' th'oo de place, one on 'em a gener'l, and turrs dem whar ride wid 'em, our mens, and dee stop at de gate to 'quire de way to de hewn-tree ford down on de river

and Meh Lady she went down to de gate to ax 'em
to 'light, and to tell 'em de way down by de pond ;
and when she standin' dyah shadin' de sun from her
eyes wid a fan, and de rose in her hand ('cause she
ain' got on no hat), de gener'l say :

" ' You have a wounded soldier dyah ? '

" ' Yes, he's a wounded Federal officer on parole,'
she says ; and he say, teckin' off he hat :

" ' Dee ain' many soldiers dat wouldn' envy him
he prison.' And den she bows to him sort o' 'fusin'
like, and her face mos' blushin' as de rose de Cap'n
done gi' her what she holdin' ; and when dee done
rid 'long, an' ain' stop, she ain' gone back to de po'ch
toreckly ; she come out, and gi' me a whole parecel
o' directions 'bout spadin' de border whar I
standin' heahin' 't all, wid de rose done stickin' in
her bosom.

" You'd think de way Meh Lady read to him dyah
on de big po'ch, she done forgit he her pris'ner and
Virginia' enemy. She ain' do' ; she jes' as rapid to
teck up for de rebels as befo' he come ; I b'lieve she
rapider ; she call herse'f rebel, but she ain' le' him
name it. I 'member one mornin' she come in out
de fiel' an' jump off her horse, an' set down by him
in her ridin'-frock, and she call herse'f a rebel, an'
pres'n'y he name us so too, an' she say he sha'n't
call 'em so, an' he laugh an' call 'em so ag'in, jes'
dyahsen, an' she git up an' walk right straight in de
house, head up in de air. He tell her de rebels wuz

'treatin', but she ain' dignify to notice dat. He teck up a book an' 'pose hese'f, but he ain' read much: den he try to sleep, but de flies 'pear to pester him might'ly; den Hannah come out, an' he ax her is she see Meh Lady in dyah. Hannah say, ' Nor,' an' den he ax her won' she please go an' ax her to step dyah a minute; an' Hannah ain' spicion nuttin' and went, an' Meh Lady say, ' No, she won',' 'cause he done aggrivate her; an' den he write her a little note an' ax Hannah to gi' 't to her, an' she look at it an' send 't back to him widout any answer. Den he git mad. He twis' roun' in he cheer might'ly; but 'tain' do him no good, she ain' come back all day, not tell he had to teck he pencil an' write her a sho' 'nough letter; den pres'n'y she come out on de po'ch right slow, dressed all in white, and tell him sort o' forgivin' dat he ought to be 'shamed o' hisse'f, an' he sort o' laugh', an' look like he ain' 'shamed o' nuttin'.

"De sut'n'y wuz gittin' good-neighborly 'long den. And he watch over her jes' like she got her pay-role 'stid o' him. One day a party o' Yankeys, jes' prowlin' roun' after divilment, come gallopin' in th'oo de place, an' down to de stable, and had meh kerridge-horses out befo' I know dee dyah. I run in de house and tell Meh Lady. De Cap'n he wuz in he room and he heah me, and he come out wid he cap on, bucklin' on Marse Phil' s'o'de whar he done teck down off de wall, and he order me to

come 'long, and tell Meh Lady not to come out ；
and down de steps he stride and 'cross de yard out
th'oo de gate in de road to whar de mens wuz wid
meh horses at de fence, wid he face right set. He
ax' em one or two questions 'bout whar dee from
dat mornin'; den he tell 'em who he is and dat dee
cyarn' trouble nuffin' heah. De man wid meh
horses see de Cap'n mighty pale an' weak-lookin',
and he jes' laugh, an' gether up de halters gittin'
ready to go, an' call de urrs to come 'long. Well,
suh, de Cap'n' eye flash; he ain' say a wud; he jes
rip out Marse Phil' s'o'de an' clap it up 'ginst dat
man' side, an cuss him once! You ought to 'a' seen
him le' dem halters go! 'Now,' says de Cap'n,
'you men go on whar you gwine; dyah de road; I
know you, an' ef I heah of you stealin' anything I'll
have you ev'y one hung as soon as I get back.
Now go.' An' I tell you, mon! dee gone quick
enough.

"Oh! I tell you he sut'n'y had de favor o' our
folks; he ain' waste no wuds when he ready; he
quick to r'ar, an' rank when he got up, jes' like all
our fam'bly; Norf or Souf, dee ain' gwine stand no
projeckin'; dee's Jack Robinson.

"So 'twuz, Meh Lady sort o' got used to 'pendin'
on him, an' 'dout axin her he sort o' sensed when to
'vise her.

"Sometimes dee'd git in de boat on de pond, an
she'd row him while he'd steer, 'cause he shoulde*

ain' le' him row. I see 'em of a evenin' jes' sort o floatin' down deah onder de trees, nigh de bank, or 'mong dem cow-collards, pullin' dem water-flowers, —she ain' got no hat on, or maybe jes' a soldier's cap on her head,—an' hear 'em talkin' 'cross de water so sleepy, an' sometimes he'd meck her laugh jes' as clear as a bud. Dee war'n no pay-role den!

"All dis time, do', she jes' as good a rebel as befo' he come. De wagons would come an' haul corn, an' she'd 'tend to cookin' for de soldiers all night long, jes' same, on'y she ain' talk to him 'bout it, an' he sort o' shet he eye and read he book like he ain' see it. She ain' le' Cap'n Wilton nor Cap'n nuttin' else meck no diffunce 'bout dat; she jes' partic'lar to him 'cause he her cousin, dat's all, an got he pay-role; we all white folks al'ays set heap o' sto' by one nurr, dat's all she got in her mind.

"I almos' begin' to spicionate some'n' myse'f, but Hannah she say I ain' nuttin' but a ole nigger-fool, I ain' know nuttin' 'bout white folks' ways; an' sho' 'nough, she done prove herse'f. Hit come 'long todes de larst o' fall, 'bout seedin'-wheat time; de weather been mighty warm, mos' like summer, an' ev'ything sort o' smoky, hazy, like folks bunnin' bresh; an' one day d' come fum de post-office a let-ter for de Cap'n, an' he face look sort o' comical when he open it, an' he put it in he pocket; an

pres'n'y he say he got to go home, he got he ex-
changement.   Meh Lady ain' say nuttin'; but after
while she ax, kind o' perlite, is he well enough yet
to go.   He ain' meck no answer, an' she ain' say no
mo', den bofe stop talkin' right good.

"Well, dat evenin' dee come out, and set on de
po'ch awhile, she wid her hyah done smoove; den
he say some'n to her, an' dee git up an' went to
walk; an' fust he walk to dat red rose-bush an' pull
two or th'ee roses, den dee went saunterin' right
'long down dis way, he wid de roses in he han',
lookin' mighty handsome.   Pres'n'y I hed to come
down in de fiel', an' when I was gwine back to de
house to feed, I strike for dis parf, an' I wuz walkin'
'long right slow ('cause I had a misery in dis hip
heah), an' as I come th'oo de bushes I hyah somebody talkin', an' dyah dee wuz right at de gap, an'
he wuz holdin' her hand, talkin' right study, lookin'
down at her, an' she lookin' 'way fum him, ain' sayin' nuttin', jes' lookin' so miser'ble wid de roses
done shatter all over in her lap an' on de groun'.   I
ain' know which way to tu'n, an' I hyah him say he
wan' her to wait an' le' him come back ag'in, an' he
call her by her name, an' say, 'Won't you!' an' she
wait a little while an' den pull her hand away right
slow; den she say, sort o' whisperin', she cyarn'.
He say some'n' den so hoarse I ain' meck't out, an'
she say, still lookin' 'way fum him on de groun', dat
she cyarn' marry a Union soldier.   Den he le' go

her hand an' rar hese'f up sort o' straight, an' say some'n' I ain' meck out 'sep' hit would 'a' been kin-der ef she had let him die when he wuz wounded, 'stid o' woundin' him all he life. When he say dat, she sort o' squinch 'way from him like he mos' done hit her, an' say wid her back todes him he ought not to talk dat way, dat she know she been mighty wicked, but she ain' know 'bout it, an' maybe—. I ain' know what she say, 'cause she start to cryin' right easy, an' he teck her han' ag'in an' kiss it, an' I slip roun' an' come home, an' lef' 'em dyah at de gap, she cryin' an' he kissin' her han'.

"I drive him over to de depot dat night, an' he gi' me a five dollars in gold, an' say I must teck keer o' de ladies, I'se dee main' pendence ; an' I tell him I is, an' he sut'ny wuz sorry to tell me good-by.

"An' Hannah say she done tell me all 'long de chile ain' gwine mortify herself 'bout no Yankey soldier, don' keer how pretty an' tall he is, an' how straight he hole he head, an' dat she jes' sorry he gone 'cause he her cousin. I ain' know so much 'bout dat do. Dat what Hannah al'ays say she tell me.

"Well, suh, ef 'twarn' lonesome after dat! Hit 'peared like whip'o'will sing all over de place ; ev'y-whar I tu'n I ain' see him. I didn' know till he gone how sot we all dun git on him ; 'cause I ain' de on'y one dun miss him ; Hannah she worryin' 'bout him, Mistis she miss him, an' Meh Lady she gwine right study wid her mouf shet close, but she cyarn' shet her eye on me: she miss him, an' she signify it too. She tell Mistis 'bout he done ax her to marry him some day an' to le' him come back, an' Mistis ax what she say, an' she tell her, an' Mistis git up out her cheer an' went over to her, an' kiss her right sorf; and Hannah say (she wuz in de chahmber an' she hyah 'em), she say she broke out cryin', an' say she know she ought to hate him, but she don't, an' she cyarn', she jes' hate an' 'spise her- self; an' Mistis she try to comfort her; an' she teck up de plantation ag'in, but she ain' never look jes' like she look befo' he come dyah an' walk in de hall, so straight, puttin' up he s'o'de, an' when she ain' claim kin wid him back out an' say he cyarn' intrude on her, an' den ride thirty mile' to git dat paper an' come an' set on he horse at de gate so study and our mens gallopin' up in de yard to get him. She wuck mighty study, and ride Dixie over de planta- tion mighty reg'lar, 'cause de war dun git us so low, wid all dem niggers to feed, she hed to tu'n roun' right swift to git 'em victuals an' clo'es; but she ain' look jes' like she look befo' dat, an' she sut'n'y do nuss dat rose-bush nigh de gate induschus. But dem wuz de een o' de good times.

" Hit 'peared like dat winter all de good luck done gone 'way fum de place; de weather wuz so severe, an' we done gi' de ahmy ev'ything, de feed done gi'

out, an' 'twuz rank, I tell you! Mistis an' Meh
Lady sent to Richmon' an' sell dee bonds, an' some
dee buy things wid to eat, an' de rest dee gin de
Gov'ment, an' teck Confed'ate money for 'em. She
say she ain' think hit right to widhold nuttin', an'
she teck Marster' bonds an' sell 'em fur Confed'ate
Gunboat stock or some'n.' I use' to hyah 'em talkin'
'bout it.

"Den de Yankeys come an' got my kerridge.
horses! Oh! ef dat didn' hu't me! I ain' git over
it yit. When we hyah dee comin' Meh Lady tell
me to hide de horses; hit jes' as well, she reckon.
De fust time dee come, dee wuz all down in de river
pahsture, an' dee ain' see 'em, but now dee wuz up
at de house. An' so many been stealed I used to
sleep in de stalls at night to watch 'em; so I teck
'em all down in de pines on de river, an' I down
dyah jes' as s'cure as a coon in de holler, when heah
dee come tromplin' and gallinupin', an' teck 'em
ev'y one, an' 'twuz dat weevly black nigger Ananias
done show 'em whar de horses is, an' lead 'em dyah.
He always wuz a mean po' white folks nigger anyways, an' 'twuz a pity Mistis ain' sell him long ago.
Ef I couldn' a teoh him all to pieces dat day! I
b'lieve Meh Lady mo' 'sturb 'bout 'Nias showin' de
Yankeys whar de horses is den she is 'bout dee
teckin' 'em. 'Nias he ain' nuver dyah show he face
no mo', he went off wid 'em, an' so did two or th'ee
mo' 'o de boys. De folks see 'em when dee pars

th'oo Quail Quarter, an' dee 'shamed to say dee gone off, so dee tell 'em de Yankeys cyar' 'em off, but 'twarn' nothin' but a lie ; I know dee ain' cyar' me off ; de ax me ef I don' wan' go, but I tell 'em ' Nor.'

"Things wuz mons'ous scant after dat, an' me an' Meh Lady had hard wuck to meck buckle and tongue meet, I tell you. We had to scuffle might'ly dat winter.

"Well, one night a cu'yus thing happen. We had done got mighty lean, what wid our mens an' Yankeys an' all ; an' de craps ain' come in, an' de team done gone, an' de fences done bu'nt up, an' things gettin' mighty down, I tell you. And dat night I wuz settin' out in de yard, jes' done finish smokin', and studyin' 'bout gwine to bed. De sky wuz sort o' thick, an' meh mine wuz runnin' on my horses, an' pres'n'y, suh. I heah one on 'em gallopin' tobucket, tobucket, tobucket, right swif' 'long de parf 'cross de fiel', an' I thought to myself, I know Romilus' gallop ; I set right still, an' he come 'cross de branch and stop to drink jes' a moufful, an' den he come up de hill. I say, ' Dat horse got heap o' sense ; he know he hot, an' he ain' gwine hu't hese'f drinkin', don' keer how thusty he is. He gwine up to de stable now,' I say, ' an' I got to go up dyah an' le' him in ;' but 'stid o' dat, he tu'n 'roun' by de laun- dry, an' come 'roun' de house to whar I settin', an' stop, an' I wuz jes' sayin', ' Well, ef dat don' beat any horse ever wuz in de wull; how he know I heah?' when somebody say, 'Good-evenin'.' I sut'. n'y wuz disapp'inted; dyah wuz a man settin' dyah in de dark on a gre't black horse, an' say he wan' me to show him de way th'oo de place. He ax me ef I warn' sleep, an' I tell him, 'Nor, I jes' studyin';' den he ax me a whole parecel o' questions 'bout Mistis and Marse Phil an' all, an' say he kin to 'em, an' he used to know Mistis a long time ago. Den I ax him to 'light, an' tell him we'd all be mighty glad to see him; but he say he 'bleeged to git right on; an' he keep on axin' how dee wuz an' how dee been, an' ef dee sick an' all, an' so 'quisitive; pres'n'y I ain' tell him no mo' 'sep' dat dee all well 'skusin' Mistis; an' den he ax me to show him de way th'oo, an' when I start, he ax me cyarn he go th'oo de yard, dat de 'rection he warn' go, an' I tell him 'Yes,' an' le' him th'oo de back gate, an' he ride 'cross de yard on de grahss. As he ride by de rose-bush nigh de gate, he lean over, an' I thought he breck a switch off, an' I tell him not to breck dat; dat Meh Lady' rose-bush, whar she set mo' sto' by den all de res'; an' he say, ''Tis a rose-bush, sho' 'nough,' an' he come 'long to de gate, holdin' a rose in he hand. Dyah he ax me which is Mistis' room, and I tell him, 'De one by de po'ch,' an' he say he s'pose dee don' use upstyars much now de fam'bly so small; an' I tell him, 'Nor,' dat Meh Lady' room right next to Mistis' dis side, an' he stop an' look

good; den he come 'long to de gate, an' when I ax
him which way he gwine, he say, 'By de hewn-tree
ford.' An' blessed Gord! ef de wud ain' bring up
things I done mos' forgit—dat gener'l ridin' up to
de gate, an' Meh Lady standin' dyah, shadin' her
eyes, wid de rose de Cap'n done gi' her off dat same
bush, an' de gener'l say he envy him he prison. I
see him jes' plain as ef he standin' dyah befo' me,
an' heah him axin' de way to de hewn-tree ford; but
jes' den I heah some'n jingle, an' he jes' lean over
an' poke some'n heavy in my hand, an' befo' I ken
say a wud he gone gallopin' in de dark. And when
I git back to de light, I find six gre't big yaller gold
pieces in meh hand, look like gre't pats o' butter,
an' ef 't hadn' been for dat I'd 'mos' 'a' believe'
'twuz a dream; but dyah de money an' dyah de
horse-track, an' de limb done pull off Meh Lady'
rose-bush.

"I hide de money in a ole sock onder de j'ice,
and I p'int to tell Meh Lady 'bout it; but Hannah,
she say I ain' know who 'tis—jes' s'picion (and so I
ain' den); and I jes' gwine 'sturb Mistis wid folks
ridin' 'bout th'oo de yard at night, and so I ain' say
nuttin'; but when I heah Meh Lady grievin' 'bout
somebody done breck her rose-bush an' steal one of
her roses, I mighty nigh tell her who I b'lieve
'twuz, an' I would, on'y I don't orn' aggrivate Hannah. You know 'twon't do to aggrivate women
folks.

"Well, 'twarn' no gre't while after dat de war broke; 'twuz de nex' spring 'bout plantin'-corn time, on'y we ain' plant much 'cause de team so weak; stealin' an' Yankey teckin' together done clean us up, an' Mistis an' Meh Lady had to gi' a deed o' struss on de lan' to buy a new team dat spring, befo we could breck up de corn-land, an' we hadn' git mo' 'n half done fo' Richmon' fall an' de folks wuz all free; den de army parse th'oo an' some on 'em come by home, an' teck ev'y blessed Gord's horse an' mule on de place, 'sep' one mule—George, whar wuz bline, an' dee won' have him. Dem wuz turrible times, an' ef Meh Lady an' Mistis didn' cry! not 'cause dee teck de horses an' mules—we done get use' to dat, an' dat jes' meck 'em mad and high-spirited—but 'cause Richmon' done fall an' Gener'l Lee surrendered. Ef dee didn' cry! When Richmon' fall dee wuz 'stonished, but dee say dat ain' meck no diffunce, Gener'l Lee gwine whip 'em yit; but when dee heah Gener'l Lee done surrender, dee gin up; fust dee wouldn' b'lieve it, but dee sut'n'y wuz strusted. Dee grieve 'bout dat 'mos' much as when Marse Phil die. Mistis she ain' nuver rekiver. She wuz al'ays sickly and in bed like after dat, and Meh Lady and Hannah dee use' to nuss her. After de fust year or so mos' o' de folks went away. Meh Lady she tell 'em dee better go, dat dee'l fine dem kin do mo' for 'em 'en she kin now; heap on em say dee ain' gwine way, but after we so po' dee went 'way, do' Meh Lady sell some Mistis' diamonds to buy 'em some'n to eat while dee dyah.

"Well, 'twan' so ve'y long after dis, or maybe 'twuz befo', 'twuz jes' after Richmon' fall, Mistis get a letter fum de Cun'l—dat's Cap'n Wilton; he done Cun'l den—tellin' her he want her to le' him come down an' see her an' Meh Lady, an' he been love Meh Lady all de time sence he wounded heah in de war, an' al'ays will love her, an' won' she le' him help her any way; dat he owe Mistis an' Meh Lady he life. Hannah heah 'em read it. De letter 'sturb Mistis might'ly, an' she jes' put it in Meh Lady' han's an' tu'n 'way widout a wud.

"Meh Lady, Hannah say, set right still a minute an' look mighty solemn; den she look at Mistis sort o' sideways, an' den she say, 'Tell him no.' An' Mistis went over an' kiss her right sorf.

"An' dat evenin' I cyar de letter whar Mistis write to de office.

"Well, 'twarn' so much time after dat dee begin to sue Mistis on Marster's debts. We heah dee suin' her in de co't, an' Mistis she teck to her bed reg'lar wid so much trouble, an' say she hope she won' nuver live to see de place sold, an' Meh Lady she got to byah ev'ything. She used to sing to Mistis an' read to her an' try to hearten her up, meckin' out dat 'tain' meck no diffunce. Hit did do', an' she know it, 'cause we po' now, sho' 'nough; an' dee wuz po'er 'n Hannah an' me, 'cause de lan'

ain got nobody to wuck it an' no team to wuck it
wid, an' we ain' know who it b'longst to, an' hit all
done all grow up in bushes an' blackberry briers;
ev'y year hit grow up mo' an mo', an' we git po'er
an' po'er. Mistis she boun' to have flour, ain' been
use' to nuttin' but de fines' bread, jes' as white as
you' shu't, an' she so sickly now she got to have
heap o' things, tell Meh Lady fyar at her wits' een
to git 'em. Dat's all I ever see her cry 'bout, when
she ain' got nuttin' to buy what Mistis want. She
use to cry 'bout dat do. But Mistis ain' know
nothin' 'bout dat, she think Meh Lady got heap
mo'n she is, bein' shet up in her room now all de
time. De doctor say she got 'sumption, an' Meh
Lady doin' all she kin to keep 't fum her how po'
we is, smilin' an' singin' fur her. She jes' whah herse'f out wid it, nussin' her, wuckin' fur her, singin'
to her. Hit used to hu't me sometimes to heah
de chile singin' of a evenin' things she use to sing in
ole times, like she got ev'ything on uth same as
befo' de war, an' I know she jes' singin' to ease Mistis min', an' maybe she hongry right now.

"'Twuz den I went an' git de rest o' de money de
Cap'n gi' me dat night fum onder de j'ice (I had
done spend right smart chance on it gittin' things,
meckin' b'lieve I meck it on de farm), an' I put it
in meh ole hat' an' cyar it to Meh Lady, 'cause it sort
o' hers anyways; an' her face sort o' light up when
she see de gold shinin', 'cause she sut'n'y had use

for it, an' she ax me whar I git so much money, an
I tell her somebody gi' 't to me, an' she say what I
gwine do wid it. An' I tell her it hern, an' she say
how, an' I tell her I owe it to her for rent, an' she
bu'st out cryin' so she skeer me. She say she owe
us ev'ything in de wull, an' she know we jes' stayin'
wid 'em 'cause dee helpless, an' sich things, an' she
cry so I upped an' tole her how I come by de money,
an' she stop an' listen good. Den she say she cyarn'
tech a cent o' dat money, an' she oodn', mon, tell I
tell her I wan' buy de mule ; an' she say she consider
him mine now, an' ef he ain' she gi' 't to me, an' I say,
nor, I wan' buy him. Den she say how much he
wuth, an' I say a hunderd dollars, but I ain' got dat
much right now, I kin owe her de res' ; an' she breck
out laughin', like when she wuz a little girl an'
would begin to laugh ef you please her, wid de tears
on her face an' dress, sort o' April-like. Hit gratify
me so, I keep on at it, but she say she'll teck twenty
dollars for de mule an' no mo', an' I say I ain' gwine
disqualify dat mule wid no sich price ; den pres'n'y
we 'gree on forty dollars, an' I pay it to her, an' she
sont me up to Richmon' next day to git things for
Mistis, an' she al'ays meck it a p'int after dat to
feed George a little some'n' ev'y day.

"Den she teck de school ; did you know 'bout dat ?
Dat de school-house right down de road a little
piece. I reckon you see it as you come 'long. I
ain' b'lieve it when I heah 'em say Meh Lady gwine

teach it. I say, 'She teach niggers! dat she ain' ¹
not my young mistis.' But she laugh at me an'
Hannah, an' say she been teachin' de colored chil'n
all her life, ain' she? an' she wan' Hannah an' me to
ease Mistis' min' 'bout it ef she say anything. I
sut'n'y was 'posed to it, do'; an' de colored chil'n she
been teachin' wuz diffunt—dee b'longst to her. But
she al'ays so sot on doin' what she gwine do, she
meck you b'lieve she right don' keer what 'tis; an' I
tell her pres'n'y, all right, but ef dem niggers impident to her, jes' le' me know an' I'll come down dyah
an' wyah 'em out. So she went reg'lar, walk right
'long dis ve'y parf wid her books an' her little basket.
An' sometimes I'd bring de mule for her to ride home
ef she been up de night befo' wid Mistis; but she
wouldn' ride much, 'cause she think George got to
wuck.

"Tell 'long in de spring Meh Lady she done breck
down, what wid teachin' school, an' settin' up, an'
bein' so po', stintin' for Mistis, an' her face gittin'
real white 'stid o' pink like peach-blossom, as it used
to be, on'y her eyes dee bigger an' prettier'n ever,
'sep' dee look tired when she come out o' Mistis'
chahmber an' lean 'g'inst de do', lookin' out down de
lonesome road; an' de doctor whar come from Richmon' to see Mistis, 'cause de ain' no doctor in de
neighborhood sence de war, tell Hannah when he
went 'way de larst time 'tain' no hope for Mistis, she
mos' gone, an' she better look mighty good after

Meh Lady too; he say she mos' sick as Mistis, an
fust thing she know she'll be gone too.   Dat 'sturb
Hannah might'ly.   Well, so 'twuz tell in de spring.
I had done plant meh corn, an' it hed done come
up right good; 'bout mos' eight acres, right below
the barn whar de lan' strong (I couldn' put in no mo'
'cause de mule he wuz mighty ole); an' come a man
down heah one mornin', riding a sway-back sorrel
horse, an' say dee gwine sell de place in 'bout a
mon'.   Meh Lady hed gone to school, an' I ain' le'
him see Mistis, nor tell him whar Meh Lady is
nuther; I jes' teck de message an' call Hannah so
as she kin git it straight; an' when Meh Lady come
home dat evenin' I tell her.   She sut'n'y did tu'n
white, an' dat night she ain' sleep a wink.   After she
put her ma to sleep, she come out to her mammy'
house, an' fling herself on Hannah' bed an' cry an'
cry.   'Twuz jes' as ef her heart gwine breck; she
say 'twould kill her ma, an' hit did.

   "Mistis she boun' to heah 'bout it, 'cause Meh
Lady 'bleeged to breck it to her now; and at fust it
'peared like she got better on it, she teck mo' noticement o' ev'ything, an' her eyes look bright and shiny.
She ain' know not yit 'bout how hard Meh Lady
been had to scuffle; she say she keep on after her to
git herse'f some new clo'es, a dress an' things, an' she
oont; an' Meh Lady would jes' smile, tired like, an'
say she teachin' now, and don' want no mo' 'n she got,
an' her smile meck me mos' sorry like she cryin'.

" So hit went on tell jes befo' de sale. An' one
day Meh Lady she done lef' her ma settin' in her
cheer by de winder, whar she done fix her good wid
pillows, an' she done gone to school, an' Hannah
come out whar I grazin' de mule on de ditch-bank,
an' say Mistis wan' see me toreckly. I gi' Hannah
de lines, an' I went in an' knock at de do', an' when
Mistis ain' heah, I went an' knock at de chahmber
do' an' she tell me to come in ; an' I ax her how she
is, an' she say she ain' got long to stay wid us, an' she
wan' ax me some'n, and she wan' me tell her de truth,
an' she say I al'ays been mighty faithful an' kind to
her an' hern, an' she hope Gord will erward me an'
Hannah for it, an' she wan' me now to tell her de
truth. When she talk dat way, hit sut'n'y hu't me,
an' I tole her I sut'n'y would tell her faithful. Den
she went on an' ax me how we wuz gettin' on, an' ef
we ain' been mighty po', an ef Meh Lady ain'
done stint herse'f more'n she ever know ; an' I tell
her all 'bout it, ev'ything jes' like it wuz—de fatal
truth, 'cause I done promised her ; an' she sut'n'y
was grieved, I tell you, an' the tears roll down an'
drap off her face on de pillow ; an' pres'n'y she say
she hope Gord would forgive her, an' she teck out
her breast dem little rocks Marster gi' her when she
married, whar hed been ole Mistis', an' she say she
gin up all the urrs, but dese she keep to gi' Meh
Lady when she married, an' now she feared 'twuz
pride, an' Gord done punish her, lettin' her chile

starve, but she ain' know hit 'zactly, an' ign'ance he
forgive; an' she went on an' talk 'bout Marster an'
ole times when she fust come home a bride, an' 'bout
Marse Phil an' Meh Lady, tell she leetle mo' breck
my heart, an' de tears rain down my face on de flo'.
She sut'n'y talk beautiful. Den she gi' me de dia
monds, an' dee shine like a handful of lightning-
bugs! an' she tell me to teck 'em an' teck keer on
'em, an' gi' 'em to Meh Lady some time after she
gone, an' not le' nobody else have 'em; an' would
n' me an' Hannah teck good keer o' her, an' stay
wid her, and not le' her wuck so hard, an' I tell her
we sut'n'y would do dat. Den her voice mos' gin
out an' she 'peared mighty tired, but hit look like
she got some'n still on her min', an' pres'n'y she say
I mus' come close, she mighty tired; an' I sort o'
ben' todes her, an' she say she wan' me after she
gone, as soon as I kin, to get the wud to Meh Lady's
cousin whar wuz heah wounded indurin' o' de war
dat *she* dead, an' dat ef he kin help her chile, an' be
her pertector, she know he'll do it; an' I ain' to le'
Meh Lady know nuttin' 'bout it, not nuttin' 't all,
an' to tell him he been mighty good to her, an' she
lef' him her blessin'. Den she git so faint, I run an'
call Hannah, an' she come runnin' an' gi' her some
sperrits, an' tell me to teck de mule an go after Meh
Lady toreckly, an' so I did. When she got dyah,
do', Mistis done mos' speechless; Hannah hed done
git her in de bed, which wan't no trouble, she so

light. She know Meh Lady, do', an' try to speak to her two or th'ee times, but dee ain' meck out much mo' 'n Gord would bless her and teck keer on her; an' she die right easy jes' befo' mornin'. An' Meh Lady ax me to pray, an' I did. She sut'n'y die peaceful, an' she look jes' like she smilin' after she dead ; she sut'n'y wuz ready to go.

"Well, Hannah and Meh Lady lay her out in her bes' frock, an' she sho'ly look younger'n I ever see her look sence Richmon' fell, ef she ain' look younger'n she look sence befo' de war ; an' de neighbors, de few dat's left, an' de black folks roun' cum, an' we bury her de evenin' after in the gyardin' right side Marse Phil, her fust-born, whar we know she wan' be ; an' her mammy she went in de house after dat to stay at night in the room wid Meh Lady, an' I sleep on the front po'ch to teck keer de house. 'Cause we sut'n'y wuz 'sturbed 'bout de chile ; she ain' sleep an' she ain' eat an' she ain' cry none, an' Hannah say dat ain' reasonable, which 'taint, 'cause womens dee cry sort o' 'natchel.

"But so 'twuz ; de larst time she cry wuz dat evenin' she come in Hannah' house, an' fling herse'f on de bed, an' cry so grievous 'cause dee gwine sell de place, an' 'twould kill her ma. She ain' cry no mo' !

"Well, after we done bury Mistis, as I wuz sayin', we sut'n'y wuz natchelly tossified 'bout Meh Lady. Hit look like what de doctor say wuz sut'n'y so, an' she gwine right after her ma.

"I try to meck her ride de mule to school, an' tell her I ain' got no use for him, I got to thin de corn; but she oodn't; she say he so po' she don' like to gi' him no mo' wuck 'n necessary; an' dat's de fact, he wuz mighty po' 'bout den, 'cause de feed done gi' out an' de grass ain' come good yit, an' when mule bline an' ole he mighty hard to git up; but he been a good mule in he time, an' he a good mule yit.

"So she'd go to school of a mornin', an' me or Hannah one 'd go to meet her of a evenin' to tote her books, 'cause she hardly able to tote herse'f den; an' she do right well at school (de chil'un all love her); twuz when she got home she so sufferin'; den her mind sort o' wrastlin wid itself, an' she jes' set down an' think an study an' look so grieved. Hit sut'n'y did hut me an' Hannah to see her settin' dyah at de winder o' Mistis' chahmber, leanin' her head on her han' an' jes' lookin' out, lookin' out all de evenin' so lonesome, and she look beautiful too. Hannah say she grievin' herself to death.

"Well, dat went on for mo' 'n six weeks, and de chile jes' settin' dyah ev'y night all by herse'f wid de moonlight shinin' all over her, meckin' her look so pale. Hannah she tell me one night I got to do some'n, an' I say, 'What 'tis?' An' she say I got to git de wud dat Mistis say to de Cap'n, dat de chile need a pertector, an' I say, 'How?' And she say I got to write a letter. Den I say, 'I cyarn' neither read nor write, but I can get Meh Lady to write it;'

an' she say, nor I cyarn', 'cause ain' Mistis done spressify partic'lar Meh Lady ain' to know nuttin' 'bout
it? Den I say, ' I kin git somebody at de post-
office to write it, an' I kin pay 'em in eggs ; ' an' she
say she ain' gwine have no po' white folks writin' an'
spearin' 'bout Mistis' business. Den I say, ' How I
gwine do den ?' An' she study a little while, an'
den she say I got to teck de mule an' go fine him.
I say, ' Hi ! Good Gord ! Hannah, how I gwine fine
him ? De Cap'n live 'way up yander in New York,
or somewhar or nuther, an' dat's further 'n Lynch-
bu'g, an' I'll ride de mule to death befo' I git dyah ;
besides I ain' got nothin' to feed him.'

"But Hannah got argiment to all dem wuds ; she
say I got tongue in meh head, an' I kin fine de way ;
an' as to ridin' de mule to death, I kin git down an'
le' him res', or I kin lead him, an' I kin graze him
side de road ef nobody oon le' me graze him in dee
pahsture. Den she study little while, an' den say
she got it now—I must go to Richmon' an' sell de
mule, an' teck de money an' git on de kyars an' fine
him. Hannah, I know, she gwine wuck it, 'cause
she al'ays a powerful han' to 'ravel anything. But it
sut'n'y did hu't me to part wid dat mule, he sich a
ambitious mule, an' I tell Hannah I ain' done sidin'
meh corn ; an' she say dat ain' meck no diff'unce,
she gwine hoe de corn after I gone, and de chile
grievin' so she feared she'll die, an' what good sidin'
corn gwine do den ? she grievin' mo'n she 'quainted

wid, Hannah say. So I wuz to go to Richmon' nex'
mornin' but one, befo' light, an' Hannah she wash
meh shu't nex' day, an' cook meh rations while Meh
Lady at school. Well, I knock off wuck right early
nex' evenin' 'bout two hours be sun, 'cause I wan'
rest de mule, an' after grazin' him for a while in de
yard, I put him in he stall, an' gi' him a half-peck o'
meal, 'cause dat de lahst night I gwine feed him;
and soon as I went in wid de meal he swi'ch his tail
an' hump hese'f jes' like he gwine kick me; dat's de
way he al'ays do when he got anything 'g'inst you,
'cause you sich a fool or anything, 'cause mule got
a heap o' sense when you know 'em. Well, I think
he jes' aggrivated 'cause I gwine sell him, an' I
holler at him right ambitious like I gwine cut him in
two, to fool him ef I kin, an' meck him b'lieve 'tain'
nothin' de matter.

An' jes' den I heah a horse steppin' 'long right
brisk, an' I stop an' listen, an' de horse come 'long
de pahf right study an' up todes de stable. I say,
'Hi! who dat?' an' when I went to de stall do',
dyah wuz a gent'man settin' on a strange horse wid
two white foots, an' a beard on he face, an' he hat
pulled over he eyes to keep de sun out'n 'em; an'
when he see me, he ride on up to de stable, an' ax
me is Meh Lady at de house, an' how she is, an' a
whole parecel o' questions; an' he so p'inted in he
quiration I ain' had time to study ef I ever see him
befo', but I don' think I is. He a mighty straight,

fine-lookin' gent'man do', wid he face right brown like he been wuckin', an' I ain' able to fix him no ways. Den he tell me he heah o' Mistis' death, an' he jes' come 'cross de ocean, an' he wan' see Meh Lady partic'lar ; an' I tell him she at school, but it mos' time for her come back ; an' he ax whichaways, an' I show him de pahf, an' he git down an' ax me ef I cyarn feed he horse, an' I tell him of co'se, do' Gord knows I ain' got nuttin' to feed him wid 'sep' grahss ; but I ain' gwine le' him know dat, so I ax him to walk to de house an' teck a seat on de po'ch tell Meh Lady come, an' I teck de horse and cyar him in de stable like I got de corn-house full o' corn. An' when I come out I look, an' dyah he gwine stridin' 'way 'cross de fiel' 'long de pahf whar Meh Lady comin'.

"Well, I say, 'Hi! now he gwine to meet Meh Lady, an' I ain' know he name nur what he want,' an' I study a little while wherr I should go an' fin' Hannah or hurry myse'f an' meet Meh Lady. Not dat I b'lieve he gwine speak out de way to Meh Lady, 'cause he sut'n'y waz quality, I see dat ; I know hit time I look at him settin' dyah so straight on he horse, 'mindin' me of Marse Phil, and he voice hit sholy wuz easy when he name Meh Lady' name and Mistis' ; but I ain' know but what he somebody wan' to buy de place, an' I know Meh Lady ain' wan' talk 'bout dat, an' ain' wan' see strangers no way ; so I jes' lip out 'cross de fiel' th'oo a nigher way to hit de pahf at dis ve'y place whar de gap wuz, an' whar I thought Meh Lady mighty apt to res' ef she tired or grievin'.

"An' I hurry 'long right swift to git heah befo' de white gent'man kin git heah, an' all de time I tu'nnin' in meh min' whar I heah anybody got voice sound deep an' cl'ar like dat, an' ax questions ef Meh Lady well, dat anxious, an' I cyarn' git it. An' by dat time I wuz done got right to de tu'n in de pahf dyah, mos out o' breaf, an' jes' as I tu'nned round dat clump o' bushes I see Meh Lady settin' right dyah on de 'bankment whar de gap use' to be, wid her books by her side on de groun', her hat off at her feet, an' her head leanin' for'ard in her han's, an' her hyah mos' tumble down, an' de sun jes' techin' it th'oo de bushes ; an' hit all come to me in a minute, jes' as clear as ef she jes' settin' on de gap dyah yistidy wid de rose-leaves done shatter all on de groun' by her, an' Cap'n Wilton kissin' her han' to comfort her, an' axin' her oon' she le' him come back some time to love her. An' I say, ' Dyah ! 'fo Gord ! ef I ain' know him soon as I lay meh eyes on him ! De pertector done come !' Den I know huccome dat mule act so 'sponsible.

"An' jes' den he come walkin' long down de pahf, wid he hat on de back o' he head an' he eyes on her right farst, an' he face look so tender hit look right sweet. She think hit me, an' she ain' move nor look up tell he call her name ; den she mos' jump out her

seat, and look up right swift, an' give a sort o' cry,
an' her face light up like she tu'n't to de sun, an' he
retch out bofe he han's to her ; an' I slip' back so he
couldn' see me, an' come 'long home right quick to
tell Hannah.

"I tell her I know him soon as I see him, but she
tell me I lie, 'cause ef I had I'd 'a' come an' tell her
'bout hit, an' not gone down dyah interferin' wid
white folks ; an' she say I ain' nuver gwine have no
sense 'bout not knowin' folks, dat he couldn' fool
her; an' I don' b'lieve he could, a'tho' I ain' 'low dat
to Hannah, 'cause hit don' do to 'gree wid wimens
too much ; dee git mighty sot up by it, an den dee
ain' al'ays want it, nuther. Well, she went in de
house, an dus' ev'ything, an' fix all de furniture
straight, an' set de table for two, a thing ain' been
done not sence Mistis tooken sick ; an' den I see her
gwine 'roun' Meh Lady' rose-bush mighty busy, an'
when she sont me in de dinin'-room, dyah a whole
parecel o' flowers she done put in a blue dish in de
middle o' de table. An' she jes' as 'sumptious 'bout
dat thing as ef 'twuz a fifty-cents somebody done gi'
her. Well, den she come out, an' sich a cookin' as
she hed ; ef she ain' got more skillets an' spiders on
dat fire den I been see dyah fur I don' know how
long. It fyah do' me good!

"Well, pres'n'y heah dee come walkin' mighty
aged-like, an' I think it all right, an' dee went up on
de po'ch an' shake hands a long time, an' den, meb

Gord! you know he tu'n roun' an' come down de steps, an' she gone in de house wid her handcher to her eyes, cryin'. I call Hannah right quick an' say, 'Hi, Hannah, good Gord A'mighty! what de motter now?' an' Hannah she look; den widout a wu'd she tu'n roun' an' walk right straight 'long de pahf to de house, an' went in th'oo de dinin'-room an' into de hall, an' dyah she fine de chile done fling herself down on her face on de sofa, cryin' like her heart broke; an' she ax her what de matter, an' she say nuttin', an' Hannah say, 'What he been sayin' to you?' an' she say, 'Nuttin';' an' Hannah say, 'You done sen' him 'way?' an' she say, 'Yes.' Den Hannah she tell her what Mistis tell me de day she die, an' she say she stop cryin' sort o', but she cotch hold de pillar right tight like she in agony, an' she say pres'n'y, 'Please go 'way,' an' Hannah come 'way an' come outdo's.

"An' de Cap'n, when he come down de steps, he went to Meh Lady' rose-bush an' pull a rose off it, an' put 't in a little book in he pocket; an' den he come down todes we house, an' he face mighty pale an' 'strusted lookin', an' he sut'n'y wuz glad to see me, an' he laugh' a little bit at me for lettin' him fool me; but I tell him he done got so likely an' agreeable lookin', dat de reason I ain' know him. An' he ax me to git he horse, an' jes' den Hannah come out de house, an' she ax him whar he gwine; an' he 'spon' he gwine home, an' he don' reckon he'll

ever see us no mo'; an' he say he thought when he
come maybe 'twould be diff'unt, an' he had hoped
maybe he'd 'a' been able to prove to Meh Lady
some'n he wan' prove, an' get her to le' him teck
keer o' her an' we all; dat's what he come ten thousand miles fur, he say; but she got some'n in her
mine, he say, she cyarn' git over, an' now he got to
go 'way, an' he say he want us to teck keer on her,
an' stay wid her al'ays, and he gwine meck it right,
an' he gwine lef' he name in Richmon' wid a gent'-
man, an' gi' me he 'dress, an' I mus' come up dyah
ev'y month an' git what he gwine lef' dyah, and report how we all is; an' he say he ain' got nuttin' to
do now but to try an' reward us all fur all our kind-
ness to him, an' keep us easy, but he wa'n' nuver
comin' back, he guess, 'cause he got no mo' hope now
he know Meh Lady got dat on her mine he cyarn'
git over. An' he look down in de gyardin todes the
graveyard when he say dat, an' he voice sort o'
broke. Hannah she heah him th'oo right study, an'
he face look mighty sorrowful, an' he voice done mos'
gin out when he say Meh Lady got that on her mine
he cyarn' git over.

"Den Hannah she upped an' tole him he sut'n'y
ain' got much sense ef he come all dat way he
say, an' gwine 'way widout Meh Lady; dat de chile
been dat pesterin' herse'f sence her ma die she ain'
know what she wan' mos', an' got in her mine; an'
ef he ain' got de dictation to meck her know, he

better go 'long back whar he came fum, an' he better ain never set he foot heah; an' she say he sut'n'y done gone back sence he driv dem Yankeys out de do' wid he s'o'de, an' settin' dyah on he horse at de gate so study, an' she say ef 'twuz dat man he'd be married dis evenin'. Oh! she was real savigrous to him, 'cause she sut'n'y wuz outdone; an' she tell him what Mistis tell me de day she 'ceasted, ev'y wud jes like I tell you settin' heah, an' she say now he can go' long, 'cause ef he ain' gwine be pertector to de chile de plenty mo' sufferin' to be, dat dee pesterin' her all de time, an' she jes' oon' have nuttin' 't all to do wid 'em, dat's all. Wid dat she tu'n 'roun' an' gone in her house like she ain' noticin' him, an he, suh! he look like day done broke on 'im. I see darkness roll off him, an' he tu'n roun' an' stride 'long back to de house, an' went up de steps th'ee at a time.

"An' dee say when he went in, de chile was dyah on de sofa still wid her head in de pillow cryin', 'cause she sut'n'y did care for him all de time, an' ever sence he open he eyes an' look at her so cu'yus, settin' dyah by him fannin' him all night to keep him fum dyin', when he layin' dyah wounded in de war. An' de on'y thing is she ain' been able to get her premission to marry him 'cause he wuz fightin' 'g'inst we all, an' 'cause she got 't in her mine dat Mistis don' wan' her to marry him for dat account. An' now he gone she layin' dyah in de gre't hall cryin' on de sofa to herse'f, so she ain' heah him come up de steps, tell he went up to her, and kneel down by her, an' put he arm 'roun' her and talk to her lovin'.

"Hannah she went in th'oo de chahmber pres'n'y to peep an' see ef he got any sense yit, an' when she come back she ain' say much, but she sont me to de spring, an' set to cookin' ag'in mighty induschus, an' she say he tryin' to 'swade de chile to marry him to-morrow. She oon' tell me nuttin' mo' 'sep' dat de chile seem mighty peaceable, an' she don' know wherr she marry him toreckly or not, 'cause she heah her say she ain' gwine marry him *at all*, an' she cyarn' marry him to-morrow 'cause she got her school, an' she ain' got no dress; but she place heap o' 'pendence in him, Hannah say, an' he gone on talkin' mighty sensible, like he gwine marry her wherr or no, an' he dat protectin' he done got her head on he shoulder an' talk to her jes' as 'fectionate as ef she b'longst to him, an'—she ain' say he kiss her, but I done notice partic'lar she ain' say he ain'; an' she say de chile sut'n'y is might' satisfied, an' dat all she gwine recite, an' I better go 'long an' feed white folk's horse 'stid o' interferin' 'long dee business; an' so I did, an' I gi' him de larst half-peck o' meal Hannah got in de barrel.

"An' when I come back to de house, Hannah done cyar in de supper an' waitin' on de table, an dee settin' opposite one nurr talkin', an' she po'in

out he tea, an' he tellin' her things to make het
laugh an' look pretty, 'cross Hannah' flowers in de
blue bowl twix' 'em. Hit meck me feel right
young.

"Well, after supper dee come out an' went to
walk 'bout de yard, an' pres'n'y dee stop at dat red
rose-bush, and I see him teck out he pocket-book
an' teck some'n out it, and she say some'n, an' he
put he arm—ne'm' mine, ef Hannah ain' say he kiss
her, I know—'cause de moon come out a little piece
right den an' res' on 'em, an' she sut'n'y look
beautiful wid her face sort o' tu'nned up to him,
smilin'.

"You mine, do', she keep on tellin' him she ain'
promise to marry him, an' of co'se she cyarn' marry
him to-morrow like he say; she ain' nuver move
fum dat. But dat ain' 'sturb he mine now; he keep
on laughin' study. Tell, 'bout right smart while
after supper, he come out an' ax me cyarn' I git he
horse. I say, 'Hi! what de matter? Whar you
gwine? I done feed yo' horse.'

"He laugh real hearty, an' say he gwine to de
Co'te House, an' he wan' me to go wid him; don' I
think de mule kin stan' it? an' her mammy will teck
keer Meh Lady.

"So in 'bout a hour we wuz on de road, an' de
last thing Meh Lady say wuz she cyarn' marry
him; but he come out de house laughin', an' he
sut'n'y wuz happy, an' he ax me all sort o' ques-

tions 'bout Meh Lady, an' Marse Phil, an' de ole times.

"We went by de preacher's an' wake him up befo' day, an' he say he'll drive up dyah after break-fast; an' den we went on 'cross to de Co'te House, an' altogether 'twuz about twenty-five miles, an' hit sut'n'y did push ole George good, 'cause de Cun'l wuz a hard rider like all we all white folks; he come mighty nigh givin' out, I tell you.

"We got dyah befo' breakfast, an' wash up, an' pres'n'y de cluck, Mr. Taylor, come, an' de Cun'l went over to de office. In a minute he call me, an' I went over, an' soon as I git in de do' I see he mighty pestered. He say, 'Heah, Billy, you know you' young mistis' age, don't you? I want you to prove it.'

"'Hi! yes, suh, co'se I knows it,' I says. 'Mistis got her an' Marse Phil bofe set down in de book at home.'

"'Well, jes' meck oath to it,' says he, easy like. 'She's near twenty-three, ain't she?'

"'Well, 'fo' Gord! Marster, I don' know 'bout dat,' says I. 'You know mo' 'bout dat 'n I does, 'cause you kin read. I know her age, 'cause I righ* dyah when she born; but how ole she is, I don' know,' I says.

"'Cyarn' you swear she's twenty-one?' says he, right impatient.

"'Well, nor, suh, dat I cyarn',' says I.

"Well, he sut'n'y looked aggrivated, but he ain'
say nuttin', he jes' tu'n to Mr. Taylor an' say:

"'Kin I get a fresh horse heah, suh? I kin ride
home an' get de proof an' be back heah in five hours,
ef I can get a fresh horse; I'll buy him and pay well
for him too.'

"'It's forty miles dyah an' back,' says Mr.
Taylor.

"'I kin do it; I'll be back heah at half-past twelve
o'clock sharp,' says de Cun'l, puttin' up he watch an'
pullin' on he gloves an' tu'nnin' to de do'.

"Well, he look so sure o' what he kin do, I feel
like I 'bleeged to help him, an' I say:

"'I ain't know wherr Meh Lady twenty-th'ee or
twenty-one, 'cause I ain' got no learnin', but I know
she born on Sunday de thrashin'-wheat time two
years after Marse Phil wuz born, whar I cyar' in dese
ahms on de horse when he wuz a baby, an' whar
went in de ahmy, an' got kilt leadin' he bat'ry
in de battle 'cross de oat-fiel' down todes Wil-
liamsbu'g, an' de gener'l say he ruther been him
den President de Confederate States, an' he's 'sleep
by he ma in de ole gyardin at home now; I bury
him dyah, an' hit's "Cun'l" on he tomb-stone dyah
now.'

"De Cun'l tu'n roun' an' look at Mr. Taylor, an'
Mr. Taylor look out de winder ('cause he know
'twuz so, 'cause he wuz in Marse Phil' bat'ry).

"'You needn' teck you' ride,' says he, sort o'

whisperin'. An' de Cun'l pick up a pen an' write a little while, an' den he read it, an' he had done write jes' what I say, wud for wud; an' Mr. Taylor meck me kiss de book, 'cause 'twuz true, an' he say he gwine spread it in de 'Reecord' jes' so, for all de wull to see.

"Den we come on home, I ridin' a horse de Cun'l done hire to rest de mule, an' I mos' tired as he, but de Cun'l he ridin' jes' as fresh as ef he jes' start; an' he bring me a nigh way whar he learnt in de war, he say, when he used to slip th'oo de lines an' come at night forty miles jes' to look at de house an' see de light shine in Meh Lady' winder.

"De preacher an' he wife wuz dyah when we git home; but you know Meh Lady ain' satisfied in her mine yit. She say she do love him, but she don' know wherr she ought to marry him, 'cause she ain' got nobody to 'vise her. But he says he gwine be her 'viser from dis time, an' he lead her to de do' an' kiss her; an' she went to git ready, an' de turr lady wid her, an' her mammy wait on her, while I wait on de Cun'l, an' be he body-servant, an' git he warm water to shave, an' he cut off all he beard 'sep' he mustache, 'cause Meh Lady jes' say de man she knew didn' hed no beard on he face. An' Hannah she sut'n'y wuz comical, she ironin' an' sewin' dyah so induschus she oon' le' me come in meh own house.

"Well, pres'n'y we wuz ready, an' we come out in

de hall, an' de Cun'l went in de parlor whar dee wuz
gwine be married, an' de preacher he wuz in dyah,
an' dee chattin' while we waitin' fur Meh Lady; an'
I jes' slip out an' got up in de j'ice an' git out dem
little rocks whar Mistis gin' me an' blow de dust off
'em good, and good Gord! ef dee didn' shine! I put
'em in meh pocket an' put on meh clean shu't an'
come 'long back to de house. Hit right late now,
todes evenin', an' de sun wuz shinin' all 'cross de
yard an' th'oo de house, an' de Cun'l he so impatient he cyarn' set still, he jes' champin' he bit; so
he git up an' walk 'bout in de hall, an' he sut'n'y
look handsome an' young, jes' like he did dat day
he stand dyah wid he cap in he hand, an' Meh Lady
say she ain' claim no kin wid him, an' he say he
cyarn' intrude on ladies, an' back out de front do',
wid he head straight up, an' ride to git her de letter,
an' now he walkin' in de hall waitin' to marry her.
An' all on a sudden Hannah fling de do' wide open,
an' Meh Lady walk out!

"Gord! ef I didn' think 'twuz a angel.

" She stan dyah jes' white as snow fum her head to
way back' down on de flo' behine her, an' her veil done
fall roun' her like white mist, an' some roses in her
han'. Ef it didn' look like de sun done come th'oo
de chahmber do' wid her, an' blaze all over de styars,
an' de Cun'l he look like she bline him. An' twuz
Hannah an' she, while we wuz 'way dat day, done
fine Mistis' weddin' dress an' veil an' all, down to de

fan an' little slippers 'bout big as two little white
ears o' pop-corn; an' de dress had sort o' cobwebs
all over it, whar Hannah say was lace, an' hit jes'
fit Meh Lady like Gord put it dyah in de trunk for
her.

"Well, when de Cun'l done tell her how beautiful
she is, an' done meck her walk 'bout de hall showin'
her train, an' she lookin' over her shoulder at it an'
den at de Cun'l to see ef he proud o' her, he gin her
he arm; an' jes' den I walk up befo' her an' teck
dem things out meh pocket, an' de Cun'l drap her
arm an' stan' back, an' I put 'em 'roun' her thote an'
on her arms, an' gin her de res', an' Hannah put 'em
on her ears, an' dee shine like stars, but her face
shine wus'n dem, an' she leetle mo' put bofe arms
'roun' meh neck, wid her eyes jes' runnin' over. An'
den de Cun'l gi' her he arm, an' dee went in de parlor, an' Hannah an' me behine 'em. An' dyah,
facin' Mistis' picture an' Marse Phil's (tooken when
he wuz a little boy), lookin' down at 'em bofe, dee
wuz married.

"An' when de preacher git to dat part whar ax
who give dis woman to de man, he sort o' wait an'
he eye sort o' rove to me disconfused like he ax me
ef I know; an' I don' know huccome 'twuz, but I
think 'bout Marse Jeems an' Mistis when he ax me
dat, an' Marse Phil, whar all dead, an' all de scufflin'
we done been th'oo, an' how de chile ain' got no
body to teck her part now 'sep' jes' me; an' now,

when he wait an' look at me dat way, an' ax me
dat, I 'bleeged to speak up, I jes' step for'ard an'
say:.

" ' Ole Billy.'

" An' jes' den de sun crawl roun' de winder
shetter an' res' on her like it pourin' light all over
her.

" An' dat night when de preacher was gone wid
he wife, an Hannah done drapt off to sleep, I wuz
settin' in de do' wid meh pipe, an' I heah 'em settin' dyah on de front steps, dee voices soun'in' low
like bees, an' de moon sort o' meltin' over de yard,
an' I sort o' got to studyin', an' hit 'pear like de
plantation 'live once mo', an' de ain' no mo' scufflin',
an' de ole times done come back ag'in, an' I heah
meh kerridge-horses stompin' in de stalls, an' de
place all cleared up ag'in, an' fence all roun' de
pahsture, an' I smell de wet clover-blossoms right
good, an' Marse Phil an' Meh Lady done come back,
an' runnin' all roun' me, climbin' up on meh knees,
callin' me ' Unc' Billy,' an' pesterin' me to go fishin',
while somehow Meh Lady an' de Cun'l, settin' dyah
on de steps wid dee voice hummin' low like water
runnin' in de' dark—

＊　　＊　　＊　　＊　　＊　　＊　　＊

An' dat Phil, suh," he broke off, rising from the
ground on which we had been seated for some time,
" dat Phil, suh, he mo' like Marse Phil 'n he like he

pa ; an' Billy—he ain' so ole, but he ain' fur behine him."

"Billy," I said ; "he's named after—"

"Go 'way, Marster," he said deprecatingly, " who gwine name gent'man after a ole nigger?"

OLE 'STRACTED.

"AWE, little Ephum! *awe*, little E-phum! ef you don' come 'long heah, boy, an' rock dis chile, I'll buss you haid open!" screamed the high-pitched voice of a woman, breaking the stillness of the summer evening. She had just come to the door of the little cabin, where she was now standing, anxiously scanning the space before her, while a baby's plaintive wail rose and fell within with wearying monotony. The log cabin, set in a gall in the middle of an old field all grown up in sassafras, was not a very inviting-looking place; a few hens loitering about the new hen-house, a brood of half-grown chickens picking in the grass and watching the door, and a runty pig tied to a "stob," were the only signs of thrift; yet the face of the woman cleared up as she gazed about her and afar off, where the gleam of green made a pleasant spot, where the corn grew in the river-bottom; for it was her home, and the best of all was she thought it belonged to them.

A rumble of distant thunder caught her ear, and she stepped down and took a well-worn garment from the clothes-line, stretched between two dogwood forks, and having, after a keen glance down

the path through the bushes, satisfied herself that
no one was in sight, she returned to the house, and
the baby's voice rose louder than before.   The
mother, as she set out her ironing table, raised a
dirge-like hymn, which she chanted, partly from
habit and partly in self-defence.   She ironed carefully the ragged shirt she had just taken from the
line, and then, after some search, finding a needle
and cotton, she drew a chair to the door and proceeded to mend the garment.

"Dis de on'ies' shut Ole 'Stracted got," she
said, as if in apology to herself for being so
careful.

The cloud slowly gathered over the pines in the
direction of the path; the fowls carefully tripped
up the path, and after a prudent pause at the hole,
disappeared one by one within; the chickens picked
in a gradually contracting circuit, and finally one or
two stole furtively to the cabin door, and after a
brief reconnoissance came in, and fluttered up the
ladder to the loft, where they had been born, and
yet roosted.   Once more the baby's voice prevailed,
and once more the woman went to the door, and,
looking down the path, screamed, "Awe, little
Ephum! awe, little Ephum!"

"Ma'm," came the not very distant answer from
the bushes.

"Why 'n't you come 'long heah, boy, an' rock dis
chile?"

"Yes'm, I comin'," came the answer. She waited, watching, until there emerged from the bushes a queer little caravan, headed by a small brat, who staggered under the weight of another apparently nearly as large and quite as black as himself, while several more of various degrees of diminutiveness struggled along behind.

"Ain't you heah me callin' you, boy? You better come when I call you. I'll tyah you all to pieces!" pursued the woman, in the angriest of keys, her countenance, however, appearing unruffled. The head of the caravan stooped and deposited his burden carefully on the ground; then, with a comical look of mingled alarm and penitence, he slowly approached the door, keeping his eye watchfully on his mother, and, picking his opportunity, slipped in past her, dodging skilfully just enough to escape a blow which she aimed at him, and which would have "slapped him flat" had it struck him, but which, in truth, was intended merely to warn and keep him in wholesome fear, and was purposely aimed high enough to miss him, allowing for the certain dodge.

The culprit, having stifled the whimper with which he was prepared, flung himself on to the foot of the rough plank cradle, and began to rock it violently and noisily, using one leg as a lever, and singing an accompaniment, of which the only words that rose above the noise of the rockers were "By-a-by, don't you cry; go to sleep, little baby;" and sure enough the baby stopped crying and went to sleep.

Eph watched his mammy furtively as she scraped away the ashes and laid the thick pone of dough on the hearth, and shovelled the hot ashes upon it. Supper would be ready directly, and it was time to propitiate her. He bethought himself of a message.

"Mammy, Ole 'Stracted say you must bring he shut; he say he marster comin' to-night."

"How he say he is?" inquired the woman, with some interest.

"He ain' say—jes say he want he shut. He sutny is comical—he layin' down in de baid." Then, having relieved his mind, Eph went to sleep in the cradle.

"'Layin' down in de baid?'" quoted the woman to herself as she moved about the room. "I 'ain' nuver 'hearn 'bout dat befo'. Dat sutny is a comical ole man anyways. He say he used to live on dis plantation, an' yit he al'ays talkin' 'bout de gret house an' de fine kerridges dee used to have, an' 'bout he marster comin' to buy him back. De 'ain' nuver been no gret house on dis place, not sence I know nuttin 'bout it, 'sep de overseer house whar dat man live. I heah Ephum say Aunt Dinah tell him de ole house whar used to be on de hill whar dat gret oak-tree is in de pines bu'nt down de year he wuz born, an' he ole marster had to live in

de overseer house, an' hit break he heart, an' dee
teck all he niggers, an' dat's de way *he* come to
blongst to we all; but dat ole man ain' know nuttin 'bout dat house, 'cause hit bu'nt down. I wonder whar he did come from?" she pursued, "an'
what he sho' 'nough name? He sholy couldn' been
named ' Ole 'Stracted,' jes so; dat ain' no name 'tall.
Yit ef he ain' 'stracted, 'tain' nobody is. He ain'
even know he own name," she continued, presently.
" Say he marster 'll know him when he come—ain'
know de folks is free; say he marster gwi buy him
back in de summer an' kyar him home, an' 'bout de
money he gwine gi' him. Ef he got any money, I
wonder he live down dyah in dat evil-sperit hole."
And the woman glanced around with great compla-
cency on the picture-pasted walls of her own by no
means sumptuously furnished house. " Money!"
she repeated aloud, as she began to rake in the
ashes, " He ain' got nuttin. I got to kyar him
piece o' dis bread now," and she went off into a
dream of what they would do when the big crop on
their land should be all in, and the last payment
made on the house; of what she would wear, and
how she would dress the children, and the appearance she would make at meeting, not reflecting that
the sum they had paid on the property had never,
even with all their stinting, amounted in any one
year to more than a few dollars over the rent
charged for the place, and that the eight hundred

dollars yet due on it was more than they could make at the present rate in a lifetime.

"Ef Ephum jes had a mule, or even somebody to help him," she thought, " but he ain' got nuttin. De chil'n ain' big 'nough to do nuttin but eat; he ain' got no brurrs, an' he deddy took 'way an' sold down Souf de same time my ole marster whar dead buy him; dat's what I al'ays heah 'em say, an' I know he's dead long befo' dis, 'cause I heah 'em say dese Virginia niggers carn stan' hit long deah, hit so hot, hit frizzle 'em up, an' I reckon he die befo' he ole marster, whar I heah say die of a broked heart torectly after dee teck he niggers an' sell 'em befo' he face. I heah Aunt Dinah say dat, an' dat he might'ly sot on he ole servants, spressaly on Ephum deddy, whar named Little Ephum, an' whar used to wait on him. Dis mus' 'a' been a gret place dem days, 'cordin' to what dee say." She went on: "Dee say he sutny live strong, wuz jes rich as cream, an' weahed he blue coat an' brass buttons, an' lived in dat ole house whar wuz up whar de pines is now, an' whar bu'nt down, like he owned de wull. An' now look at it; dat man own it all, an' cuttin' all de woods off it. He don' know nuttin 'bout black folks, ain' nuver been fotch up wid 'em. Who ever heah he name 'fo' he come heah an' buy de place, an' move in de overseer house, an' charge we all eight hundred dollars for dis land, jes 'cause it got little piece, o' bottom on it. an' forty-eight dollars rent besides, wid he ole stingy wife whar oon' even gi' 'way buttermilk!" An expression of mingled disgust and contempt concluded the reflection.

She took the ash-cake out of the ashes, slapped it first on one side, then on the other, with her hand, dusted it with her apron, and walked to the door and poured a gourd of water from the piggin over it. Then she divided it in half; one half she set up against the side of the chimney, the other she broke up into smaller pieces and distributed among the children, dragging the sleeping Eph, limp and soaked with sleep, from the cradle to receive his share. Her manner was not rough—was perhaps even tender—but she used no caresses, as a white woman would have done under the circumstances. It was only toward the baby at the breast that she exhibited any endearments. Her nearest approach to it with the others was when she told them, as she portioned out the ash-cake, "Mammy 'ain't got nuttin else; but nuver min', she gwine have plenty o' good meat next year, when deddy done pay for he land."

"Hi! who dat out dyah?" she said, suddenly. "Run to de do', son, an' see who dat comin'," and the whole tribe rushed to inspect the new-comer.

It was, as she suspected, her husband, and as soon as he entered she saw that something was wrong. He dropped into a chair, and sat in moody silence

the picture of fatigue, physical and mental. After
waiting for some time, she asked, indifferently,
" What de matter ? "

" Dat man."

" What he done do now ? " The query was sharp
with suspicion.

" He say he ain' gwine let me have my land."

" He's a half-strainer," said the woman, with sud·
den anger. " How he gwine help it ? Ain' you got
crap on it ? " She felt that there must be a defence
against such an outrage.

" He say he ain' gwine wait no longer ; dat I wuz
to have tell Christmas to finish payin' for it, an' I
ain' do it, an' now he done change he min'.' "

" Tell dis Christmas comin'," said his wife, with
the positiveness of one accustomed to expound con·
tracts.

" Yes ; but I tell you he say he done change he
min'." The man had evidently given up all hope ;
he was dead beat.

" De crap's yourn," said she, affected by his sur·
render, but prepared only to compromise.

" He say he gwine teck all dat for de rent, and dat
he gwine drive Ole 'Stracted 'way too.

" He ain' nuttin but po' white trash ! " It ex·
pressed her supreme contempt.

" He say he'll gi' me jes one week mo' to pay him
all he ax for it," continued he, forced to a correction
by her intense feeling, and the instinct of a man to

defend the absent from a woman's attack, and perhaps in the hope that she might suggest some escape.

"He ain' nuttin sep po' white trash!" she repeated. "How you gwine raise eight hundred dollars at once? Dee kyarn nobody do dat. Gord mout! He ain' got good sense."

"You ain' see dat corn lately, is you?" he asked. "Hit jes as rank! You can almos' see it growin' ef you look at it good. Dat's strong land. I know dat when I buy it."

He knew it was gone now, but he had been in the habit of calling it his in the past three years, and it did him good to claim the ownership a little longer.

"I wonder whar Marse Johnny is?" said the woman. He was the son of her former owner; and now, finding her proper support failing her, she instinctively turned to him. "He wouldn' let him turn we all out."

"He ain' got nuttin, an' ef he is, he kyarn get it in a week," said Ephraim.

"Kyarn you teck it in de co't?"

"Dat's whar he say he gwine have it ef I don' git out," said her husband, despairingly.

Her last defence was gone.

"Ain' you hongry?" she inquired.

"What you got?"

"I jes gwine kill a chicken for you."

It was her nearest approach to tenderness. and he

knew it was a mark of special attention, for all the chickens and eggs had for the past three years gone to swell the fund which was to buy the home, and it was only on special occasions that one was spared for food.

The news that he was to be turned out of his home had fallen on him like a blow, and had stunned him ; he could make no resistance, he could form no plans. He went into a rough estimate as he waited.

" Le' me see : I done wuck for it three years dis Christmas done gone ; how much does dat meck ? "

" An' fo' dollars, an' five dollars, an' two dollars an' a half last Christmas from de chickens, an' all dem ducks I done sell he wife, an' de washin' I been doin' for 'em ; how much is dat ? " supplemented his wife.

" Dat's what I say ! "

His wife endeavored vainly to remember the amount she had been told it was ; but the unaccounted-for washing changed the sum and destroyed her reliance on the result. And as the chicken was now approaching perfection, and required her undivided attention, she gave up the arithmetic and applied herself to her culinary duties.

Ephraim also abandoned the attempt, and waited in a reverie, in which he saw corn stand so high and rank over his land that he could scarcely distinguish the balk, and a stable and barn and a mule, or may·

be two—it was a possibility—and two cows which his wife would milk, and a green wagon driven by his boys, while he took it easy and gave orders like a master, and a clover patch, and wheat, and he saw the yellow grain waving, and heard his sons sing the old harvest song of " Cool Water " while they swung their cradles, and—

" You say he gwine turn Ole 'Stracted out, too ? " inquired his wife, breaking the spell. The chicken was done now, and her mind reverted to the all-engrossing subject.

" Yes ; say he tired o' ole 'stracted nigger livin' on he place an' payin' no rent."

" Good Gord A'mighty ! Pay rent for dat ole pile o' logs ! Ain't he been mendin' he shoes an' harness for rent all dese years ? "

" 'Twill kill dat ole man to tu'n him out dat house," said Ephraim ; " he ain' nuver stay away from dyah a hour sence he come heah."

" Sutny 'twill," assented his wife ; then she added, in reply to the rest of the remark, " Nuver min'; den we'll see what he got in dyah." To a woman, that was at least some compensation. Ephraim's thoughts had taken a new direction.

" He al'ays feared he marster 'd come for him while he 'way," he said, in mere continuance of his last remark.

" He sen' me wud he marster comin' to-night, an' he want he shut," said his wife, as she handed him his supper. Ephraim's face expressed more than interest; it was tenderness which softened the rugged lines as he sat looking into the fire. Perhaps he thought of the old man's loneliness, and of his own father torn away and sold so long ago, before he could even remember, and perhaps very dimly of the beauty of the sublime devotion of this poor old creature to his love and his trust, holding steadfast beyond memory, beyond reason, after the knowledge even of his own identity and of his very name was lost.

The woman caught the contagion of his sympathy.

" De chil'n say he mighty comical, an' he layin' down in de baid," she said.

Ephraim rose from his seat.

" Whar you gwine ? "

" I mus' go to see 'bout him," he said, simply.

" Ain' you gwine finish eatin' ? "

" I gwine kyar dis to him."

" Well, I kin cook you anurr when we come back," said his wife, with ready acquiescence.

In a few minutes they were on the way, going single file down the path through the sassafras, along which little Eph and his followers had come an hour before, the man in the lead and his wife following, and, according to the custom of their race, carrying the bundles, one the surrendered supper and the other the neatly folded and well-patched shirt in which

Ole 'Stracted hoped to meet his long-expected loved ones.

As they came in sight of the ruinous little hut which had been the old man's abode since his sudden appearance in the neighborhood a few years after the war, they observed that the bench beside the door was deserted, and that the door stood ajar— two circumstances which neither of them remembered ever to have seen before ; for in all the years in which he had been their neighbor Ole 'Stracted had never admitted any one within his door, and had never been known to leave it open.   In mild weather he occupied a bench outside, where he either cobbled shoes for his neighbors, accepting without question anything they paid him, or else sat perfectly quiet, with the air of a person waiting for some one.   He held only the briefest communication with anybody, and was believed by some to have intimate relations with the Evil One, and his tumble-down hut, which he was particular to keep closely daubed, was thought by such as took this view of the matter to be the temple where he practised his unholy rites. For this reason, and because the little cabin, surrounded by dense pines and covered with vines which the popular belief held "pizonous," was the most desolate abode a human being could have selected, most of the dwellers in that section gave the place a wide berth, especially toward nightfall, and Ole 'Stracted would probably have suffered but for

the charity of Ephraim and his wife, who, although
often wanting the necessaries of life themselves, had
long divided it with their strange neighbor. Yet
even they had never been admitted inside his door,
and knew no more of him than the other people
about the settlement knew.

His advent in the neighborhood had been mysterious. The first that was known of him was one
summer morning, when he was found sitting on the
bench beside the door of this cabin, which had long
been unoccupied and left to decay. He was unable
to give any account of himself, except that he always declared that he had been sold by some one
other than his master from that plantation, that his
wife and boy had been sold to some other person at
the same time for twelve hundred dollars (he was
particular as to the amount), and that his master
was coming in the summer to buy him back and
take him home, and would bring him his wife and
child when he came. Everything since that day
was a blank to him, and as he could not tell the
name of his master or wife, or even his own name,
and as no one was left old enough to remember him,
the neighborhood having been entirely deserted after
the war, he simply passed as a harmless old lunatic
laboring under a delusion. He was devoted to children, and Ephraim's small brood were his chief delight. They were not at all afraid of him, and
whenever they got a chance they would slip off and

steal down to his house, where they might be found any time squatting about his feet, listening to his accounts of his expected visit from his master, and what he was going to do afterward. It was all of a great plantation, and fine carriages and horses, and a house with his wife and the boy.

This was all that was known of him, except that once a stranger, passing through the country, and hearing the name Ole 'Stracted, said that he heard a similar one once, long before the war, in one of the Louisiana parishes, where the man roamed at will, having been bought of the trader by the gentleman who owned him, for a small price, on account of his infirmity.

"Is you gwine in dyah?" asked the woman, as they approached the hut.

"Hi! yes; 'tain' nuttin' gwine hu't you; an' you say Ephum say he layin' in de baid?" he replied, his mind having evidently been busy on the subject.

"An' mighty comical," she corrected him, with exactness born of apprehension.

"Well? I 'feared he sick."

"I ain' nuver been in dyah," she persisted.

"Ain' de chil'n been in dyah?"

"Dee say 'stracted folks oon hu't chil'n."

"Dat ole man oon hu't nobody; he jes tame as a ole tomcat."

"I wonder he ain' feared to live in dat lonesome ole house by hisself. I jes lieve stay in a graveyard at once. I ain' wonder folks say he sees sperrits in dat hanty-lookin' place." She came up by her hus band's side at the suggestion. " I wonder he don' go home?"

"Whar he got any home to go to sep heaven?' said Ephraim.

" What was you mammy name, Ephum?"

" Mymy," said he, simply.

They were at the cabin now, and a brief pause of doubt ensued. It was perfectly dark inside the door, and there was not a sound. The bench where they had heretofore held their only communication with their strange neighbor was lying on its side in the weeds which grew up to the very walls of the ruinous cabin, and a lizard suddenly ran over it, and with a little rustle disappeared under the rotting ground-sill. To the woman it was an ill omen. She glanced furtively behind her, and moved nearer her husband's side. She noticed that the cloud above the pines was getting a faint yellow tinge on its lower border, while it was very black above them. It filled her with dread, and she was about to call her husband's notice to it, when a voice within ar rested their attention. It was very low, and they both listened in awed silence, watching the door meanwhile as if they expected to see something su. pernatural spring from it.

" Nem min'—jes wait—'tain' so long now—he'll be heah torectly," said the voice. " Dat's what he say—gwine come an' buy me back—den we gwine home."

In their endeavor to catch the words they moved nearer, and made a slight noise. Suddenly the low, earnest tone changed to one full of eagerness.

" Who dat?" was called in sharp inquiry.

" 'Tain' nobody but me an' Polly, Ole 'Stracted," said Ephraim, pushing the door slightly wider open and stepping in. They had an indistinct idea that the poor deluded creature had fancied them his longed-for loved ones, yet it was a relief to see him bodily.

" Who you say you is?" inquired the old man, feebly.

" Me an' Polly."

" I done bring you shut home," said the woman, as if supplementing her husband's reply. " Hit all bran' clean, an' I done patch it."

" Oh, I thought—" said the voice, sadly.

They knew what he thought. Their eyes were now accustomed to the darkness, and they saw that the only article of furniture which the room contained was the wretched bed or bench on which the old man was stretched. The light sifting through the chinks in the roof enabled them to see his face, and that it had changed much in the last twenty-four hours, and an instinct told them that he was near the end of his long waiting.

" How is you, Ole 'Stracted?" asked the woman.

"Dat ain' my name," answered the old man, promptly. It was the first time he had ever disowned the name.

"Well, how is you, Ole— What I gwine to call you?" asked she, with feeble finesse.

"I don' know—he kin tell you."

"Who?"

"Who? Marster. He know it. Ole 'Stracted ain' know it; but dat ain' nuttin. *He* know it—got it set down in de book. I jes waitin' for 'em now."

A hush fell on the little audience—they were in full sympathy with him, and knowing no way of expressing it, kept silence. Only the breathing of the old man was audible in the room. He was evidently nearing the end. "I mighty tired of waitin'," he said, pathetically. "Look out dyah and see ef you see anybody," he added, suddenly.

Both of them obeyed, and then returned and stood silent; they could not tell him no.

Presently the woman said, "Don' you warn put you' shut on?"

"What did you say my name was?" he said.

"Ole 'Str—" She paused at the look of pain on his face, shifted uneasily from one foot to the other, and relapsed into embarrassed silence.

"Nem min'! dee'll know it—dee'll know me 'dout any name, oon dee?" He appealed wistfully to them both. The woman for answer unfolded the shirt. He moved feebly, as if in assent.

" I so tired waitin'," he whispered; " done 'mos
gin out, an' he oon come; but I thought I heah
little Eph to-day?" There was a faint inquiry in his
voice.

"Yes, he wuz heah."

" Wuz he?" The languid form became instantly
alert, the tired face took on a look of eager expect.
ancy. " Heah, gi' m'y shut quick. I knowed it.
Wait ; go over dyah, son, and git me dat money.
He'll be heah torectly." They thought his mind
wandered, and merely followed the direction of his
eyes with theirs. " Go over dyah quick—don't you
heah me?"

And to humor him Ephraim went over to the
corner indicated.

" Retch up dyah, an' run you' hand in onder de
second jice. It's all in dyah," he said to the woman
—" twelve hunderd dollars—dat's what dee went
for. I wucked night an' day forty year to save dat
money for marster; you know dee teck all he land
an' all he niggers an' tu'n him out in de old fiel'? I
put 'tin dyah 'ginst he come. You ain' know he
comin' dis evenin', is you? Heah, help me on wid
dat shut, gal—I stan'in' heah talkin' an' maybe ole
marster waitin'. Push de do' open so you kin see.
Forty year ago," he murmured, as Polly jambed the
door back and returned to his side—" forty year ago
dee come an' levelled on me : marster sutny did cry.
'Nem min'.' he said, ' I comin' right down in de

summer to buy you back an' bring you home.' He's
comin', too—nuver tol' me a lie in he life—comin'
dis evenin'. Make 'aste." This in tremulous eagerness to the woman, who had involuntarily caught
the feeling, and was now with eager and ineffectual
haste trying to button his shirt.

An exclamation from her husband caused her to
turn around, as he stepped into the light and held
up an old sock filled with something.

"Heah, hol' you' apron," said the old man to
Polly, who gathered up the lower corners of her
apron and stood nearer the bed.

"Po' it in dyah." This to Ephraim, who mechanically obeyed. He pulled off the string, and poured
into his wife's lap the heap of glittering coin—gold
and silver more than their eyes had ever seen before.

"Hit's all dyah," said the old man, confidentially,
as if he were rendering an account. "I been savin'
it ever sence dee took me 'way. I so busy savin' it
I ain' had time to eat, but I ain' hongry now ; have
plenty when I git home." He sank back exhausted.
"Oon marster be glad to see me?" he asked, presently, in pathetic simplicity. "You know we growed
up togerr? I been waitin' so long I 'feared dee
'mos' done forgit me. You reckon dee is?" he
asked the woman, appealingly.

"No, suh, dee ain' forgit you," she said, comfort-
ingly.

"I know dee ain'," he said, reassured. "Dat's

what he tell me—he ain' nuver gwine forgit me."
The reaction had set in, and his voice was so feeble
now it was scarcely audible. He was talking rathei
to himself than to them, and finally he sank into a
doze. A painful silence reigned in the little hut, in
which the only sign was the breathing of the dying
man. A single shaft of light stole down under the
edge of the slowly passing cloud and slipped up to
the door. Suddenly the sleeper waked with a start,
and gazed around.

" Hit gittin' mighty dark," he whispered, faintly.
" You reckon dee'll git heah 'fo' dark?"

The light was dying from his eyes.

" Ephum," said the woman, softly, to her husband.

The effect was electrical.

" Heish! you heah dat!' exclaimed the dying
man, eagerly.

" Ephum "—she repeated. The rest was drowned
by Ole 'Stracted's joyous exclamation.

" Gord! I knowed it!" he cried, suddenly rising
upright, and, with beaming face, stretching both
arms toward the door. " Dyah dee come! Now
watch 'em smile. All y'all jes stand back. Heah
de one you lookin' for. Marster—Mymy—heah's
Little Ephum!" And with a smile on his face he
sank back into his son's arms.

The evening sun, dropping on the instant to his
setting, flooded the room with light; but as Ephraim

gently eased him down and drew his arm from around him, it was the light of the unending morning that was on his face. His Master had at last come for him, and after his long waiting, Ole 'Stracted had indeed gone home.

"NO HAID PAWN."

IT was a ghostly place in broad daylight, if the glimmer that stole in through the dense forest that surrounded it when the sun was directly over-head deserved this delusive name. At any other time it was—why, we were afraid even to talk about it! and as to venturing within its gloomy borders, it was currently believed among us that to do so was to bring upon the intruder certain death. I knew every foot of ground, wet and dry, within five miles of my father's house, except this plantation, for I had hunted by day and night every field, forest, and marsh within that radius; but the swamp and "ma'shes" that surrounded this place I had never invaded. The boldest hunter on the plantation would call off his dogs and go home if they struck a trail that crossed the sobby boundary-line of "No Haid Pawn."

"Jack 'my lanterns" and "evil sperits" only in-fested those woods, and the earnest advice of those whom we children acknowledged to know most about them was, "Don't you never go nigh dyah, honey; hit's de evil-speritest place in dis wull."

Had not Big William and Cephas and Poliam fol-lowed their dogs in there one night, and cut down

a tree in which they had with their own eyes seen
the coon, and lo! when it fell "de warn no mo' coon
dyah 'n a dog!" and the next tree they had "treed
in" not only had no coon in it, but when it was cut
down it had fallen on Poliam and broken his leg.
So the very woods were haunted. From this time
they were abandoned to the "jack 'my lanterns"
and ghosts, and another shadow was added to No
Haid Pawn.

The place was as much cut off from the rest of
the country as if a sea had divided it. The river,
with marshy banks, swept around it in a wide horseshoe on three sides, and when the hammocks dammed
it up it washed its way straight across and scoured
out a new bed for itself, completely isolating the
whole plantation.

The owners of it, if there were any, which was
doubtful, were aliens, and in my time it had not
been occupied for forty years. The negroes declared that it was "gin up" to the "ha'nts an' evil
sperits," and that no living being could live there.
It had grown up in forest and had wholly reverted
to original marsh. The road that once ran through
the swamp had long since been choked up, and the
trees were as thick and the jungle as dense now, in
its track, as in the adjacent "ma'sh." Only one
path remained. That, it was currently believed by
the entire portion of the population who speculated
on the subject, was kept open by the evil spirits.

Certain it was that no human foot ever trod the narrow, tortuous line that ran through the brakes as deviously as the noiseless, stagnant ditches that curved through the jungle, where the musk-rats played and the moccasin slept unmolested. Yet there it lay, plain and well-defined, month after month and year after year, as No Haid Pawn itself stood, amid its surrounding swamps, all undisturbed and unchanging.

Even the runaway slaves who occasionally left their homes and took to the swamps and woods, impelled by the cruelty of their overseers, or by a desire for a vain counterfeit of freedom, never tried this swamp, but preferred to be caught and returned home to invading its awful shades.

We were brought up to believe in ghosts. Our fathers and mothers laughed at us, and endeavored to reason us out of such a superstition—the fathers with much of ridicule and satire, the mothers giving sweet religious reasons for their argument—but what could they avail against the actual testimony and the blood-curdling experiences of a score of witnesses, who recounted their personal observations with a degree of thrilling realism and a vividness that over-bore any arguments our childish reason could grasp! The old mammies and uncles who were our companions and comrades believed in the existence of evil spirits as truly as in the existence of hell or heaven, as to which at that time no question had ever been raised, so far as was known, in that slumberous world. [The Bible was the standard, and all disputes were resolved into an appeal to that authority, the single question as to any point being simply, " Is it in the Bible?"] Had not Lazarus, and Mam' Celia, and William, and Twis'-foot-Bob, and Aunt Sukie Brown, and others *seen* with their own eyes the evil spirits, again and again, in the bodily shape of cats, headless dogs, white cows, and other less palpable forms! And was not their experience, who lived in remote cabins, or wandered night after night through the loneliest woods, stronger evidence than the cold reasoning of those who hardly ever stirred abroad except in daylight? It certainly was more conclusive to us; for no one could have listened to those narrators without being impressed with the fact that they were recounting what they had actually seen with their bodily eyes. The result of it all was, so far as we were concerned, the triumph of faith over reason, and the fixed belief, on our part, in the actual visible existence of the departed, in the sinister form of apparition known as " evil sperits." Every graveyard was tenanted by them; every old house and every peculiarly desolate spot was known to be their rendezvous; but all spots and places sank into insignificance compared with No Haid Pawn.

The very name was uncanny. Originally it had designated a long, stagnant pool of water lying in the centre of the tract, which marked the spot from which the soil had been dug to raise the elevation on which to set the house. More modernly the place, by reason of the filling up of ditches and the sinking of dikes, had become again simple swamp and jungle, or, to use the local expression, "had turned to ma'sh," and the name applied to the whole plantation.

The origin of the name? the pond had no source; but there was a better explanation than that. Anyhow, the very name inspired dread, and the place was our terror.

The house had been built many generations before by a stranger in this section, and the owners never made it their permanent home. Thus, no ties either of blood or friendship were formed with their neighbors, who were certainly open-hearted and open-doored enough to overcome anything but the most persistent unneighborliness. Why this spot was selected for a mansion was always a mystery, unless it was that the new-comer desired to isolate himself completely. Instead of following the custom of those who were native and to the manner born, who always chose some eminence for their seats, he had selected for his a spot in the middle of the wide flat which lay in the horseshoe of the river. The low ground, probably owing to the abundance of land in that country, had never been "taken up," and up to the time of his occupation was in a condition of primeval swamp. He had to begin by making an artificial mound for his mansion. Even then, it was said, he dug so deep that he laid the corner-stone in water. The foundation was of stone, which was brought from a distance. Fabulous stories were told of it. The negroes declared that under the old house were solid rock chambers, which had been built for dungeons, and had served for purposes which were none the less awful because they were vague and indefinite. The huge structure itself was of wood, and was alleged to contain many mysterious rooms and underground passages. One of the latter was said to connect with the No Haid Pawn itself, whose dark waters, according to the negroes' traditions, were some day, by some process not wholly consistent with the laws of physics, to overwhelm the fated pile. An evil destiny had seemed to overshadow the place from the very beginning. One of the negro builders had been caught and decapitated between two of the immense foundation stones. The tradition was handed down that he was sacrificed in some awful and occult rite connected with the laying of the corner-stone. The scaffolding had given way and had precipitated several men to the ground, most of whom had been fatally hurt. This also was alleged to be by hideous design. Then the plantation, in the process of being reclaimed, had proved unhealthy beyond all experience, and the negroes employed in the work of diking and re-

claiming the great swamp had sickened and died by
dozens. The extension of the dangerous fever to
the adjoining plantations had left a reputation for
typhus malaria from which the whole section suffered for a time. But this did not prevent the colored population from recounting year after year
the horrors of the pestilence of No Haid Pawn as a
peculiar visitation, nor from relating with blood-
curdling details the burial by scores, in a thicket just
beside the pond, of the stricken "befo' dee *daid*,
honey, befo' dee *daid!*" The bodies, it was said,
used to float about in the guts of the swamp and on
the haunted pond; and at night they might be seen,
if any one were so hardy as to venture there, rowing
about in their coffins as if they were boats.

Thus the place from the beginning had an evil
name, and when, year after year, the river rose and
washed the levees away, or the musk-rats burrowed
through and let the water in, and the strange masters cursed not only the elements but Heaven itself,
the continued mortality of their negroes was not
wholly unexpected nor unaccounted for by certain
classes of their neighbors.

At length the property had fallen to one more
gloomy more strange, and more sinister than any
who had gone before him—a man whose personal
characteristics and habits were unique in that country. He was of gigantic stature and superhuman
strength, and possessed appetites and vices in pro

portion to his size. He could fell an ox with a
blow of his fist, or in a fit of anger could tear down
the branch of a tree, or bend a bar of iron like a
reed. He, either from caprice or ignorance, spoke
only a *patois* not unlike the Creole French of the
Louisiana parishes. But he was a West Indian.
His brutal temper and habits cut him off from even
the small measure of intercourse which had existed
between his predecessors and their neighbors, and
he lived at No Haid Pawn completely isolated. All
the stories and traditions of the place at once cen-
tred on him, and fabulous tales were told of his
prowess and of his life. It was said, among other
things, that he preserved his wonderful strength by
drinking human blood, a tale which in a certain
sense I have never seen reason to question. Making all allowances, his life was a blot upon civiliza-
tion. At length it culminated. A brutal temper,
inflamed by unbridled passions, after a long period
of license and debauchery came to a climax in a
final orgy of ferocity and fury, in which he was
guilty of an act whose fiendishness surpassed belief,
and he was brought to judgment.

In modern times the very inhumanity of the
crime would probably have proved his security, and
as he had destroyed his own property while he was
perpetrating a crime of appalling and unparalleled
horror, he might have found a defence in that standing refuge of extraordinary scoundrelism—insanity

This defence, indeed, was put in, and was pressed with much ability by his counsel, one of whom was my father, who had just then been admitted to the bar; but, fortunately for the cause of justice, neither courts nor juries were then so sentimental as they have become of late years, and the last occupant of No Haid Pawn paid under the law the full penalty of his hideous crime.   It was one of the curious incidents of the trial that his negroes all lamented his death, and declared that he was a good master when he was not drunk.   He was hanged just at the rear of his own house, within sight of the spot where his awful crime was committed.

At his execution, which, according to the custom of the country, was public, a horrible coincidence occurred which furnished the text of many a sermon on retributive justice among the negroes.

The body was interred near the pond, close by the thicket where the negroes were buried; but the negroes declared that it preferred one of the stone chambers under the mansion, where it made its home, and that it might be seen at any time of the day or night stalking headless about the place. They used to dwell with peculiar zest on the most agonizing details of this wretch's dreadful crime, the whole culminating in the final act of maniacal fury, when the gigantic monster dragged the hacked and headless corpse of his victim up the staircase and stood it up before the open window in his hall.

in the full view of the terrified slaves. After these narrations, the continued reappearance of the murderer and his headless victim was as natural to us as it was to the negroes themselves; and, as night after night w' would hurry up to the great house through the darkness, we were ever on the watch lest he should appear to our frighted vision from the shades of the shrubbery-filled yard.

Thus it was that of all ghostly places No Haid Pawn had the distinction of being invested, to us, with unparalleled horror; and thus to us, no less than because the dikes had given way and the overflowed flats had turned again to swamp and jungle, it was explicable that No Haid Pawn was abandoned, and was now untrodden by any foot but that of its ghostly tenants.

The time of my story was 185–. The spring previous continuous rains had kept the river full, and had flooded the low grounds, and this had been followed by an exceptionally dense growth in the summer. Then, public feeling was greatly excited at the time of which I write, over the discovery in the neighborhood of several emissaries of the underground railway, or—as they were universally considered in that country—of the devil. They had been run off or had disappeared suddenly, but had left behind them some little excitement on the part of the slaves, and a great deal on the part of their masters, and more than the usual number of no groes had run away. All, however, had been caught, or had returned home after a sufficient interval of freedom, except one who had escaped permanently, and who was supposed to have accompanied his instigators on their flight.

This man was a well-known character. He belonged to one of our neighbors, and had been bought and brought there from an estate on the Lower Mississippi. He was the most brutal negro I ever knew. He was of a type rarely found among our negroes, who, judging from their physiognomy and general characteristics, came principally from the coast of Africa. They are of moderate stature, with dull but amiable faces. This man, however, was of immense size, and he possessed the features and expression of a Congo desperado. In character also he differed essentially from all the other slaves in our country. He was alike without their amiability and their docility, and was as fearless as he was brutal. He was the only negro I ever knew who was without either superstition or reverence. Indeed, he differed so widely from the rest of the slaves in that section that there existed some feeling against him almost akin to a race feeling. At the same time that he exercised considerable influence over them they were dreadfully afraid of him, and were always in terror that he would trick them, to which awful power he laid well-known claim. His curses in his strange dialect used to terrify them

beyond measure, and they would do anything to
conciliate him. He had been a continual source of
trouble and an object of suspicion in the neighborhood from the time of his first appearance; and
more than one hog that the negroes declared had
wandered into the marshes of No Haid Pawn, and
had " cut his thote jes' swinin' aroun' an' aroun' in de
ma'sh," had been suspected of finding its way to this
man's cabin. His master had often been urged to
get rid of him, but he was kept, I think, probably
because he was valuable on the plantation. He was
a fine butcher, a good work-hand, and a first-class
boatman. Moreover, ours was a conservative population, in which every man minded his own business
and let his neighbor's alone.

At the time of the visits of those secret agents to
which I have referred, this negro was discovered to
be the leader in the secret meetings held under
their auspices, and he would doubtless have been
taken up and shipped off at once; but when the in-
truders fled, as I have related, their convert disappeared also. It was a subject of general felicitation
in the neighborhood that he was gotten rid of, and
his master, instead of being commiserated on the
loss of his slave, was congratulated that he had not
cut his throat.

No idea can be given at this date of the excitement occasioned in a quiet neighborhood in old
times by the discovery of the mere presence of such

characters as Abolitionists. It was as if the founda
tions of the whole social fabric were undermined.
It was the sudden darkening of a shadow that al‹
ways hung in the horizon. The slaves were in a
large majority, and had they risen, though the final
issue could not be doubted, the lives of every white
on the plantations must have paid the forfeit.
Whatever the right and wrong of slavery might
have been, its existence demanded that no outside
interference with it should be tolerated. So much
was certain ; self-preservation required this.

I was, at the time of which I speak, a well-grown
lad, and had been for two sessions to a boarding-
school, where I had gotten rid of some portion—I
will not say of all—of the superstition of my boy-
hood. The spirit of adventure was beginning to
assert itself in me, and I had begun to feel a sense
of enjoyment in overcoming the fears which once
mastered me, though, I must confess, I had not
entirely shaken off my belief in the existence of
ghosts—that is, I did not believe in them at all in
the day-time, but when night came I was not so
certain about it.

Duck-hunting was my favorite sport, and the
marshes on the river were fine ground for them
usually, but this season the weather had been so
singularly warm that the sport had been poor, and
though I had scoured every canal in the marsh and
every bend in the river as far as No Haid Pawn

Hammock, as the stretch of drifted timber and treacherous marsh was called that marked the boundary-line of that plantation, I had had bad luck. Beyond that point I had never penetrated partly, no doubt, because of the training of my earlier years, and partly because the marsh on either side of the hammock would have mired a cat. Often, as I watched with envious eyes the wild duck rise up over the dense trees that surrounded the place and cut straight for the deserted marshes in the horseshoe, I had had a longing to invade the mysterious domain, and crawl to the edge of No Haid Pawn and get a shot at the fowl that floated on its black surface; but something had always deterred me, and the long reaches of No Haid Pawn were left to the wild-fowl and the ghostly rowers. Finally, however, after a spell whose high temperature was rather suited to August than April, in desperation at my ill-luck I determined to gratify my curiosity and try No Haid Pawn. So one afternoon, without telling any one of my intention, I crossed the mysterious boundary and struck through the swamp for the unknown land.

The marsh was far worse than I had anticipated, and no one but a duck-hunter as experienced and zealous as myself, and as indifferent to ditches, briers, mire, and all that make a swamp, could have penetrated it at all. Even I could never have gotten on if I had not followed the one path that led into the marsh, the reputed " parf " of the evil spirits, and, as it was, my progress was both tedious and dangerous.

The track was a mysterious one, for though I knew it had not been trodden by a human foot in many years, yet there, a veritable " parf," it lay. In some places it was almost completely lost, and I would fear I should have to turn back, but an overhanging branch or a vine swinging from one tree to another would furnish a way to some spot where the narrow trail began again. In other spots old logs thrown across the miry canals gave me an uncomfortable feeling as I reflected what feet had last crossed on them. On both sides of this trail the marsh was either an impenetrable jungle or a mire apparently bottomless.

I shall never forget my sensations as I finally emerged from the woods into the clearing, if that desolate waste of willows, cane, and swamp growth could be so termed. About me stretched the jungle, over which a greenish lurid atmosphere brooded, and straight ahead towered the gaunt mansion, a rambling pile of sombre white, with numberless vacant windows staring at me from the leafless trees about it. Only one other clump of trees appeared above the canes and brush, and that I knew by intuition was the graveyard.

I think I should have turned back had not shame impelled me forward.

My progress from this point was even more diffi-cult than it had been hitherto, for the trail at the end of the wood terminated abruptly in a gut of the swamp; however, I managed to keep on by walking on hammocks, pushing through clumps of bushes, and wading as best I could. It was slow and hot work, though.

It never once struck me that it must be getting late. I had become so accustomed to the gloom of the woods that the more open ground appeared quite light to me, and I had not paid any attention to the black cloud that had been for some time gathering overhead, or to the darkening atmosphere.

I suddenly became sensible that it was going to rain. However, I was so much engrossed in the endeavor to get on that even then I took little note of it. The nearer I came to the house the more it arrested my attention, and the more weird and un-canny it looked. Canes and bushes grew up to the very door; the window-shutters hung from the hinges; the broken windows glared like eyeless sockets; the portico had fallen away from the wall, while the wide door stood slightly ajar, giving to the place a singularly ghastly appearance, somewhat akin to the color which sometimes lingers on the face of a corpse. In my progress wading through the swamp I had gone around rather to the side of the house toward where I supposed the " pawn " itself to lie.

I was now quite near to it, and striking a little less miry ground, as I pushed my way through the bushes and canes, which were higher than my head, I became aware that I was very near the thicket that marked the graveyard, just beyond which I knew the pond itself lay. I was somewhat startled, for the cloud made it quite dusky, and, stepping on a long piece of rotten timber lying on the ground, I parted the bushes to look down the pond. As I did so the rattle of a chain grated on me, and, glancing up through the cane, before me appeared a heavy upright timber with an arm or cross-beam stretching from it, from which dangled a long chain, almost rusted away. I knew by instinct that I stood under the gallows where the murderer of No Haid Pawn had expiated his dreadful crime. His corpse must have fallen just where I stood. I started back appalled.

Just then the black cloud above me was parted by a vivid flame, and a peal of thunder seemed to rive the earth.

I turned in terror, but before I had gone fifty yards the storm was upon me, and instinctively I made for the only refuge that was at hand. It was a dreadful alternative, but I did not hesitate. Outside I was not even sure that my life was safe. And with extraordinary swiftness I had made my way through the broken iron fence that lay rusting in the swamp, had traversed the yard, all grown up as it was to the very threshold, had ascended the sunken steps, crossed the rotted portico, and entered the open door.

A long dark hall stretched before me, extending, as well as I could judge in the gloom, entirely across the house. A number of doors, some shut, some ajar, opened on the hall on one side; and a broad, dark stairway ascended on the other to the upper story. The walls were black with mould. At the far end a large bow-window, with all the glass gone, looked out on the waste of swamp, unbroken save by the clump of trees in the graveyard, and just beside this window was a break where the dark staircase descended to the apartments below. The whole place was in a state of advanced decay; almost the entire plastering had fallen with the damp, and the hall presented a scene of desolation that beggars description.

I was at last in the haunted house.

The rain, driven by the wind, poured in at the broken windows in such a deluge that I was forced in self-defence to seek shelter in one of the rooms. I tried several, but the doors were swollen or fastened; I found one, however, on the leeward side of the house, and, pushing the door, which opened easily, I entered. Inside I found something like an old bed; and the great open fireplace had evidently been used at some earlier time, for the ashes were still banked up in the cavernous hearth, and the

charred ends of the logs of wood were lying in the
chimney corners. To see, still as fresh and natural
as though the fire had but just died out, these rem-
nants of domestic life that had survived all else of a
similar period struck me as unspeakably ghastly.
The bedstead, however, though rude, was conve-
nient as a seat, and I utilized it accordingly, propping
myself up against one of the rough posts. From
my position I commanded through the open door
the entire length of the vacant hall, and could look
straight out of the great bow-window at the head of
the stairs, through which appeared, against the dull
sky, the black mass of the graveyard trees, and a
stretch of one of the canals or guts of the swamp
curving around it, which gleamed white in the glare
of the lightning.

I had expected that the storm would, like most
thunder-storms in the latitude, shortly exhaust itself,
or, as we say, "blow over;" but I was mistaken, and
as the time passed, its violence, instead of diminish-
ing, increased. It grew darker and darker, and presently the startling truth dawned on me that the
gloom which I had supposed simply the effect of the
overshadowing cloud had been really nightfall. I
was shut up alone in No Haid Pawn for the night!

I hastened to the door with the intention of braving
the storm and getting away; but I was almost blown
off my feet. A glance without showed me that the
guts with which the swamp was traversed in every

direction were now full to the brim, and to attempt
to find my way home in the darkness would be sheer
madness; so, after a wistful survey, I returned to
my wretched perch. I thought I would try and light
a fire, but to my consternation I had not a match,
and I finally abandoned myself to my fate. It was
a desolate, if not despairing, feeling that I experienced. My mind was filled, not only with my own
unhappiness, but with the thought of the distress my
absence would occasion them at home; and for a
little while I had a fleeting hope that a party would
be sent out to search for me. This, however, was
untenable, for they would not know where I was.
The last place in which they would ever think of
looking for me was No Haid Pawn, and even if they
knew I was there they could no more get to me in
the darkness and storm than I could escape from it.

I accordingly propped myself up on my bed
and gave myself up to my reflections. I said my
prayers very fervently. I thought I would try and
get to sleep, but sleep was far from my eyes.

My surroundings were too vivid to my apprehension. The awful traditions of the place, do what I
might to banish them, would come to mind. The
original building of the house, and its blood-stained
foundation stones; the dead who had died of the
pestilence that had raged afterward; the bodies
carted by scores and buried in the sobby earth of
the graveyard, whose trees loomed up through the

broken window; the dreadful story of the dead paddling about the swamp in their coffins; and, above all, the gigantic maniac whose ferocity even murder could not satiate, and who had added to murder awful mutilation: he had dragged the mangled corpse of his victim up those very steps and flung it out of the very window which gaped just beyond me in the glare of the lightning. It all passed through my mind as I sat there in the darkness, and no effort of my will could keep my thoughts from dwelling on it. The terrific thunder, outcrashing a thousand batteries, at times engrossed my attention; but it always reverted to that scene of horror; and if I dozed, the slamming of the loose blinds, or the terrific fury of the storm, would suddenly startle me. Once, as the sounds subsided for a moment, or else I having become familiar with them, as I was sinking into a sleepy state, a door at the other end of the hall creaked and then slammed with violence, bringing me bolt upright on the bed, clutching my gun. I could have sworn that I heard footsteps; but the wind was blowing a hurricane, and, after another period of wakefulness and dreadful recollection, nature succumbed, and I fell asleep.

I do not know that I can be said to have lost consciousness even then, for my mind was still enchained by the horrors of my situation, and went on clinging to them and dwelling upon them even in my slumber.

I was, however, certainly asleep; for the storm must have died temporarily away about this hour without my knowing it, and I subsequently heard that it did.

I must have slept several hours, for I was quite stiff from my constrained posture when I became fully aroused.

I was awakened by a very peculiar sound; it was like a distant call or halloo. Although I had been fast asleep a moment before, it startled me into a state of the highest attention. In a second I was wide awake. There was not a sound except the rumble and roll of the thunder, as the storm once more began to renew itself, and in the segment of the circle that I could see along the hall through my door, and, indeed, out through the yawning window at the end, as far as the black clump of trees in the graveyard just at the bend of the canal, which I commanded from my seat whenever there was a flash of lightning, there was only the swaying of the bushes in the swamp and of the trees in the graveyard. Yet there I sat bolt upright on my bed, in the darkness, with every nerve strained to its utmost tension, and that unearthly cry still sounding in my ears. I was endeavoring to reason myself into the belief that I had dreamed it, when a flash of lightning lit up the whole field of my vision as if it had been in the focus of a sun-glass, and out on the canal, where it curved around the graveyard, was a boat—a something—

small, black, with square ends, and with a man in it, standing upright, and something lying in a lump or mass at the bow.

I knew I could not be mistaken, for the lightning, by a process of its own, photographs everything on the retina in minutest detail, and I had a vivid impression of everything from the foot of the bed, on which I crouched, to the gaunt arms of those black trees in the graveyard just over that ghostly boatman and his dreadful freight. I was wide awake.

The story of the dead rowing in their coffins was verified!

I am unable to state what passed in the next few minutes.

The storm had burst again with renewed violence and was once more expending itself on the house; the thunder was again rolling overhead; the broken blinds were swinging and slamming madly; and the dreadful memories of the place were once more besetting me.

I shifted my position to relieve the cramp it had occasioned, still keeping my face toward that fatal window. As I did so, I heard above, or perhaps I should say under, the storm a sound more terrible to me—the repetition of that weird halloo, this time almost under the great window. Immediately succeeding this was the sound of something scraping under the wall, and I was sensible when a door on the ground-floor was struck with a heavy thud. It was pitch-dark, but ᴛ heard the door pushed wide open, and as a string of fierce oaths, part English and part Creole French, floated up the dark stair-way, muffled as if sworn through clinched teeth, I held my breath. I recalled the unknown tongue the ghostly murderer employed; and I knew that the murderer of No Haid Pawn had left his grave, and that his ghost was coming up that stair. I heard his step as it fell on the first stair heavily yet almost noiselessly. It was an unearthly sound—dull, like the tread of a bared foot, accompanied by the scrap-ing sound of a body dragging. Step by step he came up the black stairway in the pitch darkness as steadily as if it were daytime, and he knew every step, accompanied by that sickening sound of drag-ging. There was a final pull up the last step, and a dull, heavy thud, as, with a strange, wild laugh, he flung his burden on the floor.

For a moment there was not a sound, and then the awful silence and blackness were broken by a crash of thunder that seemed to tear the foundations asunder like a mighty earthquake, and the whole house, and the great swamp outside, were filled with a glare of vivid, blinding light. Directly in front of me, clutching in his upraised hand a long, keen, glit-tering knife, on whose blade a ball of fire seemed to play, stood a gigantic figure in the very flame of the lightning, and stretched at his feet lay, ghastly and bloody, a black and headless trunk.

I staggered to the door and, tripping, fell prostrate over the sill.

*　　*　　*　　*　　*　　*　　*

When we could get there, nothing was left but the foundation. The haunted house, when struck, had literally burned to the water's edge. The changed current had washed its way close to the place, and in strange verification of the negroes' traditions. No Haid Pawn had reclaimed its own, and the spot with all its secrets lay buried under its dark waters.

POLLY.

A CHRISTMAS RECOLLECTION.

IT was Christmas Eve. I remember it just as if it
was yesterday. The Colonel had been pretend-
ing not to notice it, but when Drinkwater Torm *
knocked over both the great candlesticks, and in
his attempt to pick them up lurched over himself
and fell sprawling on the floor, he yelled at him.
Torm pulled himself together, and began an explanation, in which the point was that he had not
"teched a drap in Gord knows how long," but the
Colonel cut him short.

"Get out of the room, you drunken vagabond!"
he roared.

Torm was deeply offended. He made a low,
grand bow, and with as much dignity as his unsteady
condition would admit of, marched very statelily
from the room, and passing out through the dining-
room, where he stopped to abstract only one more
drink from the long, heavy, cut-glass decanter on the
sideboard, meandered out to his house in the back-

---

* This spelling is used because he was called "Torm" until it
became his name.

yard, where he proceeded to talk religion to Charity, his wife, as he always did when he was particularly drunk.   He was expounding the vision of the golden candlestick, and the bowl and seven lamps and two olive-trees, when he fell asleep.   The roarer, as has been said, was the Colonel ; the meanderer was Drinkwater Torm.   The Colonel gave him the name, " because," he said, " if he were to drink water once he would die."   As Drinkwater closed the door, the Colonel continaed, fiercely :

" Damme, Polly, I will !   I'll sell him to-morrow morning ; and if I can't sell him I'll give him away."

Polly, with troubled great dark eyes, was wheed- ling him vigorously.

"No ; I tell you I'll sell him.   'Misery in his back' the mischief !   he's a drunken, trifling, good- for-nothing nigger, and I have sworn to sell him a thousand—yes, ten thousand times ; and now I'll have to do it to keep my word."

This was true.   The Colonel swore this a dozen times a day—every time Torm got drunk, and as that had occurred very frequently for many years before Polly was born, he was not outside of the limit.   Polly, however, was the only one this threat ever troubled.   The Colonel knew he could no more have gotten on without Torm than his old open- faced watch, which looked for all the world like a model of himself, could have run without the main- spring.   From tying his shoes and getting his shav·

ing-water to making his juleps and lighting his
candles, which was all he had to do, Drinkwater
Torm was necessary to him. (I think he used to
make the threat just to prove to himself that Torm
did not own him ; if so, he failed in his purpose—
Torm did own him.) Torm knew it as well as he,
or better ; and while Charity, for private and wifely
reasons, occasionally held the threat over him when
his expoundings passed even her endurance, she
knew it also.

Thus Polly was the only one it deceived or frightened. It always deceived her, and she never rested
until she had obtained Torm's reprieve " for just
one more time." So on this occasion, before she
got down from the Colonel's knees, she had given
him in bargain " just one more squeeze," and received
in return Torm's conditional pardon, " only till next
time."

Everybody in the county knew the Colonel, and
everybody knew Drinkwater Torm, and everybody
who had been to the Colonel's for several years past
(and that was nearly everybody in the county, for
the Colonel kept open house) knew Polly. She had
been placed in her chair by the Colonel's side at the
club dinner on her first birthday after her arrival,
and had been afterward placed on the table and
allowed to crawl around among and in the dishes to
entertain the gentlemen, which she did to the ap-
plause of every one, and of herself most of all ; and

from that time she had exercised in her kingdom the functions of both Vashti and Esther, and whatever Polly ordered was done. If the old inlaid piano in the parlor had been robbed of strings, it was all right, for Polly had taken them. Bob had cut them out for her, without a word of protest from any one but Charity. The Colonel would have given her his heart-strings if Polly had required them.

She had owned him body and soul from the second he first laid eyes on her, when, on the instant he entered the room, she had stretched out her little chubby hands to him, and on his taking her had, after a few infantile caresses, curled up and, with her finger in her mouth, gone to sleep in his arms like a little white kitten.

Bob used to wonder in a vague, boyish way where the child got her beauty, for the Colonel weighed two hundred and fifty pounds, and was as ugly as a red head and thirty or forty years of Torm's mint-juleps piled on a somewhat reckless college career could make him; but one day, when the Colonel was away from home, Charity showed him a daguerreotype of a lady, which she got out of the top drawer of the Colonel's big secretary with the brass lions on it, and it looked exactly like Polly. It had the same great big dark eyes and the same soft white look, though Polly was stouter; for she was a great tomboy, and used to run wild over the place with Bob, climbing cherry-trees, and fishing in the creek, and looking as blooming as a rose, with her hair all tangled over her pretty head, until she grew quite large, and the Colonel got her a tutor. He thought of sending her to a boarding-school, but the night he broached the subject he raised such a storm, and Polly was in such a tempest of tears, that he gave up the matter at once. It was well he did so, for Polly and Charity cried all night, and Torm was so overcome that even next morning he could not bring the Colonel his shaving-water, and he had to shave with cold water for the first time in twenty years. He therefore employed a tutor. Most people said the child ought to have had a governess, and one or two single ladies of forgotten age in the neighborhood delicately hinted that they would gladly teach her; but the Colonel swore that he would have no women around him, and he would be eternally condemned if any should interfere with Polly; so he engaged Mr. Cranmer, and invited Bob to come over and go to school to him also, which he did; for his mother, who had up to that time taught him herself, was very poor, and was unable to send him to school, her husband, who was the Colonel's fourth cousin, having died largely indebted, and all of his property, except a small farm adjoining the Colonel s, and a few negroes, having gone into the General Court.

Bob had always been a great favorite with the Colonel, and ever since he had been a small boy he

had been used to coming over and staying with
him.

He could gaff a chicken as well as Drinkwater
Torm, which was a great accomplishment in the
Colonel's eyes; for he had the best game-chickens in
the county, and used to fight them, too, matching
them against those of one or two of his neighbors
who were similarly inclined, until Polly grew up and
made him stop. He could tame a colt quicker than
anybody on the plantation. Moreover, he could
shoot more partridges in a day than the Colonel,
and could beat him shooting with a pistol as well,
though the Colonel laid the fault of the former on
his being so fat, and that of the latter on his spectacles. They used to practice with the Colonel's old
pistols that hung in their holsters over the tester of
his bed, and about which Drinkwater used to tell so
many lies; for although they were kept loaded, and
their brass-mounted butts peeping out of their
leathern covers used to look ferocious enough to
give some apparent ground for Torm's story of how
"he and the Colonel had shot Judge Cabell spang
through the heart," the Colonel always said that
Cabell behaved very handsomely, and that the matter was arranged on the field without a shot. Even
at that time some people said that Bob's mother
was trying to catch the Colonel, and that if the
Colonel did not look out she would yet be the mistress of his big plantation. And all agreed that the

boy would come in for something handsome at the Colonel's death; for Bob was his cousin and his nearest male relative, if Polly *was* his niece, and he would hardly leave her all his property, especially as she was so much like her mother, with whom, as everybody knew, the Colonel had been desperately in love, but who had treated him badly, and, not-withstanding his big plantation and many negroes, had run away with his younger brother, and both of them had died in the South of yellow fever, leaving of all their children only this little Polly; and the Colonel had taken Drinkwater and Charity, and had travelled in his carriage all the way to Mississippi, to get and bring Polly back. It was Christmas Eve when they reached home, and the Colonel had sent Drinkwater on a day ahead to have the fires made and the house aired for the baby; and when the carriage drove up that night you would have thought a queen was coming, sure enough.

Every hand on the plantation was up at the great house waiting for them, and every room in the house had a fire in it. (Torm had told the overseer so many lies that he had had the men cutting wood all day, although the regular supply was cut.) And when Charity stepped out of the carriage with the baby all bundled up in her arms, making a great show about keeping it wrapped up, and walked up the steps as slowly as if it were made of gold, you could have heard a pin drop; even the Colonel fell

13

back, and spoke in a whisper. The great chamber was given up to the baby, the Colonel going to the wing room, where he always stayed after that. He spoke of sitting up all night to watch the child, but Charity assured him that she was not going to take her eyes off of her during the night, and with a promise to come in every hour and look after them, the Colonel went to his room, where he slept until nine o'clock the next morning. But I was telling what people said about Bob's mother.

When the report reached the Colonel about the widow's designs, he took Polly on his knees and told her all about it, and then both laughed until the tears ran down the Colonel's face and dropped on his big flowered vest and on Polly's little blue frock; and he sent the widow next day a fine short-horned heifer to show his contempt of the gossip.

And now Bob was the better shot of the two; and they taught Polly to shoot too, and to load and unload the pistols, at which the Colonel was as proud as if one of his young stags had whipped an old rooster.

But they never could induce her to shoot at anything except a mark. She was the tenderest-hearted little thing in the world.

If her taste had been consulted she would have selected a crossbow, for it did not make such a noise, and she could shoot it without shutting her eyes; besides that, she could shoot it in the house, which

indeed, she did, until she had shot the eyes out of
nearly all the bewigged gentlemen and bare-necked,
long-fingered ladies on the walls. Once she came
very near shooting Torm's eye out also; but this
was an accident, though Drinkwater declared it was
not, and tried to make out that Bob had put her up
to it. "Dat's de mischievouses' boy Gord ever
made," he said, complainingly, to Charity. Fortunately, his eye got well, and it gave him an excuse
for staying half drunk for nearly a week; and afterward, like a dog that has once been lame in his hind-
leg, whenever he saw Polly, and did not forget it,
he squinted up that eye and tried to look miserable.
Polly was quite a large girl then, and was carrying
the keys (except when she lost them), though she
could not have been more than twelve years old; for
it was just after this that the birthday came when the
Colonel gave her her first real silk dress. It was blue
silk, and came from Richmond, and it was hard to
tell which was the proudest, Polly, or Charity, or
Drinkwater, or the Colonel. Torm got drunk before
the dinner was over, "drinking de healthsh to de
young mistis in de sky-blue robes what stands befo'
de throne, you know," he explained to Charity, after
the Colonel had ordered him from the dining-room,
with promises of prompt sale on the morrow.

Bob was there, and it was the last time Polly ever
sucked her thumb. She had almost gotten out of
the habit anyhow, and it was in a moment of forget-

fulness that she let Bob see her do it. He was a great tease, and when she was smaller had often worried her about it until she would fly at him and try to bite him with her little white teeth. On this occasion, however, she stood everything until he said that about a girl who wore a blue silk dress sucking her thumb; then she boxed his jaws. The fire flew from his eyes, but hers were even more sparkling. He paused for a minute, and then caught her in his arms and kissed her violently. She never sucked her thumb after that.

This happened out in front of her mammy's house, within which Torm was delivering a powerful exhortation on temperance; and, strange to say, Charity took Bob's side, while Torm espoused Polly's, and afterward said she ought to have "tooken a stick and knocked Marse Bob's head spang off." This, fortunately, Polly did not do (and when Bob went to the university afterward he was said to have the best head in his class). She just turned around and ran into the house, with her face very red. But she never slapped Bob after that. Not long after this he went off to college; for Mr. Cranmer, the tutor, said he already knew more than most college graduates did, and that it would be a shame for him not to have a university education. When the question of ways and means was mooted, the Colonel, who was always ready to lend money if he had it, and to borrow it if he did not, swore he would give him all the money he wanted; but, to his astonishment, Bob refused to accept it, and although the Colonel abused him for it, and asked Polly if she did not think he was a fool (which Polly did, for she was always ready to take and spend all the money he or any one else gave her), yet he did not like him the less for it, and he finally persuaded Bob to take it as a loan, and Bob gave him his bond.

The day before he left home he was over at the Colonel's, where they had a great dinner for him, and Polly presided in her newest silk dress (she had three then); and when Bob said good-by she slipped something into his hand, and ran away to her room, and when he looked at it, it was her ten-dollar gold piece, and he took it.

He was at college not quite three years, for his mother was taken sick, and he had to come home and nurse her; but he had stood first in most of his classes, and not lower than third in any; and he had thrashed the carpenter on Vinegar Hill, who was the bully of the town. So that although he did not take his degree, he had gotten the start which enabled him to complete his studies during the time he was taking care of his mother, and until her death, so that as soon as he was admitted to the bar he made his mark. It was his splendid defence o the man who shot the deputy-sheriff at the court-house on election day that brought him out as the Democratic candidate for the Constitutional Con

vention, where he made such a reputation as a
speaker that the *Enquirer* declared him the rising
man of the State ; and even the *Whig* admitted that
perhaps the Loco-foco party might find a leader to
redeem it. Polly was just fifteen when she began
to take an interest in politics ; and although she
read the papers diligently, especially the *Enquirer*,
which her uncle never failed to abuse, yet she never
could exactly satisfy herself which side was right ;
for the Colonel was a stanch Whig, while most people must have been Democrats, as Bob was elected
by a big majority. She wanted to be on the Colonel's side, and made him explain everything to
her, which he did to his own entire satisfaction, and
to hers too, she tried to think ; but when Bob came
over to tea, which he very frequently did, and the
Colonel and he got into a discussion, her uncle
always seemed to her to get the worst of the argument ; at any rate, he generally got very hot. This,
however, might have been because Bob was so cool,
while the Colonel was so hot-tempered.

Bob had grown up very handsome. His mouth
was strong and firm, and his eyes were splendid.
He was about six feet, and his shoulders were as
broad as the Colonel's. She did not see him now
as often as she did when he was a boy, but it was
because he was kept so busy by his practice. (He
used to get cases in three or four counties now, and
big ones at that.) She knew, however, that she was

just as good a friend of his as ever; indeed, she
took the trouble to tell herself so. A compliment
to him used to give her the greatest happiness, and
would bring deeper roses into her cheeks. He was
the greatest favorite with everybody. Torm thought
that there was no one in the world like him. He
had long ago forgiven him his many pranks, and
said " he was the grettest gent'man in the county
skusin him [Torm] and the Colonel," and that " he
al'ays handled heself to he raisin'," by which Torm
made indirect reference to regular donations made
to him by the aforesaid " gent'man," and particularly to an especially large benefaction then lately
conferred. It happened one evening at the Colonel's, after dinner, when several guests, including
Bob, were commenting on the perfections of various
ladies who were visiting in the neighborhood that
summer. The praises were, to Torm's mind, somewhat too liberally bestowed, and he had attempted
to console himself by several visits to the pantry;
but when all the list was disposed of, and Polly's
name had not been mentioned, endurance could
stand it no longer, and he suddenly broke in with
his judgment that they "didn't none on 'em hol' a
candle to his young mistis, whar wuz de ve'y pink
an' flow'r on 'em all."

The Colonel, immensely pleased, ordered him out,
with a promise of immediate sale on the morrow.
But that evening, as he got on his horse, Bob

slipped into his hand a five-dollar gold piece, and he
told Polly that if the Colonel really intended to sell
Torm, just to send him over to his house; he wanted
the benefit of his judgment.

Polly, of course, did not understand his allusion,
though the Colonel had told her of Torm's speech;
but Bob had a rose on his coat when he came out of
the window, and the long pin in Polly's bodice was
not fastened very securely, for it slipped, and she
lost all her other roses, and he had to stoop and
pick them up for her. Perhaps, though, Bob was
simply referring to his having saved some money,
for shortly afterward he came over one morning,
and, to the Colonel's disgust, paid him down in full
the amount of his bond. He attempted a somewhat formal speech of thanks, but broke down in it
so lamentably that two juleps were ordered out by
the Colonel to reinstate easy relations between
them—an effect which apparently was not immediately produced—and the Colonel confided to Polly
next day that since the fellow had been taken up
so by those Loco-focos he was not altogether as he
used to be.

" Why, he don't even drink his juleps clear," the
old man asserted, as if he were charging him with,
at the least, misprision of treason. " However," he
added, softening as the excuse presented itself to
his mind, " that may be because his mother was
always so opposed to it. You know mint never

would grow there," he pursued to Polly, who had
heard him make the same observation, with the
same astonishment, a hundred times. "Strangest
thing I ever knew. But he's a confoundedly clever
fellow, though, Polly," he continued, with a sudden
reviving of the old-time affection. "Damme! I like
him." And, as Polly's face turned a sweet carmine,
added : "Oh, I forgot, Polly ; didn't mean to swear ;
damme if I did. It just slipped out. Now I haven't
sworn before for a week ; you know I haven't. Yes,
of course, I mean except then." For Polly, with
softly fading color, was reading him the severest of
lectures on his besetting sin, and citing an ebullition
over Torm's failing of the day before. "Come and
sit down on your uncle's knee and kiss him once as
a token of forgiveness. Just one more squeeze," as
the fair girlish arms were twined about his neck, and
the sweetest of faces was pressed against his own
rough cheek. "Polly, do you remember," asked the
old man, holding her off from him and gazing at the
girlish face fondly—"do you remember how, when
you were a little scrap, you used to climb up on my
knee and squeeze me just once more to save that
rascal Drinkwater, and how you used to say you
were going to marry Bob and me when you were
grown up ? "

Polly's memory, apparently, was not very good.
That evening, however, it seemed much better,
when, dressed all in soft white, and with cheeks

reflecting the faint tints of the sunset clouds, she was strolling through the old flower-garden with a tall young fellow whose hat sat on his head with a jaunty air, and who was so very careful to hold aside the long branches of the rose-bushes. They had somehow gotten to recalling each in turn some incident of the old boy and girl days. Bob knew the main facts as well as she, but Polly remembered the little details and circumstances of each incident best, except those about the time they were playing "knucks" together. Then Bob recollected most. He was positive that when she cried because he shot so hard, he had kissed her to make it well. Curiously, Polly's recollection failed again, and was only distinct about very modern matters. She remembered with remarkable suddenness that it was tea-time.

They were away down at the end of the garden, and her lapse of memory had a singular effect on Bob ; for he turned quite pale, and insisted that she did remember it ; and then said something about having wanted to see the Colonel, and having waited, and did so strangely that if that rose-bush had not caught her dress, he might have done something else. But the rose-bush caught her dress, and Polly, who looked really scared at it, or something, ran away just as the Colonel's voice was heard calling them to tea.

Bob was very silent at the table, and when he left,

the Colonel **was** quite anxious about him. He asked Polly if she had not noticed his depression. Polly had not.

"That's just the way with you women," said the Colonel, testily. "A man might die under your very eyes, and you would not notice it. I noticed it, and I tell you the fellow's sick. I say he's sick!" he reiterated, with a little habit he had acquired since he had begun to grow slightly deaf. "I shall advise him to go away and have a little fling somewhere. He works too hard, sticks too close at home. He never goes anywhere except here, and he don't come here as he used to do. He ought to get married. Advise him to get married. Why don't he set up to Sally Brent or Malviny Pegram? He's a likely fellow, and they'd both take him—fools if they didn't. I say they are fools if they didn't. What say?"

"I didn't say anything," said Polly, quietly going to the piano.

Her music often soothed the Colonel to sleep.

The next morning but one Bob rode over, and instead of hooking his horse to the fence as he usually did, he rode on around toward the stables. He greeted Torm, who was in the backyard, and after extracting some preliminary observations from him respecting the "misery in his back," he elicited the further facts that Miss Polly was going down the road to dine at the Pegrams', of which he had some intimation before, and that the Colonel was down on the river farm, but would be back about two o'clock. He rode on. At two o'clock promptly Bob returned. The Colonel had not yet gotten home. He, however, dismounted, and, tying his horse, went in. He must have been tired of sitting down, for he now walked up and down the portico without once taking a seat.

"Marse Bob 'll walk heself to death," observed Charity to Torm, from her door.

Presently the Colonel came in, bluff, warm, and hearty. He ordered dinner from the front gate as he dismounted, and juleps from the middle of the walk, greeted Bob with a cheeriness which that gentleman in vain tried to imitate, and was plumped down in his great split-bottomed chair, wiping his red head with his still redder bandana handkerchief, and abusing the weather, the crops, the newspapers, and his overseer before Bob could get breath to make a single remark. When he did, he pitched in on the weather. That is a safe topic at all times, and it was astonishing how much comfort Bob got out of it this afternoon. He talked about it until dinner began to come in across the yard, the blue china dishes gleaming in the hands of Phœbe and her numerous corps of ebon and mahogany assistants, and Torm brought out the juleps, with the mint looking as if it were growing in the great silver cans. with frosted work all over the sides.

Dinner was rather a failure, so far as Bob was concerned. Perhaps he missed something that usually graced that table; perhaps only his body was there, while he himself was down at Miss Malviny Pegram's; perhaps he had gone back and was unfastening an impertinent rose-bush from a filmy white dress in the summer twilight; perhaps— But anyhow he was so silent and abstracted that the Colonel rallied him good-humoredly, which did not help matters. They had adjourned to the porch, and had been there for some time, when Bob broached the subject of his visit.

"Colonel," he said, suddenly, and wholly irrelevant to everything that had gone before, "there is a matter I want to speak to you about—a—ah—we—a little matter of great importance to—ah—myself." He was getting very red and confused, and the Colonel instantly divining the matter, and secretly flattering himself, and determining to crow over Polly, said, to help him out:

"Aha, you rogue, I knew it. Come up to the scratch, sir. So you are caught at last. Ah, you sly fox! It's the very thing you ought to do. Why, I know half a dozen girls who'd jump at you. I knew it. I said so the other night. Polly—"

Bob was utterly off his feet by this time. "I want to ask your consent to marry Polly," he blurted out desperately. "I love her."

"The devil you do!" exclaimed the Colonel. He

could say no more : he simply sat still, in speechless, helpless, blank amazement. To him Polly was still a little girl climbing his knees, and an emperor might not aspire to her.

"Yes, sir, I do," said Bob, calm enough now—growing cool as the Colonel became excited. "I love her, and I want her."

' Well, sir, you can't have her," roared the Colonel, rising from his seat in the violence of his refusal. He looked like a tawny lion whose lair had been invaded.

Bob's face paled, and a look came on it that the Colonel recalled afterward, and which he did not remember ever to have seen on it before, except once, when, years ago, some one shot one of his dogs—a look made up of anger and of dogged resolution. "I shall," he said, throwing up his head and looking the Colonel straight in the eyes, his voice perfectly calm, but his eyes blazing, the mouth drawn close, and the lines of his face as if they had been carved in granite.

"I'll be —— if you shall !" stormed the Colonel ; "the King of England should not have her !" and, turning, he stamped into the house and slammed the door behind him.

Bob walked slowly down the steps and around to the stables, where he ordered his horse. He rode home across the fields without a word, except, as he jumped his horse over the line fence, "I shall have her," he repeated, between his fast-set teeth.

That evening Polly came home all unsuspecting anything of the kind; the Colonel waited until she had taken off her things and come down in her fresh muslin dress. She surpassed in loveliness the rose-buds that lay on her bosom, and the impertinence that could dare aspire to her broke over the old man in a fresh wave. He had nursed his wrath all the evening.

"Polly!" he blurted out, suddenly rising with a jerk from his arm-chair, and unconsciously striking an attitude before the astonished girl, "do you want to marry Bob?"

"Why, no," cried Polly, utterly shaken out of her composure by the suddenness and vehemence of the attack.

"I knew it," declared the Colonel, triumphantly. "It was a piece of cursed impertinence;" and he worked himself up to such a pitch of fury, and grew so red in the face, that poor little Polly, who had to steer between two dangers, had to employ all her arts to soothe the old man and keep him out of a fit of apoplexy. She learned the truth, however, and she learned something which, until that time, she had never known; and though, as she kissed her uncle " good-night," she made no answer to his final shot of, " Well, I'm glad we are not going to have any nonsense about the fellow; I have made up my mind, and we'll treat his impudence as it deserves," she locked her door carefully when she was within her own room, and the next morning she said she had a headache.

Bob did not come that day. If the Colonel had not been so hot-headed—that is, if he had not been a man—things would doubtless have straight-ened themselves out in some of those mysterious ways in which the hardest knots into which two young people's affairs contrive to get untangle themselves; but being a man, he must needs, man-like, undertake to manage according to his own plan, which is always the wrong one.

When, therefore, he announced to Polly at the breakfast-table that morning that she would have no further annoyance from that fellow's impertinence— for he had written him a note apologizing for leav-ing him abruptly in his own house the day before, but forbidding him, in both their names, to continue his addresses, or indeed to put his foot on the place again—he fully expected to see Polly's face brighten, and to receive her approbation and thanks. What, then, was his disappointment to see her face grow distinctly white. All she said was, "Oh, uncle!"

It was unfortunate that the day was Sunday, and that the Colonel went with her to church (which she insisted on attending notwithstanding her headache), and was by when she met Bob. They came on each other suddenly. Bob took off his hat and stood like

a soldier on review, erect, expectant, and a little
pale. The Colonel, who had almost forgotten his
" impertinence," and was about to shake hands with
him as usual, suddenly remembered it, and drawing
himself up, stepped to the other side of Polly, and
handed her by the younger gentleman as if he were
protecting her from a mob. Polly, who had been
looking anxiously everywhere but in the right place,
meaning to give him a smile which would set things
straight, caught his eye only at that second, and felt
rather than saw the change in Bob's attitude and
manner. She tried to give him the smile, but it
died in her eyes, and even after her back was turned
she was sensible of his defiance ; and she went into
church, and dropped down on her knees in the far
end of her pew, with her little heart needing all the
consolations of her religion.

The man she prayed hardest for did not come
into church that day. Things went very badly after
that, and the knots got tighter and tighter. An attempt which Bob made to loosen them failed disas-
trously, and the Colonel, who was the best-hearted
man in the world, but whose prejudices were made
of wrought iron, took it into his head that Bob had
insulted him, and Polly's indirect efforts at pacifica-
tion aroused him to such an extent that for the first
time in his life he was almost hard with her. He
conceived the absurd idea that she was sacrificing
herself for Bob on account of her friendship for him.

14

and that it was his duty to protect her against herself, which, man-like, he proceeded to do in his own
fashion, to poor little Polly's great distress.

She was devoted to her uncle, and knew the
strength of his affection for her.   On the other hand,
Bob and she had been friends so long.   She never
could remember the time when she did not have
Bob.   But he had never said a word of love to her
in his life.

On that evening in the garden she had known it
just as well as if he had fallen on his knees at her
feet.   She knew it was just because he had owed her
uncle the money ; and oh ! if she just hadn't gotten
frightened ; and oh ! if her uncle just hadn't done
it ; and oh ! she was so unhappy !   The poor little
thing, in her own dainty, white-curtained room,
where were the books and things he had given her,
and the letters she had written her, used to—but that
is a secret.   Anyhow, it was not because he was gone.
She knew that was not the reason—indeed, she very
often said to herself—but because he had been
treated so unjustly, and suffered so, and she had
done it all.   And she used to introduce many new
petitions into her prayers, in which, if there was not
any name expressed, she felt that it would be under-
stood, and the blessings would reach him just the
same.   The summer had gone, and the Indian summer had come in its place, hazy, dreamy, and sad.
It always made her melancholy, and this year

although the weather was perfect, she was affected
she said, by the heat, and did not go out of doors
much. So presently her cheeks were not as blooming as they had been, and even her great eyes lost
some of their lustre; at least, Charity thought so,
and said so too, not only to Polly, but to her master,
whom she scared half to death; and who, notwithstanding that Dr. Stopper was coming every other
day to see a patient on the plantation, and that the
next day was the time for his regular visit, put a boy
on a horse that night and sent him with a note urg-
ing the doctor to come the next morning to breakfast. The doctor came, and spent the day: examined Polly's lungs and heart, prescribed out-door
exercise, and left something less than a bushel-
basketful of medicines for her to take.

Polly was, at the time of his visit, in a very excited
state, for the Colonel had, with a view of soothing
her, the night before delivered a violent philippic
against marriage in general, and in particular against
marriage with "impudent young puppies who did
not know their places;" and he had proposed an ex-
tensive tour, embracing all the United States and
Canada, and intended to cover the entire winter and
spring following. Polly, who had stood as much as
she could stand, finally rebelled, and had with flash-
ing eyes and mantling cheeks espoused Bob's cause
with a courage and dash which had almost routed
the old Colonel. "Not that he was anything to her

except a friend," she was most careful to explain, but she was tired of hearing her " friend " assailed, and she thought that it was the highest compliment a man could pay a woman, etc., etc., for all of which she did a great deal of blushing in her own room afterward.

Thus it happened that she was both excited and penitent the next day, and thinking to make some atonement, and at the same time to make the prescribed exercise, which would excuse her from taking the medicines, she filled a little basket with goodies to take old Aunt Betty at the Far Quarters; and thus it happened that, as she was coming back along the path that ran down the meadow on the other side of the creek, which was the dividing line between the two plantations, and was almost at the foot-bridge that Somebody had made for her so carefully with logs cut out of his own woods, and the long shadows of the willows made it gloomy, and everything was so still that she had grown very lonely and unhappy—thus it happened that just as she was thinking how kind he had been about making the bridge and hand-rail so strong, and about everything, and how cruel he must think her, and how she would never see him any more as she used to do, she turned the clump of willows to step up on the log, and there he was standing on the bridge just before her, looking down into her eyes. She tried to get by him—she remembered that afterward—but he was so mean; it was always a little confused in her memory, and she could never recall exactly how it was. She was sure, however, that it was because he was so pale that she said it, and that she did not begin to cry until afterward, and that it was because he would not listen to her explanation; and that she didn't let him do it, she could not help it, and she did not know her head was on his shoulder.

Anyhow, when she got home that evening her improvement was so apparent that the Colonel called Charity in to note it, and declared that Virginia country doctors were the finest in the world, and that Stopper was the greatest doctor in the State. The change was wonderful indeed; and the old gilt mirror with its gauze-covered frame would never have known for the sad-eyed Polly of the day before the bright, happy little maiden that stood before it new and smiled at the beaming face which dimpled at its own content. Old Betty's was a protracted pleurisy, and the good things Polly carried her daily did not tend to shorten the sickness. Ever afterward she blessed the Lord for " dat chile " whenever Polly's name was mentioned. Had she known how sympathetic Bob was during this period, she would doubtless have included him in her benison.

But although he was inspecting that bridge every afternoon regularly, notwithstanding Polly's oft-reiterated wish and express orders as regularly declared. no one knew a word of all this. And it was a bow drawn at a venture when, on the evening that Polly had tried to carry out her engagement to bring her uncle around, the old man said, "Why, hoity-toity! the young rascal's cause seems to be thriving." She was so confident of her success that she was not prepared for failure, and it struck her like a fresh blow; and though she did not cry until she got into her own room, when she got there she threw herself on the bed and cried herself to sleep. "It was so cruel in him," she said to herself, "to desire me never to speak to him again! And, oh! if he should really catch him on the place and shoot him!"

The pronouns in our language were probably invented by young women. The headache Polly had the next morning was not invented. Poor little thing! her last hope was gone. She determined to bid Bob good-by, and never see him again.

She had made up her mind to this on her knees, so she knew she was right. The pain it cost her satisfied her that it was right. She was firmly resolved when she set out that afternoon to see old Betty, who was, in everybody's judgment except her own, quite convalescent, and whom Dr. Stopper pronounced entirely well. She wavered a little in her resolution when, descending the path along the willows, which were leafless now, she caught sight of a tall figure loitering easily up the meadow, and she abandoned—that is, she forgot—it altogether when,

having doubtfully suggested it, she was suddenly
enfolded in a pair of strong arms, and two gray eyes,
lighting a handsome face strong with the self-confi·
dence which women love, looked down into hers.
Then he proposed it!

Her heart almost stood still at his boldness. But
he was so strong, so firm, so reasonable, so self-re-
liant, and yet so gentle, she could not but listen to
him. Still she refused—and she never did consent;
she forbade him ever to think of it again. Then she
begged him never to come there again, and told him
of her uncle's threats, and of her fears for him; and
then, when he laughed at them, she begged him
never, never, under any circumstances, to take any
notice of what her uncle might do or say, but rather
to stand still and be shot dead; and then, when
Bob promised this, she burst into tears, and he had
to hold her and comfort her like a little girl.

It was pretty bad after that, and but for Polly's
out-door exercise she would undoubtedly have succumbed. It seemed as if something had come between her and her uncle. She no longer went about
singing like a bird. She suffered under the sense of
being misunderstood, and it was so lonely! He too
was oppressed by it. Even Torm shared in it, and
his expositions assumed a cast terrific in the last
degree. It was now December.

One evening it culminated. The weather had
been too bad for Polly to go out, and she was sick.

Finally Stopper was sent for.   Polly, who, to use
Charity's expression, was "pestered till she was frac-
tious," rebelled flatly, and refused to keep her bed
or to take the medicines prescribed.   Charity backed
her.   Torm got drunk.   The Colonel was in a fume,
and declared his intention to sell Torm next morning, as usual, and to take Charity and Polly and go
to Europe.   This was well enough ; but to Polly's
consternation, when she came to breakfast next
morning, she found that the old man's plans had
ripened into a scheme to set out on the very next
day for Louisiana and New Orleans, where he proposed to spend the winter looking after some plantations she had, and showing her something of the
world.   Polly remonstrated, rebelled, cajoled.   It
was all in vain.   Stopper had seriously frightened
the old man about her health, and he was adamant.
Preparations were set on foot ; the brown hair
trunks, with their lines of staring brass tacks, were
raked out and dusted ; the Colonel got into a fever,
ordered up all the negroes in the yard, and gave in-
structions from the front door, like a major-general
reviewing his troops ; got Torm, Charity, and all the
others into a wild flutter ; attempted to superintend
Polly's matters ; made her promises of fabulous
gifts ; became reminiscent, and told marvellous
stories of his old days, which Torm corroborated ;
and so excited Polly and the plantation generally
that from old Betty, who came from the Far Quarters

for the purpose of taking it in, down to the blackest
little dot on the place, there was not one who did not
get into a wild whirl, and talk as if they were all going
to New Orleans the next morning, with Joe Rattler
on the boot. Polly had, after a stout resistance,
surrendered to her fate, and packed her modest
trunk with very mingled feelings. Under other circumstances she would have enjoyed the trip immensely ; but she felt now as if it were parting from
Bob forever. Her heart was in her throat all day,
and even the excitement of packing could not drive
away the feeling. She knew she would never see
him again. She tried to work out what the end
would be. Would he die, or would he marry Malviny Pegram? Every one said she would just suit
him, and she'd certainly marry him if he asked her.
The sun was shining over the western woods. Bob
rode down that way in the afternoon, even when it
was raining; he had told her so. He would think
it cruel of her to go away so, and never even let him
know. She would at least go and tell him good-by.
So she did.

Bob's face paled suddenly when she told him all,
and that look which she had not seen often before
settled on it. Then he took her hand and began to
explain everything to her. He told her that he had
loved her all her life ; showed her how she had inspired him to work for and win every success that
he had achieved ; how it had been her work even

more than his. Then he laid before her the life
plans he had formed, and proved how they were all
for her, and for her only. He made it all so clear,
and his voice was so confident, and his face so earnest, as he pleaded and proved it step by step, that
she felt, as she leaned against him and he clasped
her closely, that he was right, and that she could not
part from him.

That evening Polly was unusually silent; but the
Colonel thought she had never been so sweet. She
petted him until he swore that no man on earth was
worthy of her, and that none should ever have her.
After tea she went to his room to look over his
clothes (her especial work), and would let no one,
not even her mammy, help her; and when the Colonel insisted on coming in to tell her some more
concerning the glories of New Orleans in his day,
she finally put him out and locked the door on him.
She was very strange all the evening. As they were
to start the next morning, the Colonel was for retir-
ing early; but Polly would not go; she loitered
around, hung about the old fellow, petted him, sat
on his knee and kissed him, until he was forced to
insist on her going to bed. Then she said good-
night, and astonished the Colonel by throwing herself into his arms and bursting out crying.

The old man soothed her with caresses and baby
talk, such as he used to comfort her with when she
was a little girl, and when she became quiet he

handed her to her door as if she had been a duch-
ess. The house was soon quiet, except that once
the Colonel heard Polly walking in her room, and
mentally determined to chide her for sitting up so
late. He, however, drifted off from the subject
when he heard some of his young mules galloping
around the yard, and he made a sleepy resolve to
sell them all, or to dismiss his overseer for letting
them get out of the lot. Before he had quite determined which he should do, he dropped off to sleep
again.

It was possibly about this time that a young man
lifted into her saddle a dark-habited little figure,
whose face shone very white in the starlight, and
whose tremulous voice would have suggested a refusal had it not been drowned in the deep, earnest
tone of her lover. Although she declared that she
could not think of doing it, she had on her hat and
furs and riding-habit when Bob came. She did, indeed, really beg him to go away ; but a few minutes
later a pair of horses cantered down the avenue toward the lawn gate, which shut with a bang that so
frightened the little lady on the bay mare that the
young man found it necessary to lean over and throw
a steadying arm around her.

For the first time in her life Polly saw the sun
rise in North Carolina, and a few hours later a gentle-
voiced young clergyman, whose sweet-faced wife
was wholly carried away by Polly's beauty, received

under protest Bob's only gold piece, a coin which
he twisted from his watch-chain with the promise to
quadruple it if he would preserve it.

When Charity told the Colonel next morning that
Polly was gone, the old man for the first time in fifty
years turned perfectly white. Then he fell into a
consuming rage, and swore until Charity would not
have been much surprised to see the devil appear in
visible shape and claim him on the spot. He cursed
Bob, cursed himself, Torm, Charity, and the entire
female sex individually and collectively, and then,
seized by a new idea, ordered his horse, that he
might pursue the runaways, threatened an immediate sale of his whole plantation, and the instan-
taneous death of Bob, and did in fact get down his
great brass-mounted pistols, and lay them by him as
he made Torm, Charity, and a half-dozen younger
house-servants dress him.

Dressing and shaving occupied him about an
hour—he always averred that a gentleman could
not dress like a gentleman in less time—and, still
breathing out threatenings and slaughter, he marched
out of his room, making Torm and Charity follow
him, each with a pistol. Something prompted him
to stop and inspect them in the hall. Taking first
one and then the other, he examined them curiously.

"Well, I'll be ——!" he said, dryly, and flung
both of them crashing through the window. Turn

ing, he ordered waffles and hoe-cakes for breakfast, and called for the books to have prayers.

Polly had utilized the knowledge she had gained as a girl, and had unloaded both pistols the night before, and rammed the balls down again without powder, so as to render them harmless.

By breakfast time Torm was in a state of such advanced intoxication that he was unable to walk through the back yard gate, and the Colonel was forced to content himself with sending by Charity a message that he would get rid of him early the next morning. He straitly enjoined Charity to tell him, and she as solemnly promised. "Yes, suh, *I* gwi' tell him," she replied, with a faint tone of being wounded at his distrust ; and she did.

She needed an outlet.

Things got worse. The Colonel called up the overseer and gave new orders, as if he proposed to change everything. He forbade any mention of Polly's name, and vowed that he would send for Mr. Steep, his lawyer, and change his will to spite all creation. This humor, instead of wearing off, seemed to grow worse as the time stretched on, and Torm actually grew sober in the shadow that had fallen on the plantation. The Colonel had Polly's room nailed up and shut himself up in the house.

The negroes discussed the condition of affairs in awed undertones, and watched him furtively whenever he passed. Various opinions by turns prevailed.

Aunt Betty, who was regarded with veneration, owing partly to the interest the lost Polly had taken in her illness, and partly to her great age (to which she annually added three years) prophesied that he was going to die "in torments," just like some old uncle of his whom no one else had ever heard of until now, but who was raked up by her to serve as a special example. The chief resemblance seemed to be a certain "rankness in cussin'."

Things were certainly going badly, and day by day they grew worse. The Colonel became more and more morose.

"He don' even quoil no mo'," Torm complained pathetically to Charity. "He jes set still and study. I 'feard he gwine 'stracted."

It was, indeed, lamentable. It was accepted on the plantation that Miss Polly had gone for good— some said down to Louisiana—and would never come back any more. The prevailing impression was that, if she did, the Colonel would certainly kill Bob. Torm had not a doubt of it.

Thus matters stood three days before Christmas. The whole plantation was plunged in gloom. It would be the first time since Miss Polly was a baby that they had not had "a big Christmas." Torm's lugubrious countenance one morning seemed to shock the Colonel out of his lethargy. He asked how many days there would be before Christmas, and learning that there were but three, he ordered preparations to be made for a great feast and a big time generally. He had the wood-pile replenished as usual, got up his presents, and superintended the Christmas operations himself, as he used to do. But it was sad work, and when Torm and Charity retired Christmas Eve night, although Torm had imbibed plentifully, and the tables were all spread for the great dinner for the servants next day, there was no peace in Torm's discourse; it was all of wrath and judgment to come. He had just gone to sleep when there was a knock at the door.

"Who dat out dyah?" called Charity. "You niggers better go 'long to bed."

The knock was repeated.

"Who dat out dyah, I say?" queried Charity, testily. "Whyn't you go 'long 'way from dat do'?"

Torm was hard to wake, but at length he got up and moved slowly to the door, grumbling to himself all the time.

When finally he undid the latch, Charity, who was in bed, heard him say, "Well, name o' Gord! good Gord A'mighty!" and burst into a wild explosion of laughter.

In a second she too was outside of the door, and had Polly in her arms, laughing, jumping, hugging, and kissing her, while Torm executed a series of caracoles around them.

"Whar Marse Bob?" asked both negroes, finally, in a breath.

" Hello, Torm ! How are you, Mam' Charity ? "
called that gentleman, cheerily, coming up from
where he had been fastening the horses ; and Charity, suddenly mindful of her peculiar appearance
and the frosty air, "scuttled" into the house, con-
veying her young mistress with her.

Presently she came out dressed, and invited Bob
in too. She insisted on giving them something to
eat; but they had been to supper, and Polly was
much too excited hearing about her uncle to eat
anything. She cried a little at Charity's description of him, which she tried to keep Bob from see-
ing, but he saw it, and had to—however, when
they got ready to go home, Polly insisted on going
to the yard and up on the porch, and when there,
she actually kissed the window-blind of the room
whence issued a muffled snore suggestive at least of
some degree of forgetfulness. She wanted Bob to
kiss it too, but that gentleman apparently found
something else more to his taste, and her entreaty
was drowned in another sound.

Before they remounted their horses Polly carried
Bob to the greenhouse, where she groped around in
the darkness for something, to Bob's complete mys-
tification. " Doesn't it smell sweet in here ? " she
asked.

" I don't smell anything but that mint bed you've
been walking on," he laughed.

As they rode off, leaving Torm and Charity stand

ing in the road, the last thing Polly said was, " Now be sure you tell him—nine o'clock."

" Umm ! I know he gwi' sell me den sho 'nough," said Torm, in a tone of conviction, as the horses cantered away in the frosty night.

Once or twice, as they galloped along, Bob made some allusion to the mint bed on which Polly had stepped, to which she made no reply. But as he helped her down at her own door, he asked, " What in the world have you got there ? "

" Mint," said she, with a little low, pleased laugh.

By light next morning it was known all over the plantation that Miss Polly had returned. The rejoicing was clouded by the fear that nothing would come of it.

In Charity's house it was decided that Torm should break the news. Torm was doubtful on the point as the time drew near, but Charity's mind never wavered. Finally he went in with his master's shaving-water, having first tried to establish his courage by sundry pulls at a black bottle. He essayed three times to deliver the message, but each time his courage failed, and he hastened out under pretence of the water having gotten cold. The last time he attracted Charity's attention.

" Name o' Gord, Torm, you gwine to scal' hawgs ? " she asked, sarcastically.

The next time he entered the Colonel was in a fume of impatience, so he had to fix the water. He

15

set down the can, and bustled about with hypocrit.
ical industry. The Colonel was almost through ;
Torm retreated to the door. As his master finished,
he put his hand on the knob, and turning it, said,
" Miss Polly come home larse night ; sh' say she
breakfast at nine o'clock."

Slapbang ! came the shaving-can, smashing against
the door, just as he dodged out, and the roar of the
Colonel followed him across the hall.

When finally their master appeared on the portico,
Torm and Charity were watching in some doubt
whether he would not carry out on the spot his long-
threatened purpose. He strode up and down the
long porch, evidently in great excitement.

" He's turrible dis mornin'," said Torm ; "he
th'owed de whole kittle o' b'ilin' water at me."

" Pity he didn' scal' you to death," said his wife,
sympathizingly. She thought Torm's awkward-
ness had destroyed Polly's last chance. Torm re-
sorted to his black bottle, and proceeded to talk
about the lake of brimstone and fire.

Up and down the portico strode the old Colonel.
His horse was at the rack, where he was always
brought before breakfast. (For twenty years he had
probably never missed a morning.) Finally he
walked down, and, mounting, rode off in the opposite direction to that whence his invitation had come.
Charity, looking out of her door, inserted into her
diatribe against " all wuthless, drunken, fool niggers "

a parenthesis to the effect that " Ef Marster meet Marse Bob dis mornin', de don' be a hide nor hyah left o'nyah one on 'em; an' dat lamb over dyah maybe got oystchers waitin' for him too." Torm was so much impressed that he left Charity and went out of doors.

The Colonel rode down the plantation road, his great gray horse quivering with life in the bright winter sunlight. He gave him the rein, and he turned down a cross-road which led out of the plantation into the main road. Mechanically he opened the gate and rode out. Before he knew where he was he was through the wood, and his horse had stopped at the next gate—the gate of Bob's place. The house stood out bright and plain among the yard trees; lines of blue smoke curled up almost straight from the chimneys; and he could see two or three negroes running backward and forward between the kitchen and the house. The sunlight glistened on something in the hand of one of them, and sent a ray of dazzling light all the way to the old man. He knew it was a plate or a dish. He took out his watch and glanced at it; it was five minutes to nine o'clock. He started to turn around to go home. As he did so the memory of all the past swept over him, and of the wrong that had been done him. He would go in and show them his contempt for them by riding in and straight out again; and he actually unlatched the gate and went in.

As he rode across the field he recalled all that Polly had been to him from the time when she had first stretched out her arms to him; all the little ways by which she had brought back his youth, and had made his house home, and his heart soft again. Every scene came before him as if to mock him. He felt once more the touch of her little hand; heard again the sound of her voice as it used to ring through the old house and about the grounds; saw her and Bob as children romping about his feet, and he gave a great gulp as he thought how desolate the house was now. He sat up in his saddle stiffer than ever. D—— him! he would enter his very house, and there to his face and hers denounce him for his baseness: and he pushed his horse to a trot. Up to the yard gate he rode, and, dismounting, hitched his horse to the fence, and slamming the gate fiercely behind him, stalked up the walk with his heavy whip clutched fast in his hand. Up the walk and up the steps, without a pause, his face set as grim as rock, and purple with suppressed emotion; for a deluge of memories was overwhelming him.

The door was shut; they had locked it on him; but he would burst it in, and—Ah! what was that?

The door flew suddenly open; there was a cry, a spring, a vision of something swam before his eyes, and two arms were clasped about his neck, while he was being smothered with kisses from the sweetest mouth in the world, and a face made up of light and laughter, yet tearful too, like a dew-bathed flower, was pressed to his, and before the Colonel knew it he had, amid laughter and sobs and caresses, been borne into the house, and pressed down at the daintiest little breakfast-table eyes ever saw, set for three persons, and loaded with steaming dishes, and with a great fresh julep by the side of his plate, and Torm was standing behind his chair, and Bob was helping him to "oystchers," while Polly, with dimpling face, was attempting the exploit of pouring out his coffee without moving her arm from around his neck.

The first thing he said after he recovered his breath was, "Where did you get this mint?"

Polly broke into a peal of rippling, delicious laughter, and tightened the arm about his neck.

"Just one more squeeze," said the Colonel; and as she gave it he said, with the light of it all breaking on him, "Damme if I don't sell you! or, if I can't sell you, I'll give you away—that is, if he'll come over and live with us."

That evening, after the great dinner, at which Polly had sat in her old place at the head of the table, and Bob at the foot, because the Colonel insisted on sitting where Polly could give him one more squeeze, the whole plantation was ablaze with "Christmas," and Drinkwater Torm, steadying him self against the sideboard, delivered a discourse on peace on earth and good-will to men so powerful and so eloquent that the Colonel, delighted, rose and drank his health, and said, " Damme if I ever sell him again! "